PRAISE FOR PRECIOUS OYEKANMI'S

'An enthralling and exhilara[ting...]
reflections, remorse, hop[e...]
bursting out with laughte[r...]'

Fola Oluborode, CEO of Firmly Rooted Ltd

'A touching and fascinating story that not only sheds light on the trauma faced by many women but also unveils God's grace and love. I was invested from start to finish and was unable to put the book down. A must-read!'

Esi Dadzie

'This book had me HOOKED! The story touches on deep topics, which made me grow as an individual. I don't think I've ever read a work of fiction that moved me so profoundly. I would definitely recommend this book!'

Reti Adoghe, Co-founder of Women Who Know

'A tear-filling love story that should be read by many, illustrating a beautiful transition from bondage to freedom.'

Kendra Dickens, Projects Intern Lead for Anima Youth

'A heart racing, yet touching and compelling novel that focuses on family, friendship, religion and trust.'

Iniabasi Ukpong, Fund Accountant

'I felt as if I was alongside Kaya throughout every page of the book. Although various heavy topics were highlighted, I was able to relate to Kaya's emotions—betrayal, confusion, and a lack of identity. This book is an amazing read!'

Jodie Osemwegie

KAYA

PRECIOUS OYEKANMI

Copyright © 2023 Precious Oyekanmi

All rights reserved.

This is a work of fiction. Any resemblance of characters to actual persons, living or dead, is purely coincidental.

The author holds exclusive rights to this work. Unauthorised duplication is prohibited. No part of this book can be reproduced in any form or by electronic or mechanical means including information storage and retrieval systems without permission from the author. The only exception is by a reviewer who may quote short excerpts in a review.

For enquiries, please contact:
authorpreciousoyekanmi@gmail.com

First paperback edition July 2023

Edited by Onifeoluwa Adebajo

Cover Design by Daniel Thompson

ISBN 978-1-7394743-0-0 (paperback)

ISBN 978-1-7394743-1-7 (e-book)

Acknowledgements

Firstly, my deepest gratitude goes to the One who breathed creativity into us as human beings—God. In Him I live and move and have my being.

Secondly, I want to thank the women in my life who have inspired me to be more than a conqueror:

Mum, our deep and meaningful conversations through our ups and downs over the years have not only brought us into a deeper understanding of each other but also into an understanding of how we overcome many of the pains of womanhood. I love you more than my words can explain.

Esther, as another wonderful mother in my life, I am so glad that your light has shined on my heart to help me become an even more refined woman.

Zoe, my beautiful cousin, I don't even know where I would have been had it not been for your openness. You were like a God-given shield for me.

Aunty Doris, you may not have realised it, but the Queen Latifah song 'Fly Girl' you used to play in the car for Reti and I (even though we're not in the club anymore) helped me realise that I was worth so much more than any validation from a man. I'm a queen!

Truly, I want to say thank you to every woman who, whether through a good or bad experience, has helped me grow into the truth of my identity. Womanhood is not easy, but I'm thankful that I know where to look now. His name is Yahweh.

For Olivia, Reti and Tomi

To three sisters who never left me when life felt far from sunshine and rainbows.

Thank you for sticking by me through my most traumatic moments.

Thank you for choosing to see light in me even when it felt as if my light was being snuffed out.

But most of all, thank you for being faithful to me so that I was able to see a glimpse of the One who is Faithful. It is friends like you that helped me finally return to my eternal Friend.

CONTENTS

Prologue	1
Chapter 1	9
Chapter 2	14
Chapter 3	22
Chapter 4	25
Chapter 5	37
Chapter 6	41
Chapter 7	47
Chapter 8	65
Chapter 9	73
Chapter 10	98
Chapter 11	111
Chapter 12	126
Chapter 13	138
Chapter 14	150
Chapter 15	167
Chapter 16	175
Chapter 17	195
Chapter 18	203
Chapter 19	217

Chapter 20	232
Chapter 21	243
Chapter 22	247
Chapter 23	260
Chapter 24	279
Chapter 25	296
Epilogue	306

Prologue

Every time I step out onto Gogo's veranda and watch the sunset, I wonder who didn't get the chance to see it go down:

A workaholic father who is so manically stressed with trying to provide for his trophy wife and three ungrateful children that he takes up a dodgy business deal and ends up first with a bullet in his kneecap and then another in the back of his head.

A teenager who has been bullied for fifteen years for having a birthmark on her face finally reaches her limit, so to end the bullying and gain popularity, she conforms to peer pressure and takes 4 tabs of MDMA and suffers a deadly fit because of it.

A toxic couple—that cannot stand ten minutes without arguing—start bickering over who left the socks in the underwear drawer, only they don't stop fighting in time to see their child walking over a zebra crossing.

I then think to myself, *if only they knew it would be the last time they ran out of toothpaste in the morning. If only they knew it was the last time they'd complain about how there are too many beans in their coffee. If only they knew it was the last time they'd have to wave at the neighbour they didn't like. If only they knew.*

When I was eight years old, my mum sent me on my first mission. I knew Mama had some kind of importance and was absolutely brilliant, but it was only later on that day that I had a life-changing discovery.

She had said to me, "Kaya, you need to start gaining some independence. I brought you into this world as a female, but I won't allow you to submit to patriarchy. Gogo and I have survived this far without a man in the house; I need you to learn to do the same. Now, I want you to go to the shops and buy me a batch of eggs. Got it?"

As I strolled along the street to the shops, all that was on my mind was the word *patriarchy*. I had no idea what it meant, but I didn't want my mum to think I wasn't ready for my first mission.

As I picked out the batch of eggs to take home, I pondered on the word further. I sensed that it had something to do with men as that seemed to be the context of the conversation. However, men were a taboo topic in our very female household. I knew my father was not a good man and, although no one ever spoke about him, I had a growing suspicion that my grandfather probably wasn't either.

Whatever, I thought. The mission was more important than my mysterious family history at this moment in time. I had to carry these eggs like they were baby chickens, ready to hatch.

A few yards away from home, I saw my best friend, Thato, coming down the street, only this time, he wasn't coming on foot. I was completely amazed—a new bicycle! Mama and Gogo had forbidden me from riding any such inventions until I was at least a teenager.

The paint work on the bike was absolutely astonishing—I'd only seen plain-coloured bicycles in the neighbourhood. It had flames of fury that rode up the bike; one of the most beautiful things I'd ever laid eyes upon.

"Check out what my dad bought me for my birthday!" he exclaimed. "Sit in the basket and I'll give you a ride down the street."

I knew Thato was excited because whenever he got excited, his left eye would get teary, and he would rub the back of his neck with the palm of his hand. (Well, I thought it was his left eye, but it could have also been his right. I would have to hold out my hands and make an 'L' shape to be sure.)

Regardless, I knew that if I'd said I couldn't join him for a quick ride, he'd have been disappointed. I thought about the mission and how annoyed Mama and Gogo would be if they knew what I was about to do; but then again, after the summer break, I'd be able to tell everyone at school about what Thato and I did!

Why couldn't I do this *and* complete the mission? I didn't want to disappoint anyone so, this way, everyone could be happy—including myself. I jumped into the basket and kept the precious eggs close to my chest.

As we soared through the air, I couldn't understand why Gogo hated bikes so much; they had much more in common than she knew. Gogo always told me that life for her started off so slowly, days felt like months sometimes—she couldn't wait to grow up. But then, there came a time when everyday felt like a second to her.

This is no different from a bike. The pedalling may start off slow, but it eventually picks up speed and everything feels so fast. I couldn't wait to get home and present my well-thought-out argument about why I needed a bike to the leader of the house (which is Gogo).

Everything was perfect until I saw a pothole in the road.

"Thato! THATO!" I shrieked. It was too late. I landed headfirst onto the asphalt road, but all I could think about were the eggs. I got up immediately hoping that they were still okay. To my disappointment, they were all splattered and frying on the road.

Thato had already begun sobbing when I got up; his new bike was completely ruined. I felt an overwhelming sense of guilt about everything, so I didn't even have the courage to comfort him. I started wondering what I would tell Mama and Gogo about my cut knees, my scraped elbows, and the failed mission. I had disappointed everyone.

***

I'm not sure why, but mums love playing intense games with their children at the most inconvenient times. The most common one my mother likes to play is the eye contact game.

Often, when we visit people, they ask us if we want something to eat or drink. Logically, it makes sense that when you're hungry or thirsty, you would accept this offer. However, I soon understood that when Mama begins to play the eye contact game, it means we must politely decline. Her eyes squint a little bit as she telepathically communicates with me. I thought adults would have outgrown playing games at their age, but, for the sake of peace, I always play along.

This was the same game she was playing with me as I entered the kitchen—she wasn't saying anything; instead, she was trying to telepathically communicate her anger with me. Our gaze slowly drifted to the wooden spoon on the kitchen counter. In order to escape a red bottom, I told her, "Mama, it wasn't my fault! The big boys were chasing me down the street. I tripped over and they ran away with the eggs. I'm sorry, Ma…"

"Kaya Imka Khumalo," she said. I became even more scared at this point because not only were we playing the eye contact game, but also the full-name game. Both of those meant I was in serious trouble. She continued, "We *do not* lie in this household. Kuyacaca lokho?"

"Yes Ma, I understand. It won't happen again." I could just about get the words out.

To my surprise, she put the wooden spoon in the drawer, and I breathed a sigh of relief. However, I was also surprised that I got away with it—was she disappointed or did she just expect this of me?

It was at this moment that I had a life-changing epiphany. My jaw dropped open as I watched my mother carry on with the cooking. How could she tell me not to lie in this household when she had done it all along? She had always told me how important it was to be open and honest about everything yet, she couldn't even stick to her own words. She knew everything I was thinking, my every move— she had miraculously predicted all those lies I'd told and instead called it 'motherly instinct'. It all made sense now.

Mama was a mind-reader.

***

For weeks after my discovery, I completely resented her. I decided I'd keep her secret safe but I wasn't going to make it easy for her. Dinner times were my favourite moments to test her abilities. I'd think to myself, *I'm not going to touch my vegetables.* Straight away, she'd complain and say, "Ingane, you are not leaving this table until you finish everything on that plate. Do you hear me?"

After that, I'd think to myself, *I'm going to pour myself a glass of juice instead of water*. Miraculously, the next thing that would come out of her mouth would be, "And don't even think about touching the apple juice; I don't want you hyper before bed." I decided I was going to keep thinking about all the things that annoyed her until she let up and told me what she had been hiding.

***

It took me exactly three weeks to realise that my mum wasn't actually a mind-reader. Mama had just bought a brand-new ebony oak-veneered mirror, quite boring looking actually. She had saved up for a while to buy it as she was trying to change the décor in her bedroom. I had snuck into her room to try and find some new evidence I could use against her at a later date.

As I rummaged through her wardrobe, I saw a black widow spider. I leapt up and fell straight into the mirror. The shards of glass were all over the floor and some pieces were in my hair. I knew that Mama and Gogo were going to *kill* me. I quickly brushed the pieces from my hair as Mama ran into the corner of the room.

"Kaya, what happened? Oh no! Are you okay? Those wretched technicians; I knew they didn't fix the mirror onto the wall properly. They will be hearing from me on Monday morning!"

She picked me up and carried me over the broken glass. Instantly, the same sense of guilt I'd felt from the failed mission came over me. Mama was not a mind-reader; I had got it all wrong.

Although I was completely insane to believe my mum was a mind-reader, she must've still been able to envision the sort of person I'd become. My name means *restful place* and my middle name, Imka, means *water*. I think that's why I'm so at ease with the concept of death. I know that there is more than what the world tells us about dying. There must be eternal peace somewhere.

Gogo must have played a huge role in it too; she's basically my soulmate. Gogo once told me that when I was born, I carried the darkness away from her life—I set free the past that had once consumed her.

Another time, Gogo told me that for the first three years of my life, I called her 'Mumoo' and referred to my mum as 'Lady'. I must have known that my mum and I lacked any genuine connection from birth. Gogo used to call me her 'golden child', and I would call her my 'lamp of light' in Zulu. We try to avoid saying all of this around my mum as we know that deep down it's hard for her to see what Gogo and I have—something they never did and something *we* never did.

Nevertheless, I wouldn't trade what me and Gogo have for anything. She completely understands me. She never questions why I use mouthwash before I brush my teeth, or why I pour milk in my bowl before the cereal, or even why I can't eat my food until I've found something suitable to watch on Netflix. My mum, on the other hand, nags at me for everything. All she knows how to do is complain. The only thing she's completely fine with is that I don't have a man in my life—if it were up to her, I'd die alone with eleven cats.

1

2021

Tomorrow morning is Gogo's 67th birthday. It's a struggle figuring out what to get her as she's never been good with presents, but I still love spoiling her.

When I was ten, I thought it was high time I got Gogo my own personal gift, rather than the yearly flowers and chocolate Mama always made me give her. At that time, we had this overly friendly guy in our neighbourhood who I was never allowed to stop and talk to. I'd just assumed it was because of my mother's weird hatred for men. So, the day of Gogo's birthday, I decided I would go and find out what he was all about. I was still unsure what her present would be, but I knew something would come to me.

On the way to get some groceries for Mama (at this point, she could now trust me with groceries again), he was sitting next to the bins behind the corner shop. He seemed to be really happy, so happy that he was singing. A wave of fear came over me as I turned in his direction ready to disobey Mama's instructions. As I approached him, he smiled gleefully.

What a lovely man, I thought. *Gogo would love him.*

He then looked away from me and started babbling about the word's 'recession' and 'economy'. I had literally no clue what those words meant but he seemed so passionate about them due to his repetition.

Gogo loves passion, I thought.

An amazing idea suddenly hit me: I could make him Gogo's date! What an amazing birthday present—Gogo could have a spectacular birthday and she could also find love again. I asked him to go and pick some flowers from the fields nearby whilst I went into the shop to buy some groceries. He seemed very willing and excited merely by the fact that someone had actually spoken to him for once. Poor man. I waited ten minutes or so after I came out of the shop, nervously awaiting my fabulous birthday present for Gogo. I was so relieved to see him come back.

I asked him to follow me back to my house and present the flowers to Gogo at dinner, which was in an hour. Whenever I wanted to sneak back into the house, when I had stayed out and played with Thato more than I was supposed to, I always used the back window that led into the bathroom. That way, I could avoid Mama and Gogo.

This time, I wanted Gogo to be surprised at dinner, so the man and I snuck in through the back. I was very surprised by his willingness to do whatever I said. Mama was wrong about him. *She's always wrong*, I thought to myself angrily.

As I distracted Mama and Gogo in the kitchen, he obediently sat down on my bed until dinner was ready. I couldn't wait! I was so excited and, somehow, Mama could tell.

"Kaya," Mama chuckled, "why are you so jittery today?"

Slightly annoyed at the fact that she had misjudged the man and kept us from friendship, her comment irritated me. "It's Gogo's birthday," I replied bluntly.

"You never act this excited on my birthday!" she said, still highly amused.

"Well, yeah…because it's *your* birthday…" I felt bad as soon as I'd said it, more so because I had brought down the whole mood rather than just upsetting Mama.

I saw Gogo's face dim after I made that rude comment to Mama. So, to save the day, I quickly arranged the table. During my smooth recovery, I managed to get a small compliment out to Mama.

"You look so beautiful today, Ma." She turned to me and gave me a half-hearted hug and kiss and tried to hide her smile. I'd always found it weird that showing my mother a little love could make her day. The air felt slightly less thick so I was filled with excitement again.

Gogo's birthday food *is* and always has been a selection of different barbecued meats with rice, a stew, and corn-on-the-cob. A thought that flashed through my mind was the fact that the man was missing *a lot* of teeth and was definitely going to struggle to chew.

Ah, whatever. Rice will do him.

As we sat down, we all held hands and shared a prayer of thanksgiving. This was something I never understood because God was something we didn't talk about in this household, probably because he is a man. Yet, it was something that was clearly personal to Mama and Gogo because, although it was an unspoken belief, it seemed that the existence of this deity was what held their lives together.

"One second, Khumalo ladies, I just need to grab Gogo's present," I said as soon as the prayer was over. I ran to my room and beckoned for my new friend to come and join me. He hadn't moved an inch since I left him there, but the smell of the room had certainly changed.

Yuck! It smells like dying cats.

I was so excited; I literally couldn't stop grinning. We crept slowly towards the dining area.

"Gogo, happy birthday!" I exclaimed gleefully. I turned towards him and nudged him forcefully, "Go on then, give her the flowers."

"Kaya. Imka. Khumalo. What have you done bringing this *sick*, smelly, old man to my house? To *our* home, Kaya? Did I born you as a mad woman for you to befriend this sicko? You are in so much trouble that you'd be lucky if I'm done dealing with you by Gogo's next birthday." Mama was absolutely raging. I could feel her blood boiling as she screamed at me.

I wanted to cry, but I didn't. She was not worth my tears. I looked at Gogo with huge embarrassment and regret. However, her response completely shocked me.

"Ah, relax Nandi. I love my birthday present, Kaya. Old man, come sit! Come join us; we have enough to feed four families. You know what, Kaya? If he was white, though, I would be even angrier than your mother!" she laughed.

I breathed the hugest sigh of relief with a small smile, just about holding back the tears of what could have been the biggest mistake I'd ever made. I ran over and gave Gogo a big hug.

"Ma, Kaya is *my* child. I understand that you don't want her to be upset but she has to learn how to respect my authority," Mama said with lightning still burning through her toffee complexion.

"Oh, shut it, Nandi! All you ever do is shout at the poor girl. Now, let me enjoy my birthday. Old man, come, come!" Gogo replied.

Watching Gogo speak to my mother like this provided me with a certain kind of happiness that I knew I should've been guilty to have. I thought, *let her have it, Gogo*. Who was she to always make me feel so rubbish all the time? I didn't even care when she stormed away from the table into her sad, boringly designed bedroom. During that moment, I wished she'd known it was me who ruined the brand-new mirror she had saved up for all those years ago.

2

2021

Now that I'm home, I've been in the middle of cancelling all my meetings so that I can give Gogo my undivided attention.

I felt especially relieved to cancel my meeting with my new client, Mr Underwood, at 3pm tomorrow as I was not ready for his plans for us to do business together. He's been throwing around all these proposals that I'm not used to, so I needed much more time to think about his suggestions.

A few weeks ago, I was first introduced to Mr Underwood through our mutual friend, Mandy. Mandy and I met at university nearly ten years ago and she is my most trusted friend in the whole world—someone I'd classify as family. When we became business partners at university, we grew so close. She deals with most of the client side of things, so I trust her when she adds someone new to the list.

However, something about Mr Underwood just didn't sit right with me and I needed some time to be able to process the business proposals he'd suggested to me a few nights ago over dinner.

At 8pm on Tuesday night, we met up at Marble Restaurant—a beautiful rooftop location in Joburg for dinner and drinks. It was a lovely evening, and I must say that Mr Underwood is certainly charming in all his ways, especially his charisma and his smile. But something about that made me think I couldn't trust him. There was not one thing I could fault about him, and, after running my own business successfully (*very* successfully) for the last nine years, I'd learnt that perfection is a big fat red flag.

From what I remember, our dinner went along the lines of something like this:

"I like the way you run your business, Ms Khumalo, but I think I could help you improve some of your business operations, such as the PR and social media pages," he said hesitantly.

"You want to help me with PR and social media?" I asked.

"Mmhmm," he added.

"What's wrong with the PR and social media pages?" I replied defensively.

"Nothing's *wrong* with it, I just think it could be better," he continued.

"Better how?"

"I'm not trying to step on your toes or anything but…it's just that some people are saying it's kind of outdated you know."

"Some people? Who are 'some people'?" I interjected.

"Look, I don't want to kick up a fuss about it. All I'm saying is when we go into business together—"

"*If* we go into business together," I interrupted rudely.

"*If* we go into business together," he corrected himself quickly, "I think it would be good to have a rebrand, something more fun and light-hearted…maybe even getting the school kids involved now rather than just the young adults. Also, some of the celebrities promoting your pages are pretty old news now. I have some friends who are much more current, and I think it could make us a lot more money," he finally managed to get out without me interrupting.

"Well, even if you're right Mr Underwood, which I don't think you are, I've signed contracts with these celebrities that you're saying we should just toss aside which still need to be paid for. Also, why would we get the kids involved when they're not old enough to come to nightclubs? That could shut down my whole business," I said irritatedly.

"Ms Khumalo, calm down. I just think you should consider what I'm saying. If you think about it, the celebrities you would be getting rid of are losing you money anyway. Pay them off and you'll make it all back and more. As for the kids, don't you know that your clubs are already full of them?"

"What do you mean?" I replied, feeling insulted.

"Let me not say too much. Just stand outside by your bouncers during one of your club nights and you'll see how many fake IDs are sliding through your clubs."

That's the way I remember it going, anyway.

But, when I realised that Mr Underwood was annoyingly and painstakingly right in every way, it made it even harder not to want to do business with him. That same night after our dinner, I stood by the bouncers in one of my clubs and saw how many kids under the age of 18 were making their way in. Annoyingly, there was nothing I could do about it.

To make my ego hurt even more, when I asked my friends and colleagues what they truly thought about the celebrities on our social media pages, they said they had wanted to tell me they were outdated for a while but thought I'd get offended. How could I *not* work with someone like Mr Underwood? We'd be able to make more money, and nothing would pass by me without me knowing if he was around. But something still told me I couldn't trust him.

The point is, I'm glad I've got more time to process this business decision I may undertake with Mr Underwood as a new client. Why was it *my* investment that he needed in particular? I understood his perspective of being able to grow his consumer base with my social media platforms, PR and, perhaps, the people that came to my clubs, but I didn't get why he wanted *me* specifically to invest. It was weird.

The way I run my business is also very private and I don't know if I trust him to know the details of how I'm running it.

I thought it best to FaceTime Mandy to clear up some of the questions going round and round in my head about this man. Also, I was surprised that I hadn't met him before now because Mandy and I share everything about our lives with each other, even down to which type of socks we're wearing. What was the mystery behind Mr Underwood?

"Hey sis," I said as our FaceTime call connected.

"Hey friend," Mandy said. "You okay?"

"Yeah…all good. What are you up to this weekend?"

"I have my nieces coming over which I'm both excited about but also terrified that they'll spill kids' stuff all over my new carpet. How is it being back home with the fam?" Mandy asked.

"Um, it feels weird to be home after so long to be honest. I haven't seen Gogo yet as I think she's sleeping, and my mum is still at work. Is it bad if I say I miss Joburg already?"

"Awhhh, do you mean you're missing *me*?" she teased.

I rolled my eyes and pretended to puke. "Gross, Mandy. But, um, can I quickly ask you some questions about this Underwood guy?" I asked, hoping she was ready to listen to all the unreasonable excuses I had so we didn't have to do business with him.

"Mmhmm, listening," Mandy said, bracing herself. She always knew when I was about to rant about someone or something that I didn't like because she let out a deep sigh that was only reserved for these moments—I knew it too well, because I complain like I get paid to do it.

"Can you first of all remind me where you know him from?" I began.

"I've *explained* this to you, Kaya. I met him at a networking event a few years ago when I was still thinking of veering off into tech. We talked for a while and became…friends."

"Okay…there seems to be some hesitation on the 'friends' part," I speculated, with my eyebrows raised.

"You're too nosey!" Mandy laughed.

"Just tell me—" I began.

"Hush now," she interrupted me with a huge secretive grin on her face. "Let me finish what I was saying."

"Fine," I agreed.

"He reached out to me a few months ago about this start-up he was thinking of setting up. He ran me through the whole business model and showed me how he planned to obtain funding, expand, and make a profit.

"After a few times of explaining it to me, I understood why it would be so successful. His platform will be an all-in-one app that allows people to make their 'want-to-be' lifestyle a reality. And… since you own three of the hottest clubs in Joburg; this is going to get you from rich to super-duper rich."

"Mmhmm," I sighed. "Mandy, you know that I would normally be straight in for something like this, but I don't understand why, out of all the lifestyle business owners, he's asking *us* for the largest investment seed? I mean, I know my business is doing well but there are certainly other investors that are making much more money than me," I persisted.

"Kaya, you seriously don't know why? Think about it…" Mandy said. "He's not as legal as you think."

It suddenly clicked for me. I knew Mr Underwood was not all the charm and smiles he had made himself out to be. He was just like the rest of us—sweet and attractive on the outside—but there was *way* more than what meets the eye on the inside. I knew I couldn't trust him; you can't trust anyone in this business.

"Who does he know that is useful for us? And how did you find out?" I asked.

"Now, here are the good questions!" Mandy smiled. "Underwood and I were…dating for a while and he enjoyed showing me off to his friends. He started by just introducing me to one or two people but then, after some months, the more he took me out, the more conversations I was involved in, and one of those conversations involved Alexander Petrov."

"The Russian guy?!" I asked in excitement. "Please, tell me it's the Russian guy."

"Yes, Kaya, it's the Russian guy," she said and we both started screaming on the phone.

"But don't get too excited yet; we have a lot of work to do before Alexander will start doing business with us, and the first step we need to take is positioning ourselves rightly with Daniel," Mandy instructed.

"Who's Daniel?" I asked.

"Underwood," Mandy clarified. "His full name is Daniel Underwood."

"Oh, right."

"From our conversations, I feel like he's pushing investment from you because he wants to be just as involved with Alexander as we want to be, and if we are already working closely together with Underwood, it will be much easier to simultaneously get into business with Petrov."

"Consider it done. Can you arrange another meeting for me and Underwood first thing on Monday morning?" I replied.

"Of course. This is going to take you to the next level, Kaya. Get ready for what you've been dreaming of. I'll speak with you when you're back."

"You're a gem, Mandy. Love you forever. Speak soon," I said as I ended the phone.

Alexander Petrov…this feels like a dream.

But why didn't I know that Mandy dated Underwood for a while? We never hide anything from each other….

3

2021

It was weird being back in my childhood bedroom—all the old memories started flooding back. I looked at my carpet and saw the blue nail varnish stain that never came out after my 16th birthday. It was a silly idea that day to let Thato play football in my room whilst I painted my nails. With his sloppy kick-ups, the ball landed straight on the nail varnish and onto the carpet.

Another memory I had was the sandalwood-scented candle I never lit because I had read *way* too many things online about people falling asleep with candles on and getting carbon monoxide poisoning. This is hilarious now because I somehow forgot all about that fear and light about a thousand candles a day—my apartment basically looks like a Catholic church everyday.

I also felt like it was insulting to bring my pretty 'non-humble' belongings (as I call them) back to my *very* humble surroundings, such as my Apple products, designer bags and expensive jewellery. It just felt odd. I definitely missed my childhood though; not realising how quickly it went makes me appreciate it even more.

As I began to drift off to sleep, I heard a soft knock on the door.

"Come in," I said, clearing my sleepy throat. I really hoped it was Gogo so we could start having our long-awaited catch up.

"Hey Kaya." I was disappointed to open my sleepy eyes to see my mum standing there with a huge grin on her face.

"Oh, hey Mum," I said.

She walked over, perched on my bed, and seemed to swallow hard as the next thing came out of her mouth; super scripted as always.

"I just got in from work and saw your bags at the door. It's really nice to have you home."

Yeah, right.

"Thanks, Mum," I said sarcastically. "I'm actually kind of tired though; maybe we can catch up another time this weekend?"

"Yes, of course. No stress at all," she said. I could see she was trying to find a way to stall and make a new conversation.

"Oh, and Mum…" I replied as she started slowly making her way to the door.

"Yes, dear!" she said quickly, trying to hide the excited look on her face of thinking she was a wanted mother.

"Could you close my door?" I said, feeling guilty at the disappointment I had just caused.

I could see it all over her, what I'd said really stung. As bad as I felt, my mother and I could not just mend our relationship in the space of five minutes; it was going to take a *long* time.

4

2012

Every year since I was young, Gogo would always make such a big deal in the build-up to my birthday as she said it was her 'second birthday of the year'. The house would always get extra loud about a week before my birthday as she would fill it with her atrocious opera singing and pot-banging due to all her weird prototype meals.

To top it off, she always starts suggesting these really strange birthday party ideas. Last year, she asked me if we should put on a speed dating party for myself (and her) for my 17th. So, now that it's the week of my big 18th, I just wanted to be out of the house and away from Gogo because this is the birthday she has been waiting for. Who knew what crazy thing she would try and arrange this year? So, I decided I would study elsewhere after school until my birthday was over.

My favourite restaurant in town was run by an Indian family in my neighbourhood. They served *amazing* home-cooked Indian food and they had the perfect study corner. It was initially created for their three children but, due to their kids' lazy negligence, I managed to take complete ownership of it by the time I was fourteen.

To my surprise, there was a young black girl I had never seen before making her way over from my study corner to the till. She looked no older than fifteen and stared inquisitively at the menu. As I watched her closely, slightly annoyed that she had gone to my study spot, I realised that she was really puzzled by the menu. I could see by the look of hopelessness on her face that she had given up trying to figure it out by herself. She slowly beckoned Mr Singh to come over so that she could find out what she wanted to know.

"Sir, can I ask you what the difference between butter chicken and chicken korma is because on the menu the pictures look exactly the same," she asked him with a puzzled look on her face.

Mr Singh, seemingly taken aback but also a bit offended at her enquiry, remained silent thinking about how he was going to answer the question. However, his wife, Mrs Singh quickly jumped in and whispered to him whilst hitting him with a cloth, "Go and answer the telephone dear!" She probably did that to save them from losing any customers in case he replied rudely to her.

With a smile on her face, she explained that they used different ingredients and bases to cook the food; however, as an excellent businesswoman that she was, she assured her that 'they all taste like heaven' and perhaps she should 'try both of them to see which she prefers.'

As I quietly observed the exchange from my study corner (which I had reclaimed by the way), the girl's response topped off this encounter for me. She said, "Actually, you can never compare anything to heaven as heaven is much nicer and much better than your food. It's an insult to God to say that curry is like heaven."

Mrs Singh's moment of charisma and etiquette quickly turned into a prolonged silence that felt like a brewing volcano of rage. One thing I learnt quickly from Mrs Singh's children is that you should *never* insult her food; it was extremely dear to her heart.

The girl did not even hesitate to continue, showing either an extreme lack of emotional intelligence or just a sheer sense of not caring. "I would happily starve all my life and not taste your food just for a glimpse of heaven. Jesus died for me so I could experience heaven and it certainly doesn't involve curry."

"Well then, perhaps *Mrs Glimpse-of-Heaven*," she replied angrily, "you should leave my shop. Go and starve in heaven and never come back!"

At that point, I realised it must've been a lack of emotional intelligence because she seemed shocked at Mrs Singh's response and left the shop in tears. Poor girl. I felt bad for her but I was also curious as to who she was. I've lived here my whole life and I know those who come and go from here as our town is really small.

In addition, no one in this town ever really spoke about God or went to church; if they had a belief, it was quiet and hidden inside their homes so as not to irritate or offend anyone. In my house, God was rarely ever brought up; I'm sure Mama and Gogo would think I'm insane if I brought God up to them. However, I thought the boldness in her belief was admirable.

When I went home that evening, I couldn't stop thinking about that girl. She really was epic in my opinion. I decided to call her Mrs Glimpse-of-Heaven (Mrs GOF for short) because she was still unnamed in my head. I think what struck me the most about Mrs GOF was that she was sure about the reason for her existence, something that most of us struggle to comprehend. It's like she was living in her own little world whilst the rest of us were extreme realists.

My house reeks of realism from the foundation to the roof—if it's Monday, it's a bad day; if it's Friday, it's a good day. The laws of our house are dictated by realism and I hate it—a girl's gotta dream sometimes!

When I got into Stellenbosch University a few weeks ago, it was a huge sign of hope for me to change the dictates of my family; but, although I could tell Mama and Gogo were happy and proud of me for getting in, I could also tell that in the back of their minds they were bracing themselves for the worst…just as it happened for them.

In a sense, even though I don't believe in the god of any kind of religion, I was amazed by her assurance of life and the hope she had which I didn't have. I wanted that, and I was determined to have that.

***

The next day, I went back to the Singhs' restaurant to see if I could draw on any more information about Mrs GOF and her ideas on the world and life. I struggled to focus all day in school because of Mrs GOF's fanatical wisdom; it seemed to really be doing something to my soul and I wanted to be her friend.

Friendship is something I do not take lightly, but there was really something that drew me to this girl. Even though she seemed so much younger than me, I felt like mentally, she was nearing a middle-aged woman. I could just tell.

As I entered the Singhs' restaurant, I could smell Mrs Singh's delightful chicken biryani being served to some customers and my belly immediately groaned. Sometimes it felt like torture coming here after school because I knew that if I ate Mrs Singh's food, I wouldn't have any room left for Mama's dinner which was a fight I'd had one too many times. Instead, I remembered what I was there for and began to enquire about the young girl I was so interested in.

"Good evening, Mrs Singh. How are you today? And how was your sister's baby shower last week?" I asked so sweetly.

"Hi gorgeous," Mrs Singh replied. "I'm doing fine—very well actually. And the baby shower was wonderful; it's a boy which is what we were hoping for since all the men in that family are so handsome and intelligent! I was actually going to ask if you could help my Sarjan with his upcoming spelling test because his siblings are so busy at the moment."

"Not a problem at all, Mrs Singh—happy to help. I also wanted to ask you a question…if that's okay?" She nodded enthusiastically to my query. "I wanted to know if you know who that young girl was yesterday, the one who rubbed you the wrong way a little bit," I added.

"I'm sorry, dear, you'll have to remind me," she said, seeming puzzled. I knew exactly how to refresh her memory.

"You called her 'Mrs Glimpse-of-Heaven?'" I quoted. As I said those words her expression grew annoyed and full of contempt. Mrs Singh always does this thing when she remembers something that annoys her where she breathes in dramatically and widens her eyes at the exact same time. It was just so funny and predictable; she was like a movie character.

"I spoke with her mother this morning because I thought what she did yesterday was completely out of order and not the way I would expect a young lady of her age to behave. How can you just move into *my* town and come and insult *my* food? Nobody asked you to come and try anything and you just walk in like you own the place. I was not at all amused! Not at all." I had to turn around for like two seconds because I found it so funny; she was literally just going on and on.

"Of course, Mrs Singh; completely unacceptable! Not lady-like. I suppose I should give her some lessons on how to act and behave in this town; do you know where she lives so I can get in contact with her?" I asked, trying to keep the laughter in.

"Good of you, Kaya. Good of you. You were raised properly and you are an example for all the young, indecent girls in this town. She lives opposite the butcher shop by the big park. You can't miss the house as it's not got anything beside it but trees," she concluded, giving me everything I needed and more. Mrs Singh doesn't even know how much I love her—she's just so hilarious honestly.

I didn't waste any time. This was the best time because it's rare for anyone's parents to be home around this hour. I had about an hour before the influx of the town's adults from work.

It's about a fifteen-minute walk up to the butchers from the Singhs' place, and it really did me well to just take in the scenery and the fresh air. It was a walk I didn't usually take which was all the more fascinating.

If I'm honest, the last few weeks have just been really tough on my mind—my 18th birthday coming up, an Induction Day at

Stellenbosch which I feel anxious about, and the fact that I hadn't heard anything from Thato in at least two weeks. I just felt overwhelmed. I wanted to get my mind off myself and just think about something new.

I didn't realise that I hadn't at all thought this through until I actually got to the street of her house. What was I going to say or do? *Hi. I really think you're cool because you laid down some marvellous ideas at the Singh's restaurant yesterday. Let's be friends.* Definitely not. I began to feel like it was such a bad idea and I should have put more thought into it.

Their door was quite extreme in my opinion—they had this hanging sign that said, 'And Whosoever Believes in Him Shall Be Saved.' Obviously, I knew it was a quote that Christians say because it's not like I'd never been to a church with Gogo or Mama but I just thought it was very over the top to hang on a door. Anyway, I rang the doorbell.

Mrs GOF opened the door, squinting her eyes at me for a few seconds or so, clearly wondering who I was and why I had appeared on her doorstep.

She looked different close up—her demeanour was so much more chilled out than I was expecting. Also, I loved her choice of outfit; it was like something you'd expect a 27-year-old woman to wear to a football game date in an American rom-com, if that makes any sense at all.

To avoid any trouble, I thought I would just pretend to live nearby and welcome her to the town.

"Hi. My name is Kaya. Just thought I would stop by and say hello," I exclaimed with a huge grin on my face, hoping it seemed convincing enough.

Much to my surprise, she replied by putting her finger to her mouth and shook her head as if I was late for something. In the seconds following, she motioned for me to be quiet. I mustn't lie, I was so confused. When she signalled for me to come in, I breathed a quiet sigh of relief, realising that she hadn't yet caught me in my hoax to befriend her.

I followed her into the house and, being my typically nosey self, began to look around. The house was nice and simple—not the kind that was boring but in a way that every piece of decoration was well-thought out and immaculate. It certainly smelled great, like scented diffusers and fresh linen.

Immediately, I could tell she had a mother that was the sort to spend four food shopping's worth of money on an expensive diffuser or candle. My favourite part of this place was that it felt like life jumped out of every corner, even though it was so simple. I can't even explain it, it just felt like everything was peaceful and alive—I'd love to have a place like this one day. I also noticed a massive family picture in the hallway—a man, a woman, Mrs GOF and another boy.

"Hey Kaya, I thought I lost you for a sec!" Mrs GOF said as she came and tapped me on the shoulder. "Follow me this way. We're in the living room."

We're? Who's 'we'?! Was someone expecting me? Gosh, if Mrs Singh ratted me out to Mrs GOF's mum, I was going to look like an absolute creep.

I followed her into the living room and, even though I was glad not to find her Mum waiting for me on the couch, I was all the more shocked at what I actually saw—there were like ten people praying and kneeling on her living room floor.

I felt like I had interrupted whatever was going on because they all stopped praying and looked at me. To think that one hour earlier I had this whole exciting plan underway for myself and that just completely failed in an instant.

Feeling embarrassed, I tried to turn around and leave the room, but a man interrupted my plan.

"I think that's actually where we should conclude fellowship for today everyone. I see that there's a young lady here that I believe the Holy Spirit has drawn into our midst; can we all just pray for her quickly before we wrap up in prayer?"

What. Was. Going. On? Was I being initiated into a cult? I wanted to go home immediately.

"Lord, we thank you for the life of this precious soul that you have drawn into your presence. We bless you and we pray that you will fill her up with peace and love as she is welcomed into this family of believers. Amen."

After he said this prayer, everyone said "Amen" in unison. I was completely and utterly shaken.

"Er…yeah, thanks guys. Nice of you to do a prayer to the big G-O-D for me," I muttered nervously.

People began to come up to me one by one as if a loved one of mine had just died, giving me hugs and smiling at me. I just wanted to know what was happening.

"Hi Kaya!" Mrs GOF boomed. "Now, I can give myself a proper introduction. My name is Genesis. I'm 15 and I just moved into this town. Who are you? Do you live around here?" *Ah, that's like the Mrs GOF I knew—up close and personal.* It was weird to think that she actually had a name though. *Genesis. Nice name.*

"Hello. Um, yes. I just stopped by to introduce myself. Not really sure what just happened to me…can you tell me?"

"Yeah, sure. We're not aliens though; no need to be afraid," she giggled.

Hmm.

"My family and I just moved to this town from Pretoria as we felt God calling us to start up a church here."

"But it's a weekday?" I replied, feeling confused.

"Yeah…well, I guess the people who weren't at work are the ones who came," she said, smiling.

"But what about you? Shouldn't you be at school?"

"Yup, but for now, my brother and I are still settling in. I'm going to start first thing on Monday morning," she answered.

"Ah okay, cool." It got a bit awkward after this and we just stared and smiled at each other in silence. She turned around and headed towards the water cooler, but I quickly followed her as I had one more question.

"How did you get these people to come over for your 'fellowship'? I don't know anyone here who goes to church."

"Oh, we posted some flyers through people's doors yesterday and had our first meeting today." She seemed excited by our conversation again. "It's been truly epic! You came literally at the end so you missed the whole thing but today's session was only an hour anyway and I guess we did it at a bit of an awkward time. Hopefully, you can make the longer service on Sunday."

Woah, a lot of information at once. It suddenly felt like I was in a romantic relationship that started this morning and is already becoming a marriage proposal. I regretted the whole thing and just wanted to be at home with Mama and Gogo.

"Oh, nice. Cool…I'm actually gonna go now because I think my family will be expecting me. Thanks for letting me stop by," I waffled.

"Oh, okay. No pressure," she smiled calmly. "Before you go, it would be nice for you to meet my parents. Oh, and my older brother —they're all super friendly," she responded, not really giving me any choice in the matter. I reluctantly followed her as she took me along to meet her parents.

Introducing me to her dad first, my initial thought was that he looked like Kobe Bryant with glasses and a thick grey beard; it was very amusing. "Hello! How are you? I hear your name is Kaya!" he said as he gave me a big fat hug.

"Er…yeah. Great, thank you. Just on my way out actually but thank you for your hospitality—"

"Good evening, young lady!" interrupted a woman I assumed to be Mrs GOF's mother. They literally looked like twins, and she certainly looked like she had spent lots of money on house scents. "So lovely for you to come to our fellowship this evening. It's a shame you couldn't be here from the beginning but we loved having you all the same!"

I could barely get any words out because they were making such a fuss about me for a good five minutes. I just nodded and smiled for the most part until I could finally make my exit.

As I tried to sneak out through the front door, I was pushed aside by a young man carrying water bottles in from his car. I felt like a nuisance even in my desperation to leave.

"Oops, I'm so sorry," he said, not even seeing who he pushed out of the way as he was carrying so much.

"No problem," I replied, frustrated and in much of a hurry to leave. He put the bottles down so he could see who I was, staring at me with the same squint Mrs GOF did when she opened the door.

"Sorry, I realise I'm staring. My sister and I are still waiting for our contact prescription from the opticians in town," he sighed lightheartedly. "My name is Luke; nice to meet you. I'm assuming you're from around here?"

"Yes, I am actually. I'm Kaya. I noticed you were new in town so I just came by to introduce myself. I didn't intend to come to the fellowship actually—I don't believe in anything," I told him, not bothering to lie for the sake of the nice people I'd just met.

"Oh, okay. No pressure," he said, just like his sister. "Hope to see you around though, K. You've got a great smile."

He picked up the bottles and continued with what he was doing before. I liked that he didn't try to put on an act for me. Wow, and he had already given me a nickname!

I decided I kinda liked this family.

5

2012

"*Kaya!*" I heard someone whisper from my bedroom window the next day. I looked at my clock and it was 4.58 am, 2 minutes before my alarm goes off on a weekday. This was certainly annoying because the older you get, the more you realise that 2 minutes of sleep is to be savoured.

I just about managed to get my head off the pillow to look outside and I could see the shadowy silhouette of a tall-ish male with shaggy, curly hair.

Thato.

Sometimes I wonder how I don't get paid for all the stress in the world this boy gives me. Who even comes to someone's window at this time in the morning as if we're in Mission Impossible?

Ever since he dropped out of our high school two years ago, we'd become more distant. He started hanging out with some other people and I got closer to my books. Thato's 'friends' had influenced him to take up a 'job' to do work for some low-level gang members in Cape Town. As frustrated as I was with him, we still tried our best to keep things between us normal and do stuff we loved doing—taking runs, watching films and, sometimes, Knock Down Ginger.

However, he hadn't replied to my texts for two weeks now and I knew he was ignoring me because he was still posting status updates on Facebook and Twitter. It definitely made me angry at first but then, I just tried to ignore it, accepting that he had probably forgotten me for his new friends. It was high time I made friends with some girls anyway.

Waving to him from my window with a very tired and grumpy face, I signalled him to come to the front door. He shook his head and told me to come outside quickly. Feeling fully awake now with panic, I put my slippers and housecoat on and ran outside onto the street.

"Hey friend. Is everything alright? You're worrying me a little with the way you're acting," I expressed worriedly.

"Hey Kaya," he gave me a hug but then struggled to look at me, probably remembering how he had been ignoring me all these weeks. "Sorry I haven't been replying to your texts but I've been really busy with work and the next stuff up and coming for me."

What a rubbish excuse.

"Great. Really happy for you, Thatz," I replied sarcastically. "Why have you come and woken me up like this? Couldn't you have just waited until the afternoon to tell me about all the cool friends you've made?"

"I can't actually stay long, Kaya. My bus leaves in an hour but I knew I had to tell you this in person."

"Tell me what? You're acting so weird."

He looked away from me again. "I'm moving to Mitchell's Plain today; I don't expect you to understand or agree with me but you know I wouldn't lie to you. Please, don't tell my dad or Jenny about what I'm doing if they come and ask you. I just want them to think I've got some casual job somewhere. I'll come back specially for your birthday next week though. Please, don't be angry with me, friend."

I was in complete disbelief and thought he had made the most selfish decision ever—both to himself and to all of us who love him. I knew exactly why he was going and the only destination he was headed was prison, or death.

"You know my opinion on this. I think you are being really, really stupid. You won't come back alive, Thato. You will never see your dad or your little brother again. If this is about your stepmother, then suck it up and learn to get along!" I shouted.

Ryan and Jenny got married five years ago when Thato and I were 12. It was the 10th year anniversary of Thato's mum's death. Ryan stated during his wedding vows, "It is a new beginning with the one I love on the day the one I loved was lost."

From that day on, it created a huge tear in him and his dad's relationship. Thato's dad and stepmother had given birth to Thato's little brother, Charlie, who was now three. However, up until now, Thato hardly ever said a word to Jenny and just about managed a "hello" to his dad when they ran into each other in the house. I felt terrible for what I had said and desperately wanted to make up for it. On the other hand, I kind of meant what I said but felt like it was too late to rephrase.

He stared at me, hurt for a few moments. Thato had never really been the sort to react in the way he was thinking. Concluding that the conversation was over, I walked back inside and went back to bed.

I decided I didn't want to go to school today.

6

2012

If there was any morning to believe in God, it was certainly this morning. I sprinted into the kitchen as I was already late, and grabbed my school bag and a rice cake.

"I'll be home a bit late, Khumalo ladies," I said to Mama and Gogo. "I've got my Induction Day at Stellenbosch."

Just as I'd said it, my stomach felt like it rolled over seven times. After all, I had no idea of what the outcome of the day would be. I also felt guilty for telling Mama and Gogo a half-truth.

"I finish up at the office around six; I'll pick you up if you want from Stellenbosch and we can even practise some driving?" my mum offered.

"I'll be fine. See you later," I replied bluntly. I could see the hurt in her eyes at my rejection. It hurt me a bit too, but I couldn't easily just dismiss her previous actions. There were consequences for being a mother that lies to her child.

***

Last week was my 18th birthday. Thato had promised me a 'birthday blaze' after I'd sincerely apologised by text for saying those horrible things to him. I'd never smoked weed before and I was super nervous, but I felt like I had to do it to make up for the way I spoke to him.

I mean, I know it can't kill you, but I thought about the possible repercussions of my actions. If my family had a history of schizophrenia I could be seeing things in the next few hours. I barely knew anything about my family history; so, all week, I had been checking online statistics about the gene that could cause schizophrenia from smoking weed.

Thankfully, no one was home, so we snuck in through the back window in case the neighbours were spying. Thato also suggested that we went into the bathroom to put a hot shower on so that no one would smell anything when they came home.

"Thato, I'm really not sure about this…I've never really been the *druggie* kind," I said.

"Oh, so *I'm* the druggie kind?"

"No, no! Thato, you know what I mean, I just meant—"

"Live a little, Kaya! All you ever do is study. You can be really boring to hang out with sometimes, you know. All the guys I hang out with can't understand why we're friends; you literally never come out on the weekend, and you act like your mum sometimes. Stop being so regimented."

It was almost as if Thato had been planning that speech for months; it really stung but I guess I deserved it after the things I said to him. I know I've never been that adventurous, but studying was my kind of fun. Anyway, I wanted to prove him otherwise, so I grabbed the blunt and took the first puff.

My chest felt like a boa constrictor had just gripped it, and my lungs felt like they were a living chimney! I could not stop coughing. It made me even more angry when Thato was hysterically laughing.

"The first puff is always the worst. At least you're one of us now!" Thato exclaimed.

I took a few more puffs and then I began to giggle. I giggled more and more until I realised nothing was funny which made me burst out into a complete laughing fit. I was high.

Someone began knocking on the front door midway through my laughing fit.

"Thato, leave now!" I pushed him out of the bathroom window and looked at myself in the mirror to see how sober I looked. Gosh, my eyes were *so* red.

They knocked again and rang the doorbell this time. I started to hyperventilate. Time seemed to have completely slowed down. I walked towards the door as calmly as possible, but I realised that I was twitching.

Knock, knock, knock.

Phew. It was just the postman. It was the usual—Gogo's medical bills and Mama's bank letters. I dropped them on the counter and turned to the fridge to grab some orange juice. As I started opening the bottle, I spilled the whole thing on the kitchen counter, all over the letters. *Great*, that's another predictable lecture coming from my mum about how I need to start taking more responsibility over my hands, or something like that.

It was always about responsibility over something. *Eye-roll.* As I began clearing up the mess I'd made and drying the letters, I saw one more letter addressed to *Kaya Khumalo*. My heart began to race out of my chest. I couldn't tell if it was because I was actually nervous or because I had just smoked marijuana. No one had ever sent me a handwritten letter before.

I went to sit in Gogo's living room chair. I did this every time I needed to think of something serious or solve a Maths equation; it helped me to relax. *OH MY GOSH. What if it was Stellenbosch telling me that they'd made a mistake on my application and they were rejecting me? What would I do with my life? I would simply end up a failure and single mother like Gogo and Mama. It's inevitable…absolutely inevitable.* I thought.

I was trembling as I began to open it. I hated the apprehension of not knowing so I started opening it as quickly as I could.

Phew, not from Stellenbosch.

It read:

Dear Kaya,

I'm sorry yet another year has gone by without me being able to see you. As you know, I never forget your birthday and I will continue sending you letters each year without fail even if you never stop being angry with me. I'm hoping that now you're 18 we can be reunited. I hope you will forgive me and let us build a relationship. I love you, my precious girl.

Happy birthday.

Dad.

As I know? *As I know?*

I rarely ever cry, but for some reason, after reading this letter, I began to cry. It was more than just tears; it was full blown sobbing, and I was crying even more because I was crying. I felt like a big baby. It must have been the drugs.

All these years I was made to believe that my dad hates me and if he truly loved me, he never would have left me. As always, my sadness turned into rage—rage for the one that had always been the biggest liar and manipulator in my life. *My mother*.

Every single time I asked her why he'd abandoned us, she'd told me he was just "the devil in disguise." I had every right to find answers about my bloodline. I could barely even remember what he looked like save a faint memory of his face. I could have brothers and sisters, aunties and uncles, and perhaps, even another grandma. I was so determined, at this point, to find my dad and leave behind the person who didn't have my best interest at heart.

That was exactly what I planned for the day. I would travel into the heart of Cape Town to the IP address I had tracked down of my dad and then head to Stellenbosch from there. Soon, I'd be completely free of my mother.

This will be a fresh start for me, I thought. What she did was truly unforgivable. If she could hide something like this from me then what else was she hiding? I was tired of all the lies and secrets, and if

Gogo also knew, then neither of them deserved for me to be around.

Interlude 1

I see folded laundry. It's too heavy for me. Sometimes, I make it from the laundry room to my bedroom but sometimes things fall out before I even reach the stairs. I frantically run back downstairs to get the things that fell before they get dirty again.

Sometimes, the clothes are so fragrant, like a field full of lilies and jasmine—bursting with all the vibrant colours you can think of. Sometimes, the sheets are damp, discoloured and damaged. I can never seem to get the balance right. Even if there are a thousand good washes, when things are going so well, one comes and destroys everything. The whole washing machine stinks; it needs to be purified.

Then, I see my friend. He always appears when the washing doesn't go my way. He knows me so well; how does he know me so well but I know nothing about him? Yet, he's still my very best friend. He would drop his whole work day to come and help me with my bad loads; yet, I don't even ask him for help, he just knows when to come. He takes my laundry basket and my clothes with ease, dropping nothing, and handling everything with so much care. I ask him if he needs help with anything. He replies, "No, I've got this. I've got you."

He rewashes the bad clothes and makes them new again. I can breathe now as I feel so much better. He's taken my load so now I can rest and refresh. He tells me not to worry about the next batch or any other batches ever again and that he'll always sort my washing out for me. I'm no longer overwhelmed. He's so loving.

What did I do to deserve such a friend like this?

7

2021

At bedtime when I was little, instead of counting sheep, I used to imagine what my life would be like if my white grandfather were around. I imagined him pushing me on the swings at the park or taking me on weekend holidays to big cities such as Johannesburg or Pretoria. I would wonder if he was still alive and if he'd ever tried to look for us.

As I grew older, I began to realise that I was living in a fantasy; he was probably married somewhere with his white wife, his three white children, a nice house and a big garden. His family probably didn't even know about us or the hardship he had caused us. That's when I grew up and stopped wishing for a white hero to come and save my life.

But I can't sit here and act as if I don't play pretend in *some* ways though. I scream about being *unapologetically this* and *unapologetically that* on social media when I know I'm still struggling to believe all of it for myself. But if I don't post this stuff, how else can I keep 800,000 followers happy? That's why they follow me, right? They know social media isn't real life.

However, I'm starting to feel really guilty about telling a half-truth all the time; sometimes I just want to post my bloated stomach or my mouth full of food and not give a care in the world. I know I need to stop caring about what other people think, it's just so difficult; I'm a validation seeker and I know it!

In school, it was always about proving myself to the teachers and my mum. At university, it was my friends and the professors. Now, it's my social media following and all these fake circles. I really hate living like this, but I feel like I've trapped myself in with no escape.

Another example of this is my apartment. If it were up to me, it would be dancing with colour and life—from teal blue walls to African tiled flooring, bursting with life and energy. It would look like a hippie spent the weekend at my place and exploded everywhere. There would be artwork from corner to corner made up of African beauty and history—portraits of animals, landscapes, and people.

Yet, I went and stuck with what the interior designer thought 'would be best for a woman of my age and influence in Johannesburg.' So, we went with the plain, white, modern look—more like a private hospital in my opinion. The only perk is that my furniture is like 99 percent glass and marble—a complete baby danger zone, which gives me a good excuse to stay single and avoid ever becoming a mum.

***

My mornings are always the same: I wake up at 5am, snooze my alarm for another 30 minutes, do a thirty-minute yoga exercise, brush my teeth, take a shower, eat a granola bar and grab a cup of coffee.

My wardrobe is made up of a collection of suits, but only trouser suits. I've never been a skirt or dress kind of girl. I have a suit in literally every colour—orange, blue, green, pink, white, black…you name it. I *never* wear heels either; I love my collection of trainers. Thato is normally always ready and waiting on my doorstep at 7am, constantly energetic, which irritates me because I don't have the mental capacity to get pumped that early in the morning.

However, today is a different kind of morning as I'm home with Gogo and my mum. I still felt bad for being rude to my mum last night but, again, we weren't ready to just rush into mending our relationship that quickly. Also, I was still so tired from my flight yesterday. I decided to get up at my regular routine time as today is Gogo's birthday and I hadn't seen her in months. I still don't think she's realised I'm here yet because she was sound asleep when I got in last night.

On the downside, spending the day with Gogo also meant spending the day with my mum and that, I wasn't looking forward to. My mum and I speak irregularly, mostly when she interrupts me and Gogo's FaceTime calls. She's always so busy with work and all the cases she works on that she never really makes time for me. I understand how busy work gets, especially as I myself run my own business but, the way I see it, you will always find time for the things you love the most; for her, that's her job.

I checked the time. *6.30 am.* That's about the time Gogo usually wakes up, but I felt like being a bit of a menace and giving her a fright first thing in the morning. I creeped up to her room, hoping she wouldn't hear the creaking floorboard that led up to her bedroom, and burst open the door shouting, "HAPPY BIRTHDAY LADY PRISCILLA THADIE KHUMALO!"

I was disappointed to see her staring right back at me with her granny reading glasses on (the ones with chains that hang on the sides) and the most unbothered look on her face.

"You think I didn't know you were going to burst into my room this morning?" she cackled sarcastically.

"Oh, Gogo! You're no fun. How did you know?" I said as her sarcasm completely deflated my mood.

"This generation thinks we were born yesterday, man," she replied, rolling her eyes.

I rolled my eyes back at her and stuck out my tongue, walking over with some presents in my hand to sit with her on the bed.

"Here are your presents, Gogo. Happy birthday," I smiled cheerfully, giving her a big, tight hug.

For the past month, I have been endlessly window shopping to find Gogo some nice things. I just wanted everything to be perfect, as always. I thought about maybe getting all her friends to come round for a birthday surprise, then I realised that she'd pretty much chased away all her friends. Everyone she'd ever tried to build a relationship with believed her views were far too extreme and that she still lived in the past. I feel like she got rid of them purposely though; she's always wanted to belong in her own world.

I had settled for an expensive bottle of perfume, a new case for her iPad and a Prada handbag.

"Seriously, Kaya? Who am I going to show this bag off to in this neighbourhood? It will get jacked off me the minute I step out of the house with it!"

She saw the disappointment in my face as soon as she had insulted the gift, so quickly added, "Although, I guess I can show those nasty old white ladies at my reading club how *successful* my wonderful granddaughter is. Thank you, my dear."

"Anything for you. Now, get your ass to the dining table so we can eat breakfast," I risked saying.

"Imka, just because you're taller than me now does not mean I still won't hit you when you're being cheeky." I dodged her hand as soon as she said that and stuck my tongue out again.

Over the years, Gogo's hatred for white people is what I believed aged her so quickly. For someone about to turn 67, she looked at least five years older. All she does is nag and nag about what they've done to South Africa and all the trouble they've caused us. I get it, a lot of the white settlers that came to this country were racist, but dwelling in bitterness all the time isn't healthy.

I keep telling her to join me with some of my morning *Zen Meditation* exercises but she always responds in the same way: "Kaya, you've barely lived through pain; you could never understand. Let me be a bitter old lady if I want to be!"

I'm mostly used to Gogo's insults and, trust me, I've grown used to taking what she says on the chin because, deep down, she says it out of love. However, it's hard to just sit there and take it when she says I don't know what pain is. When you've lived in a household of silence for most of your life, you become more than aware that there is a lot that has gone unsaid and most of it is unresolved pain.

As a child in a household of two women who don't openly speak about their pain, you somehow become a burden-bearer for what they're going through even if you don't know exactly what it is. Day in and day out, you become familiar with that pain until it becomes a part of you whether you've chosen to carry it or not. I don't even think they realise what I'm carrying on the inside of me. Regardless of the little information I know, I feel what they feel—it's like we all share the same body.

When I look back at what apartheid has done to my country, to my people, I can't even comprehend the pain and anger they must be feeling. Gogo can barely utter a sentence about what apartheid did to her and her family, and, most of the time, I'm too afraid to ask. I've never said it out loud but I know that Gogo hates white people because they kept her apart from the one she loved.

When I was younger, I would sometimes overhear her telling her friends about the man of her dreams that was ripped away from her because their families didn't see eye-to-eye. I didn't need to ask as I knew it must've been my white grandfather. Poor Gogo was completely exiled from her community because my mother was mixed-race. She raised her all by herself, with help from no one at all —the unfortunate yet empowering story of many women around the world.

It's crazy how you become so desensitised to a heartbreaking story because it's been repeated over and over again. I have certainly become desensitised to this story.

"Happy birthday, Umama," my mum said as she kissed Gogo on the cheek. It always feels like the house can breathe when my mum isn't around. It constantly feels like we're walking on eggshells around her because her moods are so unpredictable. I almost forgot that she existed until she came down to join us for breakfast.

"Hey Mum," I could barely make eye contact with her. I don't even know what was making me feel tense around her because we hadn't had an issue in a while. I certainly hadn't made it any less tense by calling her 'Mum' because I knew she hated it. She always loved it when I called her 'Mama', but before I can call her that again, I'd first have to feel the love between us again. It felt like all of our exchanges were formal and lacking intimacy. I wish that things were different but we simply don't understand each other the way Gogo and I do.

She sat down at the dining table and started eating her eggs. I glanced over at her as she ate. Something was different about her—she was still in her pyjamas and she had no make-up on. My mother *always* dressed up, even when nothing was happening.

She was the sort of Mum who would wear red lipstick in the house on the days we were just resting. It was one of her weird coping mechanisms from when she and my dad divorced. Then again, with how little time I spend with her, I guess this may be her new normal.

This time, I *really* stared at her. I watched as she slouched over the table and got crumbs on her dressing gown. Her mind was completely elsewhere, like someone had snatched her sanity.

We sat in silence for a while, it was definitely an awkward silence. We used to have *so* much to talk about around this dinner table. We would talk about the movies we loved, the countries we wanted to travel to, and our favourite childhood memories. Sometimes, we would even have conspiracy-theory debates about whether Nelson Mandela was secretly a white man or whether the government wanted to kill off the world's growing population, but all of that seemed to have died now.

I couldn't even remember the last time I sat at this dinner table with my family; it was such a rare occasion these days. Every short trip I take to see Gogo happens during the times my mum would be at work. I know I'm a bad daughter but, at the same time, I feel like I can't savour a relationship I feel has already been lost. I mean, what's the point? She never tells me anything about her past. She doesn't trust me, especially not after all the stunts I pulled when I was 18. For my own sake, though, I couldn't continue to sit here in awkwardness.

"Mum, how's work and the case you've been working on?" She faintly nodded, but she didn't seem to want to reply so I tried to go on further. "Gogo told me some bits and pieces about it and has been telling me that it's been dragging on for months now. Heck, by the time you get it finished, the convict may have managed to escape!"

My attempts at jokes have always been really lame but, this time, my mum started laughing. Gogo and I were so surprised that we exchanged a look and joined in. For a split second, I felt like we were a real family again.

However, the laughter then continued for a lot longer than it should have. Gogo and I slowly stopped laughing but my mum was laughing more and more; she looked sort of demonic actually.

"Mum?" I whispered. She couldn't hear me as she continued to laugh and laugh. I ran round the table and spoke firmly this time, "Mama. Stop this. Please!" I was surprised I called her 'Mama' again but I needed her to hear me because she was scaring me.

It's only as I got close to her that I realised tears had been streaming down her face this whole time. I hugged her tightly and just hoped that she would stop. I could feel her pain; I've always been able to feel it.

"Please, Mama, you're scaring me." At this point, she began to get quieter and just kept her arms wrapped around me. I haven't felt my mother hold me since I was a little girl; I felt like a little girl again now. I forgot about the worries of life, my fears and my realities. *No. I don't need to show vulnerability to her, or to anyone for that matter*, I thought. I pulled back instantly.

I helped her onto the couch and put a pillow under her head. She just continued to stare into space. She looked…older. I knew something was really wrong but, for some reason, I just didn't have the willpower to ask. I knew that Gogo had sensed it for some time too.

Sometimes I just look at my mum and see so much of her in myself. Although we don't speak about it, I know we've never seemed to understand our place in this world. With her being half-black and half-white, and myself being half-coloured and half-mixed, we don't seem to fit in anywhere.

We are too white for the blacks and too black for the whites. Our hair isn't quite puffy enough to call it an afro and not droopy enough to call it straight. The black community hates us because they see us as having 'light-skin privilege', and the white community hates us because they see us as contaminated objects. I sat there and watched her for hours; I don't think she even knew I was sitting right opposite her.

"I'm going to bed, Ma. I'm getting really tired. I probably won't see you in the morning as I'm heading out early to a spa with Gogo. Goodnight."

"I can't do the case, Kaya. I just can't do it…" I was so startled by her response as I had no idea she could hear me through her breakdown. I was silent for a moment, partly because I was still in shock but also because I didn't know what to say.

"Mum, you're the best lawyer I know here, even though I only know about three lawyers," I chuckled. "You're going to smash the case like you always do. He needs a woman like you to send him away for years. He raped his own child, he can't get away with that."

"No, Kaya, you don't understand. How am I supposed to deal with a family rape case when I couldn't even deal with my own?" She looked away from me immediately after she'd said this, afraid of what my response was going to be.

What did she mean when she said she "*…couldn't even deal with her own?*" My mind went blank. I couldn't breathe. I had to grab onto my hands because they wouldn't stop trembling. My heart was racing. I wanted to say something but no words were coming out. Who raped my mother? Was it a friend? A cousin? Was it a long lost uncle?

I finally managed to get a few words out.

"Wh-what happened, Ma?" I muttered.

She sat up and turned towards me, holding onto my trembling hands. I met her gaze for the first time in God knows how long. I realised I hadn't looked at her properly in such a long time because I'd forgotten how her chestnut-brown eyes shaped her face. They carried such an elegance and grace that I was not fortunate enough to inherit and, at this moment, it was the only thing that could comfort my unease.

2012

Stepping onto Cape Town soil was certainly different from the way I expected it to be—everyone appeared much friendlier than I had assumed. I think all the Sollywood movies had gotten into my head because they really portrayed people here to act way different. I imagined I'd have to put a brave Don't Talk To Me face on as soon as I got here in case someone tried to take advantage of me.

The greenery was lovely (although, biased, I still thought the greenery in my town was nicer), and the atmosphere just felt generally quite alive and upbeat. However, the only thing I found really weird and felt unfamiliar with was the people rushing around in different directions. There were stall-sellers shouting everywhere, kids running on the road, and—the only part I hated so far—men catcalling me in every direction. Sollywood *definitely* got that part right.

I couldn't remember the last time I'd been to Cape Town, or if I'd ever even come here before; not that I could remember. Gogo and Mama were not really fans of going too far away from home so we mostly did everything we needed to do in our town or towns close by.

As I thought about this, I realised just how unfamiliar these settings were to me. I felt so far away from my comfort zone. Fear began to take its grasp on me. The smartest thing I could think to do at this point was to refuse to ask anyone for directions even though I didn't really know my bearings. What if all those Sollywood movies were true and I shouldn't be around this place by myself? The fear of being robbed or kidnapped suddenly overwhelmed me. I kept my head down and tried not to draw any attention to myself as I could tell that I looked like an outsider.

I followed the map that led me deeper into the city and came nearer and nearer to the destination I'd found on the internet a few days earlier. After about an hour, I arrived at the location I'd circled on my map, but it didn't look how I expected it to look…at all.

I looked around at the rundown flats, the stray dogs and the sewage in the streets and concluded that I must've been in the wrong location. This place was called Bishop Lavis; there was no way that this neighbourhood could have that name.

Feeling even more nervous about being robbed or kidnapped than I did an hour ago, I looked around for a safe place where I could ask for directions. I searched around for a few minutes and saw a sign on a shop door that said it was a local bakery.

I don't think I'll be getting robbed or kidnapped here, I thought.

The smell of sewage pipes was rampant; it hit me right in the face, although when I got closer to the bakery, it was mixed with the smell of fresh bread which really confused and overwhelmed my nose. It was a sensory overload.

I followed the smell and peered my head in through the door to see if anyone was around. I couldn't see anyone in the front room but I could see a back room with a bunch of young children in. Why weren't they at school?

Suddenly, a very round and plump lady came right in front of me and blocked my view. "Why are you nosing around my shop, little girl?" she thundered.

"Oh, g-good morning, Ma'am. Sorry, I was just having a look to see if anyone was around," I stuttered like a little chicken. I felt like I was about to wet myself.

"Yeah, I'm around. What do you want?" she shouted.

"I-I was just wondering if you know where Bishop Lavis is?" I asked.

She finally relaxed, realising that I was not trying to do anything dodgy but just came to ask for help.

"Yes. This is it," she replied inexpressibly, all her anger disappearing. As she calmed down, I finally took a brave look at her face. To my shock, her four front teeth were missing and it looked pretty scary. What was that all about?

"Thank you for your help. Lovely shop," I lied.

I walked out immediately with a really strange feeling in my stomach. *This is it?* This was where my father lived? I didn't know how to react. Maybe it was one of those neighbourhoods where there was a nice side? I wanted to believe that anyway.

The name *Bishop Lavis* gave me this picture in my head that I was going to go to a place with lots of trees, parks, and the smell of fresh flowers. I don't know why I didn't do an image search. *Should I just leave?* I questioned.

I found a lady selling water on the side of the road. In the scorching heat, I felt I needed to have a rest and drink some water. This place was really hot, so much hotter than I was used to as I usually made sure to stay out of the heat during the day. After buying the water, I lay down on an open patch of grass and put my sunshades on to relax. I was too exhausted to be afraid of this environment anymore.

"Up you get, young lady! Don't just lay out here like this or you'll get yourself in some trouble. It's not Disneyland you know; these are the Cape Flats!" a woman said, looking left and right frantically as though someone was watching me. I looked at her face a bit more closely amid my shock. She seemed to be in her mid-thirties but I couldn't get the best look as she grabbed me, pushed me round the corner and dragged me by the arm into her house. My heart was certainly racing because I had no idea what she was talking about.

"Get off me!" I screeched. "I'll call the police on you!"

"Shush!" she whispered. "Don't even think about mentioning the word 'police' around here or they could *off* you any moment."

The fear came back to me again. I had to sit on the floor to stop myself from shaking so much, feeling overwhelmed with everything happening.

"I'm sorry; I didn't mean to scare you, sweetie. I could just tell you're not from around here. A girl of your sort shouldn't be lounging around outside like that," she said under her breath. "This is gang turf."

A girl of my sort? Gang Turf?

Oh. My. Gosh. I suddenly remembered that she said this was the Cape Flats. *How did I come to the Cape Flats and not realise it?!* I'm a straight-A student with a full scholarship from Stellenbosch managing to track down my long lost father and didn't realise I was in the *Cape Flats?* I felt so stupid and actually downright foolish.

"Right. Okay. It's okay, Kaya. Don't panic. You got this," I said over and over to myself, pacing up and down. I certainly felt the meaning of my name leave me at this point. Restful place? More like *stressful* place!

After a few minutes, I calmed down and sat on her sofa. I could tell she was just waiting for me to stop being a little princess and just explain to her what I was doing here.

"Sorry for all the fuss. I *clearly* didn't do my research properly before coming here," I stated bluntly with a slight attitude.

"And what exactly *are* you doing here?" she said with a concern in her voice that reminded me of Mama.

I thought about telling her the truth but then quickly reminded myself that I was in the Cape Flats and didn't know if I could trust her.

"Erm…er…I just came to look for student housing." Seriously, Kaya? What a terrible lie! Who looks for student housing in the ghetto?

She sighed and went into the kitchen. I had no idea what her sigh meant and it made me feel even more anxious. Why was I even here? She could've tricked me.

After a few minutes, during which I was greatly conflicted about whether I should leave or stay, she came back out with tea and biscuits.

"Kaya, my dear—" she began.

"How do you know my name?" I interrupted, suspecting her even more now.

"Because you said it out loud about a hundred times ten minutes ago when you were panicking for the whole neighbourhood to hear," she chuckled.

"Oh, right. Yeah. Sorry for interrupting you."

"It's okay. Look, I don't mean to be rude, but what are you doing here?"

Gosh. She was *just* like Mama. I don't know how she did it. They both had this way of making you feel so comfortably-uncomfortable that I have no choice but to cry and tell them the truth.

I blurted out in blubbery ten-year-old Kaya tears; the kind that only Mama could bring out of me. It was strange because, although I was much closer to Gogo, it was only Mama I truly felt this level of safety around when it came to my tears.

"I-I c-came t-to find my d-dad but I don't even know where he is or what he looks like or if he's alive or dead or knows about me or —"

"Okay, okay, Kaya. Calm down, my love." She gave me such a warm and gentle hug, just like Mama would do when I was younger. At that moment, I didn't know why I had made such a rash decision, but I felt safe. "Everyone knows someone who knows someone here so I'm sure we'll find him," she replied comfortingly.

Without saying anything else so that I didn't cry, I slowly brought out the birthday letter that was addressed to me. On the back, it said '*Roger Holden*' which is my dad's name.

I watched her face as she took the letter from me, ensuring she was delicate with the only part of my dad I had. Her face went from curiosity to sadness, which I thought was strange because she hadn't even opened the letter yet. Why was she holding onto it? The way she was acting was making me feel suspicious and nervous again.

As she looked up and down at the letter and at me, I realised I didn't even know her name or who she was; so, for my own safety, I gathered my things to go.

"No! Kaya, wait. Don't go, please." Immediately, tears just started coming out of her eyes. What had gotten into her? It wasn't even that dramatic of a sob story.

"I need to get going," I said as I paced towards the door frantically.

"Just give me five minutes to explain," she said, blocking the door.

"I don't know you. Please, move out of the way so I can go," I pleaded, trying to move her out of the way.

I finally managed to push my way past her and walked out of her house, ready to forget that I ever stupidly came here.

"I know Roger!" she shouted at me as I speed-walked down the road.

I turned back slowly. She could have been lying just so she could get what she needed out of me. Maybe she wanted to steal my bag or sell me to someone in the neighbourhood; who knows? But something in me told me to go back.

Just five minutes and counting, I thought to myself, annoyed.

I sat down frustratedly again on her couch, slightly embarrassed at the tussle we'd just had. I reminded myself that just because I had turned 18, it didn't mean I would grow up overnight. I was certainly still childish in some ways and my current sulkiness proved just that.

It seemed as if she was clearing her throat for the whole five minutes before she even spoke. I felt like I was going to lose it. She was really annoying me.

"Do you believe in God, or maybe even destiny?" she asked me.

My mind flashed to Mrs GOF and I laughed briefly but put my straight face right back on so that she didn't get the message that I wanted to be there. It was actually the perfect time for her to ask me because I was thinking about this on the whole bus journey here.

"Good question. I don't know if I believe in God but I think I can consider destiny being aligned by something," I considered.

"Well, *now*, I definitely do." She started crying again but, this time, I felt too bad not to comfort her so I patted her back lightly.

"Your dad has missed you so much, Kaya. So much," she sobbed.

How does she know my dad?

"Sorry, I don't mean to be rude, but who are you?" I said, standing up abruptly. "And how do you know my dad?"

She hesitated again for another few seconds, going through the clearing throat episode again.

"Don't you remember me, Kaya? I'm your dad's sister, Aunty Andrea."

Aunty Andrea. I knew that name. I had only two teddy bears in my room; one from Mama, and one from someone called Aunty Andrea.

8

2021

I couldn't sleep. I tried for hours to distract myself by watching YouTube videos, replying to comments and making a new exercise schedule, but I simply needed to know what had happened to my mum. For the first time in my life, I could say I actually felt terrified.

I decided to go to the bathroom to floss my teeth and wax my eyebrows as there was this really good dental floss Gogo had which she annoyingly *still* wouldn't tell me where she got it from. Whenever I come home, she removes all the labels so I can't search it up online. It was a hobby of hers to annoy me in these ways.

I paced up and down for a while and then sat on the toilet seat, still trying to figure out some more about what had happened to my mother. Maybe it was that 'cool' uncle that we used to visit during Christmas sometimes; but, then again, he and my mum were still friends so it couldn't be him. We literally were never around men in my childhood so I still had no clue as to who it could've been.

I looked up above the bathroom cabinet and saw my purple childhood photo album which I hadn't looked at in ages. I opened each page carefully, starting at the beginning which was the day of my birth—7th April 1994. I was so cute and I don't even say that to be vain. I was a really cute child all the way through.

It's so strange to see how I was born with blondish hair and bright green-blue eyes. I held the baby photo in the mirror and compared how those bleach blonde curls had turned fawn brown with a few golden highlights, and how my eyes were now hazel-brown with a slight tint of green. Cuteness factor is still the same but just different (so I tell myself).

I continued to flick through the years, smiling and adoring myself for a little while longer until I remembered the situation with my mum and became stressed again.

I went into the living room and sat in Gogo's chair, the chair that helped me think when I was stressed, but no thoughts came. I looked over at the old grandfather clock and remembered the days my mum and I would dance and sing to Celine Dion's songs and I'd secretly sip her wine as she closed her eyes to the song hook. Right now, I miss those days. I certainly felt odd—as though someone had fed me a strange alien recipe and then said goodbye without explaining what I'd eaten. I just needed to know who abused my mother then I would feel okay.

"Kaya, what are you still doing awake, honey?" my mum said, much to my surprise as she entered the room, clearly not able to sleep either. She looked like she'd been distressed for days. Gogo's birthday dinner was probably an explosion from a long and overwhelming build-up. I felt so bad for her, and I felt worse that no one seemed to realise it.

"Please, sit with me, Mum. I just need to know that you're okay," I pleaded.

"Thank you for checking on me, darling, but I'm really okay," she said with the fakest and most airy smile. She had her make-up on again so I knew she was back to her typical facade of being the perfect mother and home-maker.

"Please, Mama." She looked me straight in the eyes as I called her again by the name I hadn't used in nearly ten years, her eyes softening immediately. I, too, was shocked, but it just came right out…just like at the dinner table. But I needed her to be the mother I remembered her to be at this moment.

She took her time to come and join me; first procrastinating and dilly-dallying in the kitchen, pretending that she had things to do and sort out, but I knew she was just trying to gather her thoughts together. It's a bad habit I've also picked up from her—when I'm faced with confrontation, I put it off until the very last moment.

At last, she came to join me in the front room with some popcorn and a glass of wine in her hand. This combination may sound strange to most people, but it was definitely a huge coping mechanism for the Khumalo ladies.

When I was a little girl, if I came into the living room and saw my mother and Gogo with these two things in their hands, I knew not to even *dare* be a nuisance towards them.

"How's work?" she queried.

"Yeah, fine. Thanks. All good. But, Mama how are you—"

"Why do you keep lying to me about what you do?"

Woah. I was not expecting that. If this was about to be an interrogation session then I certainly didn't have the energy for it right now. I was about to come back with the same energy of bluntness but I remembered that this really wasn't the time for that.

"Why would you think I'm lying, Mum?"

"Exactly because of just that, Ingane—you just switched from calling me 'Mama' to 'Mum' again which is exactly what you've been doing to keep me from the truth of your life. Ever since you were 18 and started to keep things from me, you started calling me that. Or you thought I wouldn't notice?" Her voice was getting louder and louder with every single sentence, or maybe it was just getting harsher, I couldn't completely tell. All I knew was that I absolutely hated this.

"Why are you asking me this all of a sudden, Mum? We're here to talk about *you*, remember? This is not about me right now. Maybe you should put the alcohol down. That's enough," I responded, feeling extremely attacked. I tried to grab the bottle from her but she snatched it right back.

"How can you expect me to tell you about what happened to me when you've kept me in the dark about your whole life? I barely even hear from you these days; the most I hear about you is from the girls in this town stalking your Instagram page and asking me if I'm your mother! This so-called daughter of mine that ran away at 18 and started living with the man who treated me like crap throughout our whole marriage. How can you expect me to tell you anything, Kaya?"

Now I was really angry.

"Are you serious, Mum? You really want to know why I don't tell you anything? Because *your daughter* learnt all of this secretive behaviour from her own birth mother who lied to her about just about everything in her whole life. The apple *really* doesn't fall far from the tree Nandi Khumalo! At least, Dad never lied to me, and, for that, I respect him so much more than I will ever respect you!" She slapped me, hard.

I broke down in tears on the floor. Why couldn't anyone in this household understand that I'm the one that has suffered the most for their pain? It's always the children that have to deal with the consequences and it's like no one has even realised that Kaya Khumalo has ever been the least bit troubled by their problems?

I looked back up at her when I managed to calm down a bit to see if she had even the slightest amount of remorse in her eyes, but all I could see was bitterness and contempt towards me, her only child. It's like she had been waiting for this moment since the day I ran away at 18. I felt like an orphan then and I still feel like an orphan now.

I decided I needed to leave now, and this would be the last time I was going to see my mother for a long time.

2012

"You look just like him," this lady who claimed to be my aunty said.

Neither of us really knew what to say after this; we just sat in silence and pretended to sip our tea. Of course, I had so many questions but, for some reason, it just didn't feel right to ask them at this point.

"Can we go and sit out the back?" I asked. I had been staring at the mango tree I could see through the back window for some time now. I wanted to just be out in the open so I could be distracted by nature.

We walked into the garden, taking some chairs with us, and took shade by the mango tree, the air definitely feeling thickened by our silence.

"Where is he?" I said, finally. I could tell she was so relieved that she'd finally gotten a response out of me.

"He's on a short business trip out of town until tomorrow night. Sorry, I know that's who you came to see but I'm so glad you're here. You should stay till he's back. You're more than welcome, honey."

I certainly thought about it, but I also thought about my Induction Day at Stellenbosch. It would be stupid of me to miss it just so my dad could come back from his business trip to his uninvited daughter that he might not want to see. I started thinking about how angry Mama and Gogo would be if they found out I came to look for my dad *and* missed the Induction Day. I began to feel scared and realised what a risk it was for me to do this today. I think they would actually disown me.

"Ah, thank you, but I've actually got somewhere to be soon. It was kind of you to offer." It went silent again, I didn't even understand why this was so dramatic and awkward. I felt like we were in a really tacky housewives' drama.

I thought it would be nice to ask her one last question before I left, just in case I'd never get a chance to see my dad.

"Why did he leave me and my mum?" I could barely look at her as I asked this. I was so scared of what she might say.

Her eyes widened and she took a huge deep breath in. Instead of replying, she took our plates and cups to the kitchen so that she could think of the response she was going to give me.

She reappeared with something in her hands; although, this time, without tea and biscuits. She sat down and handed me some files.

I opened up the A4 envelope with the handwriting that I could now recognise as my father's, and delicately pulled out a bunch of beautifully crisp film photos which barely looked touched or handled.

"These were supposed to be for your father to show you, but I think it's important that you have them before you go just in case he doesn't get a chance to see you. They've never been touched," she said, holding back tears.

I picked up the first photo—it was me…and my dad. He looked *just* like me, or I guess I looked just like him. It was actually scary.

"Aunty Andrea, we are literally twins! How didn't you notice when you were telling me off on the grass?" I stressed. "Come on, it must have been so obvious!" It was kind of irritating.

"Good question. I don't even know, but I can tell you this one thing: after living in the Cape Flats for 20 odd years, you learn that registering the face of someone you don't know can be dangerous, so I guess we just learn to brush these things. I'm glad God shielded my eyes at that moment, though, because this has been such a beautiful unfolding."

I stayed there, staring at the photos for another few minutes.

I looked at my watch and realised I needed to get going. "Well, thank you for inviting me into your home and for making me feel welcome."

"Kaya, you're always, always welcome. I hope you come back to see your dad," she smiled tearfully.

And with that, I said my goodbyes and hugged her and left.

On my way to Stellenbosch, I felt a huge feeling of disappointment continuing to well up inside me. I was so close to meeting my father yet I still didn't get the chance; it just felt inevitable. I thought over and over again about whether I should go back and meet him but I just kept thinking about him seeing me face to face and not wanting anything to do with me.

I kept one of the film photos with me and simply could not stop looking at how alike we looked—we were quite literally carbon copies of each other. He even had the same colour of eyes as me, and, although the picture was slightly faded, I felt like I could faintly see that he had the same green tinted streak in his left eye. I decided I couldn't make the decision for myself so I would have to rely on a good old coin. Heads and I would go back, tails and I would never return.

Heads. I guess I'm going back.

9

2021

"Ingane, where are you going at this time of the night?" I heard Gogo shout from the porch as I tried to book my taxi to the airport.

I felt so terrible; I had come all the way here for Gogo's birthday only to leave abruptly without saying goodbye. I was planning to leave her a super detailed text message and a promised flight for her to come and see me in Johannesburg the following week to make up for such dramatic affairs my mum and I had just had, but I felt so bad just walking away.

Walking back towards her, hoping she couldn't see my puffy eyes or the still red and fresh mark on my face, I made up a silly excuse.

"Hey Gogo. Sorry, I've just got to run back to Joburg as we have some new producers coming to one of my clubs for a meeting. I was thinking you could come over to mine next weekend though?"

"Tut-tut, no need to lie, Ingane. I know this is because of all that ongoing drama you and your mother have been having. Don't worry, I'm not going to push you to talk about it," she reassured me, and I breathed a huge sigh of relief. "However, I won't be able to come to Johannesburg anytime soon because the doctors have said my blood pressure has gotten worse."

"Gogo! Come on, I told you to stop keeping your medical reports from me. I need to know these things."

"Yeah, yeah, I know I should've told you. But, in my defence, why would I tell you when instead of paying for my medical bills you buy me Prada bags that I don't need? It's like you're saying 'Gogo, even if you die, please die pretty!'" We both cracked up with laughter. Gogo always had a way of making the most serious things funny, especially when it had anything to do with her health or death. I really didn't want to leave Gogo like this but I also didn't feel like I could bear to see my mother right now.

"I know you two must have had a bad riff today but I don't want you to leave until we've at least had a good catch-up. Your mother is in bed now and absolutely sound asleep. Come in for an hour?" Gogo pleaded. I gave in and followed her back into the house, still trying to hide the mark on my face from her in shame.

We sat down and just took in the atmosphere for a few minutes. I always felt so comforted in the company of Gogo, whether silent or not.

"Have I ever told you about when I was a little girl?" Gogo asked me intently.

"What a random question, Gogo, but no, I don't think so. I guess I remember you mentioning once that your father was an English teacher or something and that's why your English is so good. That's all I remember though."

"Hmm, that's good. Now, we have something *real* to talk about other than your healthy eating stuff and your exercise nonsense," she snorted.

"Eh! It's not nonsense; it's called *enlightenment*," I defended.

"Enlightenment? I grew up knowing people like Mandela and Biko and you want to talk to me about enlightenment? Oh, God save your soul," Gogo cackled.

"Blah blah blah," I whined childishly. "Now can we get to your story?"

"Are you sure you're ready? It'll make you cry, I must warn you."

"WAIT! Let me go get the wine and the popcorn," I said as I quickly ran to the kitchen and grabbed the glasses, the wine and the popcorn.

"Okay, ready now Gogo."

1970
Priscilla Khumalo

The day my father was fired, I realised he had lost so much hope in his eyes for freedom. The voice he'd found seven years prior became muted by the realities of injustice. Martin Luther King Jr's big American speech in 1963 set my father's heart on fire. However, as hopeful as he was, he knew deep down that something would eventually extinguish his flame.

At the end of the speech, barely breathing a word to Umama, myself or my baby brother, he ran down to the local bar with glimmers of hope safely tucked behind his belt, ready to be unleashed to those who were ready to embrace the severe lashings for a future of freedom.

Back then, drinking was a complete choice for Ubaba, saved for occasions like these where each sip added to his already full excitement. He scanned the bar to find those men who shared his feelings of hope, because, although everyone was outwardly cheering for King, by the time he had reached the bar, only a few had been set apart by fire.

Once a week, my father invited these men to our home, which at first were just "...casual meetings, my darling. Nothing at all to worry about."

So, on a Friday evening, Umama and I would prepare rice and beans for the men with homemade mango juice to accompany their filling meal. My favourite was Uncle Fredrick; he would always do a magic trick and make sweets and chocolate appear behind my ears when he came through the door. It was always the same pattern with the men—the small talk would go on for a good fifteen to twenty minutes after their meal as they didn't want to digest their good food with bitter talks of injustice. They often had well-rehearsed small talk, usually about women, "Ah, I'm sure you're getting better fed than the poison my wife feeds me!"

During the small talk, one of the men would always get tired of their filthy talk of women (not that they would think it was filthy), and rage about something he'd seen that week.

Finally, when they decided to get into the real meeting, the first thing they'd do was look around the room in case an intruder had stepped into the meeting. Then when the coast was clear, usually it would begin along the lines of, "This week, I heard of another brutal killing in the centre of Joburg the other day as one of the blacks were where they shouldn't have been. We need to stand up like our fellow brothers Mandela and Tambo. This could have been one of our sons who was killed in cold blood. I suggest we start making allies across our part of town until we reach the whites. After that, we strike."

Someone would respond, "Brother, I would love to do that and my heart truly wants to, but I just think it is too dangerous. We should wait a while longer until the ANC are able to gain more power politically."

My father, with his flame still undefeated, would then rally the men together, reminding them of their unity and the rewards of their self-sacrifice. "My brothers, let's not fight or disagree on these matters. We are all here for the same reason. After King's speech, I had hope for my young children and even greater hope for South Africa. We are not here to destroy the white people. For, although what they did was wrong, they are here now and we must live in peace and harmony *together*. I agree, we should have the courage of our brothers Mandela and Tambo, so let's win this fight the right way. Time is our friend."

His smile at the end of his weekly speech would leave the men with a sense of pride for a country that had never been fair to them. It was admirable. They were encouraged to do things the 'right' way because of Ubaba's highly convincing way with words, he was truly gifted—the most talented English teacher I knew.

The men continued to silently make friends with people who had the same vision of justice, some were even extended members of the

ANC. Each Friday they would share the small progresses they made within their workplaces, churches and neighbourhoods. Everything continued to run smoothly, and my dad's glimmer of hope shined brighter and brighter each and every day.

On this particular Friday, my mother was not feeling too well and came down with her yearly case of what seemed to be a flu. Then, it was not a huge problem as Ubaba's salary was the main thing that kept us fed. Although she was recovering well, I didn't want her to use up all her strength cooking for the men who would come a couple of hours later. I was only nine, but I knew how to make the rice and beans with my eyes closed because of the countless times I had done it with Umama. Also, I knew that I would get an extra treat from Uncle Fredrick when he came through our door because of my due diligence.

As I set the table and brought the food and juice over, each man entered one by one through the door—something I found to be strange due to the normally erratic arrival times of the men. My father was the last through the door, with his head hanging low. This would be the first time I saw a sense of hope drift away from his eyes.

As they came in, I wondered why only five of the six seats from my father's so closely knit brotherhood were filled. They didn't speak for a long while and I just kept waiting there because I was hoping for my expectant treat when Uncle Fredrick came through the door.

Finally, the silence broke.

"So what are we going to do about it?" one of the men said. "They killed him, they killed him!"

Who? I thought.

"Priscilla, please go to your room, my dear," Ubaba told me solemnly.

I knew that this was a delicate moment so I didn't bother to object. Instead, I hid behind the kitchen door and listened to my father's friends.

"We do nothing," Ubaba replied.

"We do *nothing*. We do *nothing* Bonga Khumalo? Hmm? This is the same *nothing* bull-crap that all of us actually listened to you with. The same 'nothing' that just got our friend killed because we listened to you and made friends with the enemy?" One of the uncles returned. "You know what Bonga, you can continue to fight for this so-called 'freedom' in your fantasy land but for those who are with me on the true fight, I'll be taking a stand in inner Cape Town on Monday." With that, he left.

My father didn't say a word, I could sense his head falling lower and lower to the ground. His empire was crushed.

I heard the rest of the men rise to their feet as the chairs scraped the old wooden floorboards. From the quiet whispers and the slow pace in which they left the front door, I could tell that they were grieving for my father's disappointment.

As I reopened the kitchen door, not only did I see Ubaba cry for the first time, but I also realised that the white-skinned people had taken one of my dearest friends. I didn't know at the time, but this was just one of the first reasons I grew to hate them in the end.

Ubaba and I shared a moment of silence over our beloved Fredrick as we tidied away the completely untouched food I had sweated and toiled over.

Most weeks after were like this for my father; however, I still felt there was some hope left inside his eyes for a freedom he knew was to come.

On the final Friday of hope for my father, one of his friend's walked through the door at the time of what used to be their weekly Friday meetings. This brother seemed absolutely frantic and sick with worry.

"Eh, eh. My brother, what is the matter?" my father asked in a panic. I could tell that, although Ubaba was in a fret due to his friend's sudden appearance, he felt relieved that one of his friends had still honoured his existence.

"They've got us in so much trouble man, I'm really worried. I told them not to do it but they did it anyway," his friend replied.

"What have they done?" Ubaba responded.

For me, the most fascinating thing was that my father knew exactly *who* his friend was talking about, something that clearly comes with knowing your friends inside and out.

"Well, after they left the meeting all those months ago when Fredrick was murdered, they would gather and plot evil, *evil* things against the whites. After the first two meetings, I didn't come back because I was so traumatised about the things they were planning to do."

Midway through, I could see how betrayed my father felt at the thought of his friends holding meetings without him. "Just over an hour ago, my wife came to me and told me that the wives of our friends were all in tears—their husbands were arrested."

My father repeated the same question, "*What have they done?*"

"Bonga. They raped and killed the teenage daughters of those white men that killed Fredrick."

That was the first time I'd ever heard the word *rape*.

My father was absolutely distraught. I think he was more distraught because he blamed himself for making friends with such hateful, blood-thirsty people, people he had once referred to as his brothers.

My father's friends became the complete talk of the town and, although my father was guilty of nothing, to the outside world he was guilty of everything. Secretly, most people in our town were happy about what they did to those girls. However, the school my father worked for was completely disgusted. They saw the faces of the children they taught and were reminded of the brutal acts my father's friends committed. Knowing that they were his friends, they asked him to leave.

"What's the point in fighting for freedom, eh? What. Is. The. Point? If it's my own people that have pushed me out of my job when I'm fighting for their children then what hope do we have for this country? They've stripped me of my manhood. Everybody in this town has turned against me. How am I supposed to get a job now, eh?" His voice was cracking after every sentence. My mother didn't even have the words for him because, at the back of her mind, all she could think of was how the pain in her hands, knees and back were about to worsen because of the further shifts she would have to put in to provide for our family.

My father then did what he didn't know he was about to start doing best. Instead of picking up a pen, he picked up a bottle of beer.

2021

"Woah, Gogz. This is really deep, I'm loving it though." My eyes and ears were so set on every word that had just come out of her mouth, I kind of wished I made a voice memo and made it into a podcast; people would love this.

"Very deep, my darling. Although, this is truly only the beginning. Are you sure you want me to go on with the rest? The teenage years are where it became really complicated," Gogo stressed.

"Very sure and very ready. This is when you had Mum, right? I wanna hear all about it and don't miss out any of the details! Can I record this?"

"No!" she snapped instantly. "This is not at all for anyone to hear or know. I'm telling you this because I think you deserve to know. If I find out you've recorded this, Kaya…"

"Sorry, I won't. I really won't; I didn't know."

"Okay. Here it goes…" she exhaled.

1970

Priscilla Khumalo

Who created race anyway? I thought to myself in one of my spring Mathematics classes. I thought race was a really stupid idea, created by even stupider people. How could you just look at people and think, *yeah, these ones are special; or no, these ones aren't so special?* It's dumb and stupid, and I don't just say that because I am on the receiving end of it; I'm saying so because it's not even *logical*. The white people think I'm ugly, the coloured people think I'm ugly, and some of the black people think I'm ugly all because I have a darker shade? Nice!

As my Science teacher began speaking to us about politics instead of photosynthesis (since every teacher thinks they're Steve Biko these days), I began thinking of the summer of 1964, when I was ten years old.

I was out in the fields on the farm my grandfather worked. Umama never used to work on weekends, but since my father had recently lost his job, she had to work extra shifts at the Jansen's house. Prior to Ubaba losing his job, Umama's knuckles were always tough because of how many floors she scrubbed; now, they were bruised and cracked because of all the extra hours she was working.

Whilst I was on the field with my grandfather (due to the fact that Ubaba had become incapable of looking after me whilst my mother was working), I saw what looked like a group of kids playing Ring a Ring o' Roses in the distance. Excitement filled my belly because I had finally found something to do other than distract my grandfather whilst he was working. I skipped over to the children as I ran my hands through the long, yellow grass. As I got closer to them, I couldn't help but start running.

When I got there, some of them stopped playing. Those that continued were oblivious to the fact that I had just disrupted their world of fun so the kids that noticed tapped the others and pointed at me. Suddenly, I felt a bit nervous as I awaited their approval to let me join in, but it took a while before someone said something.

One of the girls whispered to those around her and they all burst out laughing. A boy in an orange t-shirt found it so funny that he felt he should share it with me. "She said you can't join in because you look like an ugly Golliwog." I did not know what a Golliwog was at the time but from the word *ugly*, I knew I had been intensely rejected.

They were all in hysterics while I felt my eyes prick with tears. My throat felt crowded with thorns. I couldn't understand because we were all black. Why was I different and ugly? I ran and ran until I reached my grandfather and hysterically said, "Umkhulu, the children over there are calling me ugly; why are they calling me ugly? Ubaba always calls me beautiful."

Lacking all emotional intelligence, as most men in my life at the time did, my grandfather replied in Zulu, "Umzukulu, there is much more in this world to worry about right now. Some people will think you're ugly, others won't—it's just the way it goes. There will always be a man we can find for you to marry, whether he thinks you're ugly or not. Now, help me hold this pig still!"

I've never understood why a man is supposed to shape a woman's existence. How can a man figure out more about me than I don't already know myself. A man is supposedly meant to give me purpose, reason and hope to continue in this hopeless world. Some days I just stare at myself in the mirror and think *who am I?* I feel so disfigured and weird for not being like all the other girls in school who swoon over Benjamin Dlamini or Kabelo Khoza because of their perfect smile and athletic physique.

Six months ago, Benjamin joined our school after making a big move from Johannesburg to Cape Town. Until he joined my Mathematics class, I had never seen so many girls care about turning up to class on time. And, to make it worse, it seemed that every time Mr Botha asked a girl a question when Benjamin was there, they would answer the question with a high-pitched, chirpy sounding voice and a pencil in their mouth. Have some shame!

I think Benjamin intrigued everyone so much because of his background; he was the only coloured guy in our school who was coloured because of interracial parents. Well, so I'd heard from the girls in my Maths class. I wasn't sure if I yet believed it because we all knew mixed marriage was illegal—people had been killed for even trying.

A month into Benjamin being in our class, we were told we would have a paired project for every lesson next week to show our proof for Pythagoras' Theorem. I kid you not, that same lunch time, there was a bidding amongst the girls in our Maths class for who was going to get paired with him. I saw make-up boxes, shoes, clothes and even a radio being bid. *This can only be madness*, I thought. That was one of the few times I was completely convinced that I was sane.

Pairing day came and Rose Dube seemed to have convinced the girls that she was most deserving based on the glow she had when she came into class. Oh, *and* the way she wore her red lipstick, wore her hair differently and left her shirt half-unbuttoned. But, in her defence, she was absolutely stunning. Not sane, but stunning. I'm sure Benjamin wouldn't hesitate to be paired with her.

I felt the air tighten when Benjamin walked in; it felt like a courting ceremony.

"Good afternoon class. If you remember, last week, I said you'd be doing group work to show proof for Pythagoras' Theorem. I'll give you a moment to get into pairs so you can begin this project. You have a total of three lessons this week to create your presentations and then in the first lesson next week, you will be presenting them."

I simply sat back and waited to see how Rose was going to use her fangs to attack Benjamin with her insanity-filled venom. She walked over to him prudently with her chest out, turning back towards her audience every second whilst giggling. She leaned over his desk and, although I couldn't hear what she was saying, I could hear the murmurs of that stupid high-pitched chirpy voice she'd been doing for the past month.

To my complete surprise, I saw him shake his head gently and watched her run out of the room with embarrassment. *What in the high school drama just happened?* Even more to my surprise, I saw his head slowly turn towards me. My heart started racing as I saw him head towards my direction. Could he read my mind or something? What did I do?

He walked over and stopped right in front of my desk.

"Hey. My name is Benjamin, or Ben for short. I was wondering if I could work with you on this project?" *WHAT?* This was worse than everyone catching me impersonating Winnie Mandela in the mirror when I skipped PE class—at least, I could run away from that one. *Help*!

"Uh, hi. I'm Priscilla," I replied hesitantly.

"Nice to meet you, Priscilla, but you didn't actually give me a reply to the second part," he chuckled.

I was chuckling too. *EW*. Less than ten seconds into his charm and I'm practically Rose Dube. I quickly corrected my facial expression and bluntly accepted.

"Yeah, sure, whatever. Not like I want to be doing this project anyway; I'll leave all the work to you," I said with a well-rehearsed eye-roll.

He was laughing, but he was also blushing. Okay, what was wrong with this guy? I'm not even funny. He didn't know I existed up until now, so I didn't understand why he was acting like this. Ah, how could I forget? He's that get-into-your-pants Prince Charming type. The only thing working in his favour is the fact that he didn't grab Rose with his easy opportunity. What do I care anyway? It's not like I'm into him.

***

Benjamin's house is really, *really* nice. From the outside, it looks like there is more than one floor…*wow*. It reminded me of the places my mother would clean when I was younger. I waited a few minutes outside before I knocked, because my friend Lesedi told me that I needed to be fashionably late, if not, I could look desperate.

The door was a beautiful glossy wood and was probably the first door I'd knocked on that was made of anything of that kind of quality. I almost wanted to lick my knuckles to see if I could taste the money. Even as I heard his footsteps coming towards the door, it sounded like expensive flooring.

I hope I look okay, I thought.

"Good afternoon Pris," he said as he kissed my cheek to greet me. I could feel my heart racing and the butterflies jolting around in my stomach.

"Afternoon Benjamin," I replied nervously. "I-I b-brought all the Maths materials we need for the presentation on Monday."

"Okay. Would you like to come in?"

I stepped into what I could only imagine the houses must look like in America. I could not believe that someone from our school would have a house that was this beautiful. The floor was made of the most beautiful white marble I had ever seen in my whole life, the walls were painted a charming frost blue with a few feature walls—my favourite being a wallpaper with silver deer all over it. Not to talk of the floral designs dotted around the ground floor—orchids, roses, lilies, irises…the list goes on. I felt like I was in paradise.

"I know what you're thinking, because I would be thinking the same," Benjamin speculated.

"What am I thinking?" I asked with a huge weight of fear. Did he know I was thinking about how I still think he's half-blind for showing an ounce of interest in me?

"You're wondering why I live in a house like this, who my parents are and how I came to be, right?"

I mean, yes, I was also thinking that. But thank goodness he didn't know what I was *really* thinking.

"Oh…yes, yes! That's exactly what I was thinking."

"Before we sit down to talk, can I get you something to drink first, maybe some tea or coffee?" he asked politely.

"Oh, lovely. Maybe some tea?"

Even the way he made the tea was unlike any of the other boys around here. He had so much grace and good manners in everything that he did. I felt like I was watching a real life porcelain doll.

As he made me tea, I decided to have a stroll around the house to see what I could figure out about him before he told me his life story. It was all kind of the same—beautiful decoration, well kept and expensive; I wouldn't say anything immediately caught my eye.

On my way back to his kitchen, I decided to have a quick look at myself in the mirror to make sure I still looked okay. Just as I stepped away from the mirror, I found a picture of what looked like a young Benjamin with his family.

A white mother and a negro father? Interesting. What was even more interesting was that I could ever so faintly see wedding bands on his parents' hands, so I just began to wonder what the story behind this could have been because this kind of marriage was strictly illegal.

Startling me as I continued to stare deeply at the picture, Benjamin said, "By the look on your face, I see you've found the photo of myself, Papa and Mum?" He gently placed the teapot on the perfectly white and round dining table and strolled over to me.

"Indeed I have. How is this possible…?"

"Let's discuss it over our tea?" he suggested.

Following him to the white table, I sat down carefully and began to pour my tea. I was scared I was going to break all of this expensive porcelain china.

"Okay…so, my father met my mother in 1950—" Benjamin was cut off by the sound of the front door opening and my heart began to race out of my chest. The first thing that went through my mind was that I was about to get arrested for being in this kind of neighbourhood. It was only for the rich black people and I'm sure these people could smell that I was not from around here.

"You need to go. *Now!* My father *cannot* catch you here," Benjamin exclaimed whilst lifting me up from my chair.

We were too late. A tall man, perhaps in his early forties, stepped into the kitchen and stared at me for a good few seconds with what looked like lightning all over his face. He then looked over at Benjamin and gave him the sternest look I'd ever seen in my whole life, as though he was going to strike him at any second. I held my breath, not daring to move an inch.

He walked closer to myself and Benjamin, giving me a closer look almost as though he was smelling me. The air was silent.

"Hahaha! We got her!" the man said as he and Benjamin sniggered uncontrollably.

"That one was so perfectly timed Papa! I was just about to tell her the story of how you and Mum met."

I couldn't really understand what was happening but I felt like peeing my pants, laughing and running away all at the same time.

"W-what was so perfectly timed?" I stuttered. "D-did I miss something? Am I in trouble?"

"No, dear, you are not at all in trouble. I'm so sorry that Ben and I just pulled that stunt on you. You're actually the first guest we've had in this house and we just felt we'd stay true to ourselves and prank you. Sorry, that was harsh. You can call me Uncle Henry," the tall man introduced.

"Nice to meet you, Uncle Henry," I answered as I moved closer to shake his hand. "My name is Priscilla Khumalo."

"It's nice to meet you also sweetheart. Please, make yourself at home, and thank you for being a friend to my son during this difficult transition in his life. There have definitely been tears on his part in terms of adjusting, so you have been a life-saver."

"Dad!" Benjamin blurted, clearly embarrassed at his father's revelation of his precious male emotions. I thought it was really funny and now, it was my turn to laugh along with Uncle Henry.

We all talked and laughed from afternoon until evening with pure happiness in our midst like the good old days in my house. I missed it when Umama and Ubaba would share story after story with me about their siblings, their schools and how they met.

Today felt like Uncle Henry and Benjamin had walked me through memory lane and given me what I didn't realise I needed, and that was simply quality time. At this moment, I felt that I had fallen hard and fast for Benjamin, and it was like I had simultaneously fallen in love with his dad in a daughter-like way. This was exactly where I wanted to be.

"Pardon me but before I go, am I permitted to ask you about the family photo…?" I proceeded to ask with caution, hoping not to offend anyone but, with the dynamics we had shared all day, it didn't feel like I was crossing a line.

Benjamin and his father exchanged looks as if to decide who was going to share the sad story this time. Clearly, many people had asked them this question in the past. It seemed that this time, Ben's dad was going to do the honours.

"It's okay, my dear. I've told you to feel free and comfortable in this house, except don't finish all the food in the fridge!" he laughed. "Yes, so you want to know how Helena and I met each other, and how it was possible that we were married?" he continued gracefully.

"Yes, if you don't mind," I smiled.

"Well, if you haven't already listened closely to Benjamin's accent, you will find that he has a slight English accent."

Woah, how did I not notice? It was clear that Benjamin's accent was not fully like someone from South Africa, but it didn't register that he may have lived in a different country. I continued to listen with intent.

"So, if you remember, I explained earlier that I am a physician by profession, but I didn't tell you my journey to becoming a doctor. As a high school graduate, I was privileged enough to be sponsored by my parents who scrimped and saved for a ticket for me to go to England to study Medicine at university. Thankfully, I had a fully paid scholarship.

"During my first few years, I was completely all eyes and ears into my books and my classes. I didn't go out much, especially because although there is no apartheid in England, it can still often feel that way. I had one or two other African friends who were also there studying but that was about as far as it went for my social interactions.

"However, one day, I decided to go to an Easter event for all the third year Medicine students as I'd started to really miss home and just needed to be cheered up a bit. Helena was the only white lady that seemed to be brave enough to speak to the African people there all night, and I just happened to be the only one reciprocating her charm.

"We met up almost everyday after that and we were married within six months. Of course, her family was absolutely disgraced but we were young and happy. It was a bitter-sweet predicament because then, I realised I probably wouldn't be coming back to live in South Africa for a long time because of the utterly foolish marriage laws, which was absolutely heartbreaking for my parents. In 1954, we had Benjamin and then in 1957, we had Amelia."

He has a sister?

"However, the sparks stopped flying, the arguments and unforgiveness grew, our families were not *at all* supportive and things just seemed easier if we went our separate ways. So, in 1968 when the divorce was finalised, I had a huge opportunity to come back to South Africa and start up business here with all the experience I had had in England, and lo and behold, it's been a mighty success. I knew it would be a jump for the children so I sat them down and asked them what they thought, and they were both very happy and supportive of me.

"At first, I suggested I would go back for a short visit every Christmas and they could come during the summer, but Benjamin insisted on coming with me. I was worried for him because, although England is not yet perfect in terms of abolishing racism, I knew it would be a lot harder and tougher on him to come into the apartheid system. As much as I warned him many times, he still insisted on coming with me. It was hard on his mother and sister but, in the end, they let him go. I'll always love Helena but I think it was the right decision for us."

Wow, what a story!

"Thank you for sharing that with me. It really means a lot to me that you have made me feel so welcome like this. My family and I used to be like your family, until…" I trailed off, not realising I had spoken too much about what I didn't plan to talk about. It felt embarrassing, especially after seeing the perfect dynamic Benjamin and his father had.

"Until what?" Benjamin couldn't help but ask, his father looking just as expectant for the story.

I twiddled my fingers over and over, wondering if I could get myself out of the haste of my tongue but I knew it wouldn't be possible, and it wouldn't be fair after they had just told me that much.

"Forgive me, I don't want to be rude, but I just need a few moments to try to talk about it because I realise I haven't ever shared this story with just about anyone," I said as my bottom lip shivered.

"Priscilla, we wouldn't want to force you if you feel uncomfortable," Uncle Henry reassured me.

"No, no, I want to tell you the story," I decided. "I had a normal childhood, a happy childhood actually. My mother worked as a maid and my father an English teacher—he always wanted to go to England actually." This made Uncle Henry and Benjamin smile. I was happy that my story brought some happiness to them because I knew it would end with them feeling far from gleeful.

I went on. "We didn't have a lot of money but we got by a lot better than many of those around us. We had food on our table and beds to sleep on. We were happy, very happy indeed." I could feel the tears trying to push themselves up but I kept them securely locked behind my eyes.

"My father was someone who was so inspired by the Martin Luther King speeches; every time he would get a chance to watch him on the television he looked like the happiest man alive. So, when I was nine years old, he took it a step further by becoming the leader of a group who wanted to execute real change within our community. The way my father saw it, whites, blacks and coloured's were supposed to be one community with no division.

"The group was doing well at first, educating those around them with their morals and ideologies. There was even some progress in what was being taught in our local church. He was excited and optimistic about the future, especially for my brother and I. However, on one particular Friday during my father's meetings, my Uncle Frederick didn't show up. Everyone was quiet. At some point,

I managed to put two and two together and realised he was probably never coming back. So, my father's friends began to rebel against my father's regime of peacefully infiltrating the system because of what happened to poor Uncle Frederick. But, they didn't realise that peace does not always mean there will be no death; it simply means *you* choose not to respond with violence.

"His friends didn't think this way. They went around spreading violence and raping young Afrikaners. Although my father was completely innocent, they still associated him with those cruel men and he lost everything. Now, he spends all his time drinking beer and acting useless. My mother kicked him out last year but he comes back every other day banging on the door at stupid hours in the morning. I think we may be moving soon so that he won't be able to find us. My mother works *tirelessly* and just about manages to make ends meet now that she has opened up her own shop but, honestly, I hate the way my life is now. I miss my father and the way things used to be." At least, I managed to get to the end before the tears spilled out. However, I was proud of myself for being able to tell my story.

Uncle Henry and Benjamin said nothing but allowed me to have my moment whilst they handed me some tissues, soaking in the atmosphere. It felt like something was breaking inside of me but also as if it was the beginning of my healing journey to what I did not realise even needed to be healed.

Eventually, Uncle Henry spoke. "You have a beautiful and pure soul, Priscilla, and I say that with total honesty from what I've seen in you today. This circumstance is just a hurdle that is going to mould you into the woman you were created to be. I know it seems hard right now, and my advice may not seem like much, but you are more than what you think of yourself; in fact, I think you would make a fantastic lawyer. You are someone who has the perfect balance of fire and compassion for others. Please, do not limit yourself to the fate of your father. Your story does not have to be like that."

"A lawyer...? I've never thought of being a lawyer; I've never really thought of being anything if I am being honest," I croaked, finally managing to get the tears to stop.

"I agree with my father, Pris; you really are going to be something special. I knew that from the moment I met you," Benjamin blushed. I was certainly blushing too, not *daring* to glance over at Uncle Henry.

"Okay children. I will certainly leave you to it now as I think this is the part the parents are not cool enough for but, seriously Priscilla, you are a delightful addition to our household. You are always welcome as I said and I will hopefully see you again soon?"

"You hopefully, definitely, certainly will see me again soon!" I giggled as he waved me goodbye and disappeared upstairs.

"I should get going now, Benjamin. Thank you so much for having me and I will see you for our *very* unprepared presentation on Monday."

"Goodness me, and I've never been one for winging it! Don't worry, I'm sure we'll be fine. Do you mind if I take you home?" My heart immediately sank as I thought of him seeing my pit of a home in comparison to his Barbie Dream house.

"Not to bother, I'll be more than okay. I'm sure no one will harass me around here; it's a beautiful neighbourhood."

"Okay...as long as you're sure. Please, stay safe and thank you again for coming, Priscilla. I've loved having you," he said. I was glad that I could save him seeing my house for another time. Hopefully never. I loved being at his house.

"Also, I meant what I said; you are special, Priscilla Khumalo."

As soon as our eyes locked, my palms immediately went clammy and my breathing intensified about fourfold. I had been told about this moment by just about every girl in school, but I didn't know mine would come this soon, or ever.

He moved closer to me and kissed me, still keeping to his Benjamin-style class, probably the way all English people did it. Anyway, I was certainly taken aback.

"W-wow, um…I don't know what to say. N-no one has ever done that to me before," I stuttered helplessly. Benjamin simply smiled. I could *really* see the English in him now.

"See you on Monday Pris." With that, I turned around and walked home with the warmest feeling I'd ever felt in my heart.

10

2021

"Gogo, I'm not trying to be rude, but this story doesn't seem sad at all. I mean, the bit about your dad was terrible, but the Uncle Henry thing, the Benjamin Dlamini thing and the *love* thing seem… amazing," I butt in.

"Well, that's why you have to be patient with the story and not just assume that things always continue the way they start. If you'd let me *finish* without interrupting me, I was about to get to the tragic part of the story. Think about it, Kaya; your mother is ten shades lighter than me so there must be more to the story!" Gogo contested.

"Yeah, Gogo. I know you had my mum when you were 17, but I guess now, I'm just assuming Benjamin was the baby daddy," I suggested, which earned me a thump on the back from Gogo.

"Don't *ever* call him my baby daddy; he was my *first love*. My only love for that matter. He was kind and caring, the most considerate man I have ever met in my whole life. Although, I can't say that about Uncle Henry," she revealed bitterly. "And again, I need not remind you that your mother is half-white."

"Yeah, I know, Gogo. I was hoping that somehow, after this story, you were counting Benjamin as white because of his English mum."

"No! I would never imply that. Benjamin was a black man and was proud to be black. His father could have afforded him to go to an expensive private school from the beginning, where he would have integrated with whites and could have pretended to be white, but Benjamin chose to be with us, in our crappy school, because he was *black*."

"Okay…so what happened Gogo? How was my mother conceived?"

1971

Priscilla Khumalo

"Happy New Year!" exclaimed Uncle Henry as he hugged both Benjamin and I, kissing me lightly on the forehead. "If everyone could raise their glasses, I would like to make a toast to this year. Firstly, a toast to these wonderful men I am about to enter into business with; it is an honour to pursue business with you and an opportunity for us to be delightfully wealthy! It is wonderful to see that things in this country are moving forward and you have not discriminated against me as a black man.

"Secondly, a toast to my brilliant son, Benjamin, for all his hard work and success. He is someone I will be so proud to one day pass my business onto. Lastly, a toast to my daughter, Priscilla, whom I love with all my heart and am so glad to have become a father-like figure to. You are a delight to all who know you, darling. Cheers everyone!"

My heart leapt at the sound of Uncle Henry calling me his *daughter*. As we clinked our glasses, my eyes welled up with tears because of the loving atmosphere; it was the most acceptance I had ever felt in my whole life—an acceptance I was so sure would last forever. Uncle Henry would be my father, Benjamin would one day become my husband and things would be perfect.

At that very moment, it was like I could see my whole life ahead of me, myself and Benjamin with our perfect marriage, our perfect house and our perfect children. Maybe we would even move away to England and set up our life there, away from the apartheid laws. And, to make things even better, the life of my whole family would change; my mother would not have to struggle anymore. Maybe we would even be able to get my father the help that he needs.

"Happy new year, my love," I said gently to Benjamin, still overwhelmed by Uncle Henry's speech. "I'm so glad that God blessed me with you, and for the rest of my life."

"Happy new year, Priscilla Thadie Khumalo. Thank you for putting up with me," he smiled.

Benjamin and I had been together for nearly a year now and my life had not been the same since. To begin with, when everyone at school found out that Benjamin and I were dating, it was like we were the black Bonnie and Clyde for a whole month. Not a single person expected it or saw it coming (nor did I).

Everyone began giving us special treatment from all over—Rose Dube was even trying to be my friend. "Heyyy, Pris. How's things? Just wondering if you wanted to do something on the weekend?" she would ask me pretty much every Maths lesson, and, every time, I would find an excuse. She just seemed to *suddenly* realise we were in the same class...after two years. It was weird, and we certainly hated the attention as we were both introverted people. Finally, we decided that, in school, we would avoid hanging out together and drawing attention to ourselves so that a sense of normality would return. Eventually, it did. Now, we were old news.

Another thing that changed was that I spent almost all my time with the Dlamini's. At least three times a week I would be at their house. Even during the summer, when Benjamin went to visit his mother in England, I would still go and spend time with Uncle Henry. We were like a little family.

Additionally, Benjamin and I began making university plans and Uncle Henry encouraged us to consider going to England to study—I mean, Benjamin didn't really seem to have a choice. For me, I loved the idea because I knew I was clever and hardworking, but I did not know how I would pay for it. Uncle Henry offered many times to sponsor me but I really didn't want him to do that.

I began looking for fully paid scholarships to study Law at Oxford University. Benjamin and I also started having some healthy rivalry as he was one hundred percent set on Cambridge and hoped to study Economics. We always joked and placed bets on who was going to turn into a snob the fastest. However, in order to do so, I would need to have a better and more 'certified' academic record than I had at the time as my school was pretty...rubbish.

Benjamin was going to move to a private school soon as Uncle Henry didn't want him to stay in our school any longer; he allowed Benjamin to have his inspirational black man moment for a while but even Ben knew that he had no chance of success by staying in our school.

Uncle Henry also gave me no option but to go to the school with Benjamin. He said, "Pris, you may not let me pay for your university fees, which I understand; I would have done the same. However, you are going to the new school with Benjamin and that's not a debate. I've already gone to speak to your mother and she has agreed. So it is decided, kuyacaca lokho?"

I'm telling you, life has felt like the most surreal movie over the past year and it's been wonderful.

***

Uncle Henry's New Year's party was the most vibrant but *strangest* party I had ever been to in my life. It was definitely illegal, I could tell you that.

His new business expansion and investors included both whites and Indians, and they had decided to come to his party. I'm sure their wives and kids didn't know they were in a black man's home, or else by now the police certainly would have been on their way; but, as they say, if you have money you can get away with just about anything.

The curtains were closed to ensure no passer-by or stranger could see our party, and all of Uncle Henry's neighbours were here so we knew they weren't going to rat. Uncle Henry was a smart man and he knew how to have a good time whilst avoiding trouble. But, if anyone did rat, it would only be us blacks and coloured folk in trouble, not the whites.

After the toast, the drinks continued to flow and everyone was having a good time. Due to my father's more than habitual drinking, I'd always been one to avoid alcohol so that I wouldn't endure the same fate. Today, however, I felt much more relaxed and as if I deserved to enjoy the night, so I joined in with everyone on the champagne.

After a while, my body began to feel lighter and warmer and, as a result, when Benjamin went to play some music on the piano and Uncle Henry joined him for a duet on his saxophone, it was like the whole atmosphere was full of even higher spirits. I began to dance with the neighbours first; there was a girl there a little younger than Ben and I, and we took turns pretending to be the man. It was really fun. However, when she went over to dance with her family, I needed another dance partner and the Dlamini's were very carried away with their instruments so I decided to leave them to it.

Much to my surprise, one of the Indian men came over and asked if I could join him for a dance. Seeing that Benjamin overheard it, I looked over to him to see if it was okay; after all, he was Uncle Henry's age and I could tell he was not trying to be weird.

After Benjamin's much approved wink and laughter, I joined the man for a dance and had a great time. However, I started to catch Uncle's Henry's business partner friends in the corner watching us dance. Prior to this, they had been minding their own business. It certainly made me feel uncomfortable and I knew Benjamin could sense it.

"Pris, come over and join me here on the piano," Benjamin said, understanding my feelings of awkwardness much to my relief. As soon as I joined Benjamin, it was like they got back to talking business. As I said, a vibrant but strange party. After failing to hold a chord on the piano and making the music in the room sound like a mess, I went to get a glass of water because my head started to spin and I felt ever so slightly nauseous.

I walked over to the kitchen, filled up a glass with water and sat on the kitchen counter, hoping for my mind to steady itself; however, the noise coming from the living room was just too much for me to bear. I stood up and just about managed to wobble my way upstairs and lie down in the guest room (which was essentially my bedroom).

I just kept thinking in my head over and over about the things Ubaba went through. Being drunk for the first time tonight helped me understand exactly why he was an alcoholic. It's like your whole mind just becomes focused on the here and now; you don't have to think about anything. You feel bold and confident, like you could take on the whole world if you really wanted to, which explains why he used to come banging on our door all the time. I now understood.

My mind slowly began to stop spinning, and I could feel normality arising again, especially as the feelings of anxiety which I had about joining the new school came flooding back. I put the glass on the side and decided it was time to join them back at the party as I had been gone a while. I also hoped it'd become less packed as I'd heard a few cars leaving.

A knock at the door? It was probably Benjamin so I quickly put myself together again and tiptoed over to the door. The one rule Uncle Henry and my mother agreed on was that Benjamin and I were not allowed to be in a bedroom unaccompanied to save us from messing up our lives anytime soon. I also thought it was a good idea as I was in *no* way ready to sleep with him; it's something I wanted in the far future, or maybe even when we were married.

I slowly opened the door to see who was on the other side but, by the time I got there, no one was there. *Oh, okay?* I thought to myself. I walked back towards the bed, making sure I laid it back to the tidiness in which I found it.

"For a second, I thought you may not have been in here, but it seems you are." I heard someone say from the other side of the room. Turning around abruptly, it was one of the white businessmen Uncle Henry had been working with.

"Sorry, Sir, but is someone looking for me downstairs?" I said, panic mixed with alcohol in my breath.

"No, not at all. I just came up to find you as you've been gone a while," he replied, greatly slurring his words.

"I see. Well, I'm coming back down now, no need to worry about me," I smiled with much fear. I turned around hoping he would leave. Thankfully, I heard footsteps followed by the sound of the door closing. I breathed out with relief.

Why did I hear the door lock? Can you lock the door from outside? I turned around immediately to see he was standing there, a drunk grin on his face. "Sorry, Sir, is there an issue?" I shouted, hoping Benjamin would come and save me.

"No issue at all, beautiful. Has anyone told you how stunning you looked as you danced tonight?"

At this point, I couldn't even reply. I was so afraid and just wanted to get out of there.

"Don't be scared, there's no need to be scared. We're just two people having fun. You wanna dance? You danced with Tahir, so it's nothing new right?"

"Does Uncle Henry know you're up here?" I threatened, trying to stay brave and free of fear.

"Why does it matter? There's nothing to hide, I know you want it anyway from the way you danced with my friend," he said as he began to undo his belt and come closer to me. "I know when a negro girl wants it; I have many maids like you."

"Want what? I do not want anything, Sir. I was just having fun, and it was not anything romantic."

"You don't need to lie to me, my dear. Let's just be mature and stop with the games," he said as he touched my cheek and tried to stroke my neck.

"Stop it!" I screamed. "I have a boyfriend! I don't want to do whatever you are trying to do, thank you very much! Now, I am going back downstairs," I sternly replied.

"Oh no, you are not little missy!" he said as he grabbed me by the arm, throwing me onto the bed and pinning me down.

"Get off me, get off! BENJAMIN! UNCLE HENRY! HELP!" I screamed and screamed with desperation, hoping someone would hear me, but all I heard was even louder music and people laughing from downstairs. No one could hear me. No one was coming to help me.

I lost all sense of self at this moment. I didn't even need to be drunk anymore to put my mind on something else. I didn't know who I was. I couldn't feel anything; I chose not to.

As soon as he was done, he kissed me on the forehead and walked straight out. I continued to lay there, still feeling nothing.

A few minutes later, Benjamin came to find me. "Pris, where have you been? My dad has been worrying about you. His friend came downstairs and told me where you are."

I still said nothing, I couldn't talk.

"Pris? Are you okay?" Benjamin whispered, looking down at my underwear that had been pulled down to my feet. "Pris…oh my goodness, Priscilla! What did he do? What did that man just do to you?" he shouted as tears began to stream from his face.

After that, it was a bit of a blur for me. Benjamin ran straight downstairs and punched the man over and over, beating him to the brink of death. At that point, reality hit me and I just started crying, thinking of all the mess that I had made. I could not bear to go downstairs and show my face to anyone as they probably all thought I was a whore. I could just feel it in my gut that this man had just ruined my whole life.

2021

"Give me a moment please, Gogo," I said, nearly having a panic attack. "So, you mean to tell me that you had my mum from a man that raped you? You're telling me a white pincher came and stole it all from you?"

"And now you see why I hate them so much," Gogo said bitterly.

"I'm so sorry, Gogo. I'm so so sorry," I began to cry and she also began to cry—something I rarely saw from myself or from Gogo.

Finally, as we got ourselves together, I realised I needed to know a few more things.

"But Gogo, you said that Uncle Henry was the worst of it all. How is that if he did nothing wrong?"

"Nothing wrong? Uncle Henry chose his business over me; he continued doing business with the man and shunned me from their lives. After that man raped me, I couldn't speak for weeks on end. I refused to let Benjamin speak to me and my mother was so worried. After Benjamin explained to her what happened, she tried her best but I refused to see him.

"In the weeks that followed, I finally plucked up the courage to see Benjamin and explain to him what had happened, although he was now attending the boarding school so it was much harder to see him. A month after I'd seen Benjamin, my mother realised I was pregnant from the way I was nauseous and reacting to her food, and the fact that I had put on some weight even though I'd barely touched anything.

"Like any angry mother would, she stormed over to the Dlamini's house and screamed and swore profusely at Uncle Henry, blaming him for messing up my life. She told him to take some responsibility but, instead, Uncle Henry called the police to remove her from his property. After that, he moved house, forced Benjamin to go back to England and continued with his business. As for me, I was left pregnant and alone with no official education and every hope and dream of a future snuffed out.

"At first, my mother tried to be brave for me but the pressure of our extended family on her got too much. They all said 'I'd brought shame on them', not only because I was pregnant, but also because there was a white man involved. So, to make it easier, I left."

I didn't even have the words for Gogo, my throat felt stiff and my mind was filled with so many emotions. I felt like finding that evil man and making him suffer for what he did to Gogo. How can you destroy someone's life like this and get away with it? He continued to get rich and have a happy life, a happy family and everything good whilst Gogo scraped her way through life. How was that fair?

"Kaya, I want you to know that I didn't just tell you this story just for the sake of you knowing my life better, although I do believe that is important. However, I told you this story so you can understand how hard it is for your mother to be able to tell you her own. Give her time; it's really not easy to talk about rape. It's something no woman ever wants to go through. Be patient with her, please," Gogo said solemnly.

I understood what she was saying, and I was glad she was able to be open with me about her story; but a part of me was still angry that no one had been more open with me, no matter how hard it was.

"Gogo, I understand that and I will be patient but…I think you and Mum struggle to understand that I also have suffered with you both. When a child is born into a household in which she's never told about who she is, where she comes from and why she exists, it's really hard too. I'm not trying to push aside your emotions in all of this, but my emotions have been pushed aside because you and Mum shut me out of everything. Up until today, I had no idea where my mum came from, and if it wasn't for me being at home at the right time on my eighteenth birthday, I wouldn't even know who my dad is.

"I guess what I'm trying to say is, Gogo, I understand how much pain you both must've been through; but, I also want you to see that I'm in pain too." I just about managed to reason, feeling proud that I'd finally found the words I'd wanted to say for years and years.

"I know, my child. You're right. No child should ever have to suffer because of their parents' silence. All this time, I thought we were protecting you, but it was stupid to assume you would be okay with ignorance. I apologise, seriously. And I hope your mother will have the courage to tell you her story one day," Gogo said patiently.

"Love you, Gogo," I said as I went over to cuddle her. I was so appreciative of her level of understanding towards me—it's such a gift. Mum really struggled with patience and understanding, and, unlike Gogo, she almost always resorted to anger or shouting. Although, after Gogo's story, I have definitely gained a greater level of understanding towards her and now feel like letting our disagreement go.

"I'm still going to make my way back to Joburg though; it was all a bit much with Mama tonight," I said.

"Ah…that's okay, my child. I never expected you to stay; I just wanted you to know my story. But hey, look, you're calling her Mama again," Gogo chuckled.

"I did not just call her Mama!" I denied, "I called her 'Mum'."

"Whatever. Not gonna argue with you little-miss-stubborn. Oh, yes, and I forgot to say that Genesis came over last week asking if she could have your number. She misses you," Gogo told me.

"Oh, wow. Genesis. I haven't seen her in…eight or maybe nine years now. She still lives around here?" I asked, feeling nostalgic.

"Hmm, I didn't ask. I guess you'll have to ask her. Do you want her number?"

"Yeah…why not? It would be good to catch up with her."

11

2012

I hadn't felt nerves like this in a while and, to top it off, the halls reeked of bleach and private school children all in one. I hated the smell of both. I immediately noticed how polished the floors were and how designer shoes were reflecting off them like a literal mirror. As well as nerves, embarrassment began to hit me as I couldn't hide my two year old Massmart trainers. I sucked it up, took a deep breath in and thought, *I'm Kaya Imka Khumalo. Let's do this.*

After being confused for a few minutes, I eventually found my way to the Engineering department and walked into the lecture hall for the first part of the Induction Day. A surreal feeling rose up in me because, for the first time ever, this was actually like the movies. The chairs were all exactly and evenly spaced out and went up at an angled slope, the room smelt like whiteboard pens with a mixture of air-freshener and chewing gum, and the people all looked so privileged. It was as though South-Africa had met High-School Musical for a university remix.

I looked around for any Thato lookalikes or anyone who looked like they could have a conversation with Gogo without crying, but instead, I felt like I was in a hall full of people who looked like they would get on with my mum—snooty, stuck-up, judgemental people. *Eye-roll*.

I took a seat on my own, right in the middle of the lecture hall. I've never had any problem being the centre of attention, especially when I don't fit in. It gives people something to talk about.

As I was climbing the stairs, I heard three black girls giggling about my Massmart trainers in a language I knew too well—Zulu. They pointed in turns and sniggered at me, trying to make it obvious enough that I noticed but not obvious enough that I could tell them to stop doing it. The fourth girl sitting with them was the only one that seemed to have common sense; she clearly didn't assume that I have no black culture in me—just because my skin is lighter and my curls are not as tight, they seemed to think I couldn't understand Zulu.

I desperately wanted to snap back at them but I was not going to stoop to their level. I'd been taught better by Gogo. Gogo always said, "Never waste your tongue on those who do not know how to use it."

However, this overwhelming sense of hope began to flood over me; I would always be remembered as the girl who came to Stellenbosch with nothing and left with more than she could ever imagine. I was created to be a trailblazer, I just knew it. So, if the most I could give them is five minutes of laughter over Massmart shoes so that I can have a lifetime of legacy, then so be it. It was a no-brainer really.

I quickly decided after the first session that I didn't want to be here and would just email the professors to find out what I'd missed, which I doubted was much at all. My mind was going hay-wire with a thousand different thoughts, and the last place I wanted to explode was the place I was about to study for the next few years. People don't forget anger outbursts very quickly.

For starters, my mind was overthinking the fact that I was moving to the university this year. Secondly, I suddenly realised I was now an adult; thirdly, when was I going to go back to see my dad? I definitely needed a break from my thoughts so I thought it would be nice to go over and see Genesis this evening. She invited me over for a girl's movie night a few days ago but I told her I wasn't sure if I would be able to commit. Now, I was sure I needed a break to wind down so I sent her a text to let her know I'd be at hers by 8.30pm.

***

Every time I went over to Genesis' house, I just felt super relaxed and my thoughts were clear and easy to dissipate. Genesis was also really good at helping you break down exactly *what* and *how* you were feeling; everyone knows someone like that, right? It's like you have a personal counsellor in a friend so you're getting free therapy sessions every time you see them. I love it.

"Hey, friend," I said, trying to look happy.

"Hey!" Genesis said as she beamed at me, but the smile on her face began to disappear as she saw how upset I was starting to look. "By the look on your face, we are totally scrapping the whole movie night thing and we're just gonna have a venting session, right?"

"Spot on," I sighed.

"Come in and sit. Tell me all about it, friend!" Genesis encouraged.

I slumped my whole body on the sofa as if I was going through a midlife crisis or paying for expensive celebrity counselling and stared up at the ceiling for a few moments, trying to think of where to start.

"I think a good place to start would be my birthday last week. Wait, Luke isn't here right?" I panicked.

"Okay, girl, check you out! This is such an improvement from a few weeks ago. At least, now, you can find a starting point to your stories without me having to spend ten minutes calming you down. And, no, Luke isn't here. Why…?" she replied.

"Oh, er…no reason. Just don't want him asking me questions about this story in school. It'd be weird that's all."

"Okay…" she said unconvinced. "Anyway, go ahead."

"Right. So, it was my birthday last week and, please don't judge me, but Thato came over and we smoked weed," I said, feeling guilty.

"Thato," she said, rolling her eyes. "Of course, I'd never judge you, friend, but I'm telling you, that boy is trouble!"

"Can I be honest with you about *just* that sis?" I replied.

"Always," Genesis reassured me.

"I think you're right—Thato is trouble. But he's been my best friend since we were out of the womb. I can't just abandon him and let him destroy his life, but I'm tired of him."

"Now, that's true, girl. I don't think we should ever give up on people but you have to apply wisdom. People who go down the wrong path *always* take others with them. I can understand why you're tired," she said, choosing her words carefully so that she wouldn't offend me.

"Yeah, I don't disagree with you, friend. I'll think about it. Anyway, back to what I was saying; so, we got high and a postman came to the door, dropping some letters. Somehow, I stumbled across this letter that had my name on it. I opened it but I was scared because it was handwritten. At first, I thought it was Stellenbosch giving me a rejection letter but, when I opened it, it was a birthday letter."

"That's sweet, right?" Genesis interrupted, eager for me to just get the story out.

"No, just wait for it. So, I read the letter and the person who wrote it told me they sent me a letter every single year. I was thinking, huh? No one sends me a letter every year. So I get to the end and guess what?"

"What?" she said anxiously.

"It was from my *dad*," I said, and from the look on Genesis' face when I said it, she now knew why I was going through it. "And, to make it even worse, my mum had been hiding the letters from me all these years."

"Oh, sis, I'm so sorry. Can I give you a hug?" Genesis asked, feeling deeply sorry for me.

"Of course, please do," I said as she leaped over the sofa to cuddle me. "I don't even know what to do. I went to find my dad today before the Stellenbosch induction but he wasn't there. Instead I met my long lost aunt who I realised gave me a teddy years and years ago."

"Okay…so you have to go back. You have to go meet your dad, Kaya, he's literally been reaching out to you," Genesis advised. "But, you also can't keep it a secret from your mum as she may be protecting you from something. Remember what I told you a few weeks ago; it's lies that tear down relationships above everything."

"Gen, I can't. I can barely look her in the eyes after I found that letter. All those years of thinking I wasn't good enough to have a dad, wondering if he even remembered me or cared about me…just to find out he's been begging to see me all this time."

"Sis, I know this is hard but you *must*. You may be trying to gain another parent but if you lie to your mum you'll lose her as a result," she warned me.

"Yeah, I know. I'll think about it," I lied, knowing full well I was not going to let my mother in on any of it.

"Can I pray with you?" Genesis asked quietly. "I believe that God will make this all okay."

"Mm, okay…" I replied hesitantly.

"Father Lord, thank you for Kaya and thank you for reuniting her with her long lost family. I pray that you will guide her and give her strength in this troublesome time. Please help her to make the right decisions. In Jesus' name, amen."

"Thanks," I said, feeling that sense of awkwardness I felt when I accidentally came to their fellowship.

Luke came home with some of his rugby friends just when we finished praying, saving me from making up an awkward excuse to escape. You could smell the smell of rugby all over them, like a sport's perfume, but I found it quite soothing.

"Hey little sis!" Luke shouted as he jumped on Genesis, which landed me in the middle of a sibling play fight.

"Be gentle with each other, guys!" I said as I tried to break them up, seeming not to understand that this is the typical sibling dynamic of showing love.

"Sorry Mum," Luke teased me, finally leaving Genesis in peace.

"Don't call me that!" I argued back defensively. "I was just trying to stop you from killing a girl that's half your size with all your rugby muscles."

"Rugby muscles…so you've been checking them out?" Luke chortled.

"N-no, I haven't at all. I was just making an…observation!" I stammered, super embarrassed. I could hear all his rugby friends laughing in the kitchen, clearly listening in on our conversation.

"It's okay to admit it, K; it's normal to check someone out," he mocked, definitely wanting all his boys to continue with the joke. He was irritating me and I was tempted to be nasty, but I was trying to improve my anger issues so I decided to stay quiet.

After Luke went to rejoin his friends in the kitchen, I felt like it was time to go home so I could have my own quiet time.

"Thank you so much for your support tonight, Gen; I really needed it. Love you sis."

"Love you too, friend."

"You should come by to see Gogo and I tomorrow afternoon?" I suggested gently.

"I will definitely come and see you and Gogo tomorrow. Gogo is a star! I'll stay praying for you too."

"Thanks," I said.

On my way out, I caught Luke taking some of his rugby things out of his car.

"You alright, K? You seemed a bit down today," Luke asked, falsely concerned in my opinion.

"Yeah, all good thanks," I said, still feeling annoyed about the way he spoke to me in front of his friends.

"I guess you're annoyed at the way I spoke to you in the house; I realised soon after that it was wrong. Sorry," Luke apologised, which was pleasantly surprising.

"All good," I mumbled, trying not to make a big deal out of his surprise apology.

"Can I walk you home? And please don't say no because I'm going to walk you home regardless—I know you'll be stubborn about it if I don't put my foot down."

"I'm not stubborn!" I said, stubbornly. He just laughed and shook his head, knowing that he'd proved his point.

We walked in silence for a while, not knowing what to say after the living room mocking situation.

"Can I tell you something I've never told anyone, K?" he asked.

"Go for it," I said with hesitation, hoping he wasn't going to tease me again.

"I don't know if I believe in God," Luke revealed.

Woah, I was not expecting that.

"Jeez, woah." I was really shocked at what had just come out of his mouth. "I mean no judgement, but why are you telling me this?"

"I trust you," Luke admitted.

"Why would you trust me when you barely know me?" I enquired.

"I don't know, I just trust you and I'm never wrong with instinct. Also, I want to get to know you more; will the stubborn lady allow me the honour of doing so?"

I was barely blushing, but I was blushing. Why would Luke suddenly want to get to know me after he'd just teased me in front of all of his friends? Maybe this was a dare from one of the boys; it had to be a dare.

"Which one of them dared you to do this?" I demanded.

"Woah, chill. No one dared me to do this, and why would I tell you my biggest secret if I was being dared?" Luke defended.

True, why *would* he tell me his biggest secret if it was a dare?

"Besides, we're just getting to know each other as friends right? No pressure," he smiled.

He and Genesis loved that phrase 'No pressure', and, indeed, it made you feel like just that when they said it.

"Yeah, just getting to know each other as friends. 'No pressure,'" I teased.

2021

When I hear people talk about drug dealers, they think they're just rich for ordering a few people about. In their heads, we can pass off all of the work to our employees so we can sit back and relax on some Greek island, but that's far from the case. You see, you find that as soon as your clients build trust and a relationship with you, passing them off to someone else that works for you is near to *impossible*; it's too lethal a business to trust just anyone.

My business really started to take off about five years ago, in 2016, when Mandy and I were invited to an exclusive club event. The business was doing well at that time—we'd just graduated and had steady income. Our client base was made up of small business owners, office managers, accountants, you name it, we had it. They were mostly middle class people from all over Cape Town.

However, we knew that 'steady' wasn't going to take us even *close* to where we wanted to go. I was still adamantly set on my initial business plan which was to grow the business into a *super* rich clientele—politicians, lawyers, consultants and, lastly, celebrities. If we could expand and develop the client base, it would be much easier to avoid trouble from law enforcement and it would make us stinking rich.

It wasn't like I really wanted to sell to these people (because I knew there would be loads of fake laughing, gossip sessions with rich middle-aged women and eating caviar for breakfast), but I just knew it would be much easier to clean our cash if it went through their accounts.

All I had to do was figure out which network of rich people were unopposed to bending the rules. Eventually, we would have a huge drug network through almost completely 'legal' means, so that no one could say that Kaya Khumalo was the one behind it. It would be a totally smooth-sailing operation—I just needed someone to help me get a foot in the door.

Mandy and I were invited to this exclusive club event by one of our favourite clients—Ms Jeffreys. She was a doctor, believe it or not, and spent many of her Friday nights out in the city instead of catching up on sleep from her exceedingly busy schedule. Mandy and I loved her so much because she always gave us life advice from her mistakes—one of which was getting married. Mandy and I wholeheartedly agreed with the divorce.

When we met Ms Jeffreys in 2015, Mandy had recently come out of her first serious relationship and was *very* heartbroken. One thing Mandy and I decided on at that point was a no-man-zone policy. We agreed that it was best for us to go through life practically single even if we were dating. So, when we met Ms Jeffreys, it was like she just understood us completely.

On the personal side of things, Ms Jeffreys enjoyed cocaine to help her with stress and to cope with her day-to-day life. But, Ms Jeffreys also started running cocaine distribution amongst her patients, so we became a needed supplier for her. She called this her 'after-work treatment', and had been doing this for the past couple of months.

On this specific night, we thought it would just be our usual with her—get there by 10pm, order a bottle to the table and catch up on our hopeless love lives and any future business agreements or changes. However, when Mandy and I turned up this time, there were some men sitting there laughing alongside Ms Jeffreys.

"Erm, who are *they*?" Mandy said in annoyance.

"I don't know, maybe some of her patients or something?" I replied with irritancy also.

We walked over to the table, putting a smile on our faces so as not to offend Ms Jeffreys, because I was sure she would have a reasonable explanation for why these men wanted to come and interfere with our night.

"Hey ladies!" Ms Jeffreys exclaimed with the most bubbly smile on her face. "Come sit down and grab a drink. These lovely guys said they wanted to join us tonight!" she shouted over the music, "*and they're paying for everything*," she mouthed.

I really wasn't feeling like being chatted up by some measly guys who probably had girlfriends or wives waiting up for them at home whilst they fooled about and never bore the consequences of their actions.

"Give it an hour and then we'll go," I whispered to Mandy.

"Deal," she agreed.

"So good to see you tonight," I said as Mandy and I kissed and hugged Ms Jeffreys, ignoring the other guys. "We'll be okay getting our own drinks though," I added, tugging Mandy's arm for us to go to the bar and get our own cocktails.

"Why'd you do that?" Mandy asked hysterically as we got to the bar. "Who cares if we didn't expect them to be here? Free drinks are free drinks!"

"It's the principle, Mandy; we agreed after Oliver broke up with you that we were never going to take anything from a guy ever again."

"Oh, Kaya. Give it a rest; we were just saying all that emotional stuff in the moment, you don't really care about that do you?" Mandy sighed.

"Oh, yes I do," I said bluntly. "Can we have two Mojitos please?" I asked the bartender.

"No problem, that's 250 Rand for both of you," the bartender replied.

"Add it to my tab!" a man shouted.

My eyes slowly followed the trail of the bartender's eyes to this man who had so rudely imposed himself. I could feel anger starting to burn up in my belly, but, to make it even worse, I realised it was the man who was wearing Air Force 1's sitting at Ms Jeffreys table.

"You can call me J," he said, beaming in my face. I was in utter shock and disbelief at what seemed to me to be arrogance and a lack of self-awareness. I certainly did not want to speak to him.

"I won't be calling you at all," I hissed.

"Ooo, burn! You're a feisty one, aren't you?" he laughed. "What's set you off in a bad mood tonight then?"

"I'm not in a bad mood!" I argued, "I just don't get why you've come to crash our night out with Ms Jeffreys."

"You're the only one with a frown on your face. Look over at the table—Ms Jeffreys is having a great time, and so is your friend," he replied. I looked back to see that Mandy had swiftly abandoned me to go and party on the table with the intruders.

"Well, someone has to be able to stand their ground," I muttered as I rolled my eyes in Mandy's direction.

"Perhaps if you would lighten up a little, I could tell you why we're actually here?" this 'J' guy responded sarcastically.

Feeling intrigued, I tried to lighten up my tone a little. "Why *are* you here?" I said less rudely.

"Well, I actually came to meet you, Kaya Khumalo. It's a pleasure," he smiled whilst fake curtsying.

"Oh…you know who I am?"

"Of course, your immaculate work is being talked about all over Joburg," he acknowledged.

"People know who I am in Joburg?" I queried.

"They do, and I am one of those people."

"So why did you come all the way to Cape Town to find me?" I questioned sceptically.

"I believe I have a great business opportunity for you if you would take me more seriously than a low life that comes to see women shake their bum on the weekend."

"How did you know I saw you like that?" I laughed.

"Because I also see those men like that," he admitted as we both continued laughing together.

"Well, what's this opportunity?" I asked with eyes wide open.

"Hmm, I'll put it like this; there's a lot of space in the market to provide this kind of 'service' to the rich," he murmured. At that point, my heart began to beat about a million miles per hour as I realised that there was an opportunity for my business plan to finally become a reality.

"What did you say your name was again?" I asked plainly.

"Jaguar," he replied.

The rest remains history. Jaguar was my foot in the door and is a huge reason for the success I'm enjoying now. He jumped on the opportunity to work with me as soon as he realised how much potential I had to make this a multi-million dollar business. But, Jaguar was shot dead last year—just the realities of this business; if you cross the wrong person, you'll pay for it with your life.

When I look back on it, I realise I didn't know exactly what I was getting myself into. The rich have really, *really* high standards for anyone they're doing business with and, if something is even slightly out of line, they won't let you rest until things have gone exactly their way. It's a burden, and no one is currently trustworthy enough to help me carry it. But, as I've said before, this business is lethal so I can't just have any random person help me. This is why I desperately needed to partner with Alexander Petrov—I couldn't do this alone anymore.

Honestly, I kind of want out of this now. Maybe I should call Genesis?

12

2021

My thumbs twiddled out of nervousness as I paced back and forth, deciding whether or not I should call Genesis. I hadn't spoken to her since my second year at Stellenbosch, and even by that point, things were just really awkward. I realised our friendship was more than just Genesis and I—it was Genesis and I *and* her whole family. So, when things got weird with her family, things got weird between the two of us.

I missed her a lot, so much so that, at times, I would go on her Facebook or Instagram, but she never had anything uploaded, so I had no idea what was going on in her life. It upset me. After trying to distract myself with Netflix, Youtube and every other thing like I always do, I knew my mind wasn't going to rest until I called her.

I called her but got no answer. But, at least, it felt like a weight had lifted off my shoulders because, now, I couldn't say I didn't try; maybe she just asked Gogo for my number because she thought that's what she had to say.

A few minutes later, the same phone number began to ring me back, so I picked it up. I stayed silent for a while, wondering what I would hear on the other side and whether it really was Genesis.

"Kaya?" I heard a croaky voice say, sounding just like Genesis.

"Gen?" I whispered.

"Oh my goodness! It's really you," she said, as I began to hear her explode with tears.

"You too, Gen. Please don't cry," I said, also failing to hold back my tears.

"Kaya, please don't call me crazy, even though I'm sure you'd remember I do *a lot* of crazy things, but I'm coming to see you right now."

"What? Genesis, slow down. Why would you do that?" I replied, feeling overwhelmed at what was happening in the first one minute of our phone conversation.

"As soon as I saw your missed call, I felt a prompting in my heart to come and see you, even though I wasn't sure if it was your number. I said, 'God, if Kaya is the one who picks up the phone, I'll go straight to the airport,' and it was you. So, let's save the tears for when I get to you tonight," she said firmly.

"Right, wow okay. I'll send you my address," I said, not bothering to be argumentative for once.

***

Seven hours later, Genesis turned up on my doorstep. We couldn't even say anything, we just threw ourselves into each other's arms and started weeping for all the lost time. I'd missed my old friend so much.

As the tears dried and the emotions in my hallway cleared up, I invited her inside my home for a long-awaited life reunion.

"I don't think I actually have the words, Kaya. I've just been praying over and over to be able to see your face, I wasn't sure I ever would see it again," Genesis admitted, still crying.

"I'm sorry, Genesis. I'm so sorry, I've been wanting to say that for years and I wasn't sure if I would ever get the chance. I know it's my fault that we didn't speak all this time, and I'm so sorry," I said, still crying as well.

"It's okay, Kaya. The past is the past; it's forgotten, seriously. Let's focus on the here and now, yeah?"

"You really are a Glimpse-of-Heaven, aren't you Mrs GOF?" I chuckled solemnly.

"You still call me by that name?" Genesis laughed, drying up her tears.

"Girl, of course. I'm never gonna stop calling you that," I giggled. "Seriously, though, you don't need to lie to me if you're still angry with me."

"I'm seriously not angry with you. We all make mistakes, friend. It hurt at first but I understood why you distanced yourself. We have to forgive and move on. You're family," she smiled. "But can we get to the glow-up talk now! You look like a million dollars, girl, and your *penthouse* certainly looks about triple that! I always knew you were going to be successful but, friend, you have gone above and beyond what I imagined."

"Success is subjective," I said, trying to talk modestly.

"Okay, let's cut that pretend humility thing out now. I see your smile behind all that! Tell me, tell me pleaseeeeee," she pestered.

"Chill, okay, okay. I'm a business owner here in Joburg."

"Nice, what kind of business? Property, fashion, lifestyle?" Genesis asked.

"Yes, lifestyle…" I hesitated, hoping she wouldn't push me to say anymore.

"Okay…finish off your sentence. It's not like I'm gonna have to force it out of you like when we were kids, right?"

"I'm a…nightlifey-kinda-clubby-kinda-owner," I sighed, staring right at the ground. I counted three seconds and looked up, and looking right back at me was the facial expression I dreaded. "What? Owning a club is not an illegal hustle and I've done lots of good things like taking people off the streets and giving them a proper job!"

"Friend, you know what? I didn't come here to lecture you today on what I believe is right and wrong, I just want us to spend time together. Now that's not me saying that I approve or that the lecture isn't coming at some point but, *today*, let's just be Genesis and Kaya again," she decided, which made me do a happy dance in my head. I just wanted it to be like old times again.

We started on our old favourite movie collection—*Rush Hour*. We laughed and giggled throughout our movie marathon, helping me relax and destress from the argument my mum and I had a few days beforehand. However, as we watched the movie, something really kept bugging me—Genesis kept hiding her phone whenever particular texts or phone calls came through. *I bet it was Luke.*

Pausing the movie, I said quietly, "Can I ask you something?"

"We were just at the best part, Kaya!" she laughed, but quickly seeing the solemn look on my face she replied, "oh, sorry, my bad! What did you say?"

"*I said*, can I ask you something?"

"Yeah, of course. Ask away," she said, giving me a comforting smile.

"How is Luke?" I asked, immediately regretting the question. I wasn't even sure if I was ready or even wanted a response to it, but it was too late now.

"He's well. I'm actually going to go and visit him tomorrow. What made you ask that?"

"Just wondering, I guess…I just thought I would ask now that you're here. And are you sure you don't want to stay in Joburg with me for a few days? You can't be doing all that flying back and forth in such a short amount of time," I said.

"Oh, sorry, Kaya, I thought you knew?" she replied, looking away from me.

"I knew what…?"

"Luke lives in Joburg now. He's been here for a few years," Genesis revealed, making my heart absolutely sink.

"Ah, okay, nice. I hope he's liking it here," I replied, trying to play it cool.

"Kaya, I'm going to give him your number because I feel as if you should both talk out what happened."

"No!" I shouted. "Please don't do that, there's no need." I really wished I hadn't brought it up.

"Sorry, friend, I didn't mean to upset you," she apologised.

"No, no. I'm sorry, you don't need to apologise. It was an overreaction, that's all. Maybe at some other point, Luke and I can talk, but I think that, for the moment, I would prefer not to as I have some important business stuff coming up," I explained.

"No pressure," she reassured me, "as long as you're sure? I'm always here for you to talk about it too?"

"I'm sure. Thank you, Gen. You're a star."

"As are you, friend. Okay, now play the movie! WA-WHO-YEAH!"

I had really missed Genesis.

2012

"Kaya!" Gogo shouted, "there's a handsome man asking for you at the door!!"

I'd never panicked so hard in my life about the way I looked. Why would Luke not tell me he was coming to see me on a Saturday morning? I'd barely just woken up as I'd treated myself to a Saturday lazy day and I looked *rough*.

"Give me like ten minutes!" I shouted as I rushed into the bathroom to brush my teeth and give myself a 30 second rinse. I was panicking so much that I may have even brushed my teeth with my mum's toothbrush. I didn't even remember to bring my towel in so I patted myself down with my pyjama top—I truly felt like I was in an apocalypse.

"H-hey. M-morning," I stuttered as I forced a smile at Gogo and Luke as if I wasn't half dishevelled and straight out of bed.

"Did you just get up?" Gogo laughed. I turned around straight away and gave her a look so that she knew not to embarrass me in front of Luke.

"What, you think I'd let you go on a date with a boy who judges my granddaughter for just waking up?" Gogo cackled.

"Gogo! Oh my, why are you so embarrassing?" I shrieked, wishing I could curl up into a little ball. "And Luke and I are *just* friends. We're not going on a date."

"Oh, we're not?" Luke smirked.

"I like this one!" Gogo exclaimed. "Yes, I approve of you, Luke. Do whatever you need to do to knock the stubbornness out of my granddaughter. You seem like one who could do it."

"I am not stubborn," I hissed.

"Oh, yes you are, Ingane," my mother said as she walked through with the laundry. Who asked for her opinion anyway?

"Let's go, Luke!" I ordered, feeling desperate to get away from my very annoying family.

"How about we spend time with your mum and Gogo? I like it here," Luke smirked, again.

"How about we leave Gogo and my mum to do what they planned to do on their Saturday morning," I said sternly.

"I have no plans—" Gogo started.

"Gogo!" I interrupted. "Fine. If you guys all wanna hang out together then let me get on with my own day and go back to bed."

"So, you *did* just wake up?" Luke teased. I suddenly couldn't remember why I'd agreed for us to be friends in the first place; he was *so* annoying. "Chill! I'm joking, I'm joking," Luke laughed as he realised I was serious about going back to bed. "I've booked us two tickets to a theatre in Cape Town. I came now so we can have enough time for us to drive down and do a few things before the show."

"Are you serious?" I asked, getting all excited and then suddenly re-remembering why we were friends. He nodded, clearly he was serious.

"Ahhhhh! I'm going to the theatre, I'm going to the theatre!" I sang right up in Gogo's face.

"Thank you so much, Luke," I said as I ran up to him, giving him a huge hug.

***

On our way down to Muizenberg, Cape Town in Luke's old blue Mazda, we listened to loads of Rhythm and Blues 80's songs, getting us ready for the theatre mood. His car was surprisingly cleaner than I expected, super clean actually; it made me wonder if he'd just cleaned it because he knew I would see it.

"Your car is really clean," I started. "Since when were rugby boys this clean?"

"Didn't you know I'm a straight up neat freak?" he marvelled.

"I just thought all boys were messy. Thato's car is super messy," I said.

"Well, yeah, that's *Thato*," he said with slight annoyance.

"How do you know anything about Thato? You haven't met him, have you?" I asked curiously, wondering why he seemed not to like him.

"No, I haven't met the guy but I know Genesis doesn't like him hanging out with you."

"Oh, right, I see. He's my best friend though, and he's a good person behind all that stuff he's doing. I don't think I'd be here without him." It was a bit of an awkward silence after that. I wasn't really sure how much Gen had told him about Thato, or why he was even brought up at all, but it still wasn't enough for Luke to be annoyed about it.

"You told your grandma we're just friends," Luke said as he broke the silence.

"I thought that's what we said? We're just getting to know each other as friends," I replied, hoping he wasn't about to make it an even weirder car journey seeing as we still had a bit of a journey to go.

"Well, we've been hanging out a lot and I spend more time with you than I do with anyone these days. So, are we really just *friends*?" Luke pressed.

"You tell me," I asked shyly. I could feel my heart rate increase to like a million heart beats an hour. I'd been wishing this moment would come for weeks but, now that it was here, I suddenly didn't want it to happen anymore. Things are always so much nicer when they're just stuck in your imagination.

"I'm a confident and straight up guy so I'll just say it as it is. You and I both know we're not just friends. I trust you and I like you a lot. There are feelings there, strong feelings. I don't think we have to make it weird or complicated and do that whole making it *dramatically official* thing, but I can definitely say you're my person and I want you to be my person. No pressure though."

I suddenly calmed down because he'd taken the lead and said the part I didn't want to say. "Okay then. Agreed," I said, not feeling brave enough to look at him after practically just becoming someone's girlfriend for the first time. I mean, not only was I becoming someone's girlfriend for the first time, but this was the first time I had even gotten to know someone in that way; it was very surreal.

The day felt like a dream, and I don't even say that to sound like I'm in a movie. It truly didn't feel real. Luke and I were just such a match for each other; we were effortlessly like a jigsaw puzzle that fit together. We laughed, we ate, we watched the performance and I didn't want to leave that moment. To be honest, something in me said that I wanted us to be forever together.

As we walked through the city after the performance, a sudden wave of curiosity came over me as I realised neither of us had spoken about his big secret since the first day we became friends.

"Luke, you never told me why you don't think you believe in God?" I asked.

"Oh, wow, we're going there after such a good day?" he sighed.

"No, no, we don't have to talk about it if you don't want to. No pressure," I winked at him as we crossed the road back to the car.

"Oh, so now that you're my girlfriend you think that you can steal my lingo!" he laughed. "You know what, I don't want us to have any secrets so I'll explain. I guess I've always been in a Christian household. I'm a pastor's kid and I've never really had an option in my belief. When I was younger, I used to pray and ask God to reveal himself to me and nothing came. As I grew older, I think I kinda just realised that God is just a made-up character that people use to try to make life make sense and a little easier. Everyone has a different reality, but I just struggle to come to terms with the fact that there is a heaven and hell; I just think once we're dead, we're dead."

"Hmm, interesting. Thanks for sharing with me. By the way, I would never judge you or whatever walk of life you choose to take," I reassured him.

"This might sound strange but, as stubborn as you are, Kaya, there's just something about your presence that feels peaceful. Can I call you 'peaceful' instead of Kaya?" he smiled.

"Woah, that's so weird because my name literally means that. Did you search that up or something?" I asked, feeling slightly freaked out.

"No, not at all. My family always says that I do things like that. It's like I just know things about people somehow. Weird right?"

"Very. Can I ask you to help me with something?" I asked.

"Anything, except homework, because I know how you are with school. I'm just trying to pass high school, not become the next Stephen Hawking," he teased.

"Whatever," I sang as I rolled my eyes. "Basically, I don't know if I ever told you, but a few months ago I found out where my dad was."

"Oh, wow, that's so dope! I know it's been tough not having him there. How's it all going?"

"That's the whole issue, Luke; it isn't. He wasn't there when I went to find him at his house here in Cape Town. But I think I may go back to find him," I revealed.

"That's deep. Sorry K," he sympathised. "So, what would you like my help with?"

"Well, I was hoping that the next time I go, you could come with me, just for moral support."

"Of course, you don't even need to ask," he said gently.

"Thank you, I appreciate it," I smiled, feeling so comforted that this time, I didn't have to go through it alone.

By the time we got in the car to drive back home, it was reaching 10pm, and my mum was ringing my phone nonstop—it was probably the first time I'd ever been out of town this late. I immediately put it on silent.

"Hey K, do you wanna do something crazy?" Luke volunteered.

"Depends on what?" I apprehended, knowing that whatever it was could land me in loads of trouble with my mum.

"Well, we're already in Cape Town, and I know Cape Town is massive, but why don't you see how far away your dad lives from here? Check it on my GPS system," Luke dared.

"What? Are you serious?!" I voiced.

"I'm serious if you're serious…" he whispered.

"Well, okay then," I smiled. "Woah! Luke, it's literally only 25 minutes away from where we are right now. What do you think?"

"Off we go. Can't believe I'm already meeting my father-in-law," Luke chortled.

13

2021

It was nearly 7pm and I was hurrying around, trying to make sure my place was in perfect condition for all the guests that were about to come over. I was hosting a celebration party for me and Mr Underwood's new business deal.

I'd made sure the DJ was already playing on my balcony so that when people came in there weren't any awkward silent moments. I'd strung beautiful bulbed lights across the ground floor of my penthouse and connected them onto the balcony. The mixologist had laid out ready-made Cosmopolitans, Pina Coladas and Mojitos —it was all set. I decided I'd turn the jacuzzi on at 10pm or so, so that people would enjoy the atmosphere and get to know each other first before jumping straight in. I also thought it'd be nice to get everyone a personalised gift bag for when they were leaving. Now, I was just feeling the nerves kicking in and hoped everyone would have a good time.

You see, when I host events at the club, there aren't nerves involved because it doesn't feel like my private zone, but now that people were coming into my home to party, it felt like they were stepping into *me*. Either way, it was about time I hosted something in this penthouse.

"CONGRATULATIONS!" Mandy screamed as she entered through my front door. "You're officially in business with Daniel Underwood, and that means we're on our way up to doing business with Alexander Petrov; isn't this a dream come true? Who said that women had to have a man in charge to be successful in this trade? We are doing so well, sis!"

"Hello to you too, Mandy! Come in first and grab a drink. See, I listened to your recommendation on the DJ," I vocalised to her.

"Ooooh nice. He was at a beach party I went to in Pretoria last summer—he's good, right? And yes, please! I would love a Mojito right now. Can I just say, you have outdone yourself with this, Kaya. You've made this place sparkle," Mandy marvelled, looking at all the decorations with eyes wide open. I was glad at her reaction as it helped me to stop overthinking that I hadn't done a good job with the set-up.

"Thank you, sis. I made it look the best I possibly could. Back to what you were screaming about…yeah, this is about to be really crazy. If Mr Underwood can partner us up with Petrov then it's going to be so much easier for us to move stuff through the borders; he has so many contacts because of how long he's been in the game. That also means we'll have less police sniffing around, not that they care anyway, they just want to be paid. But, yeah sis, I'm so excited!" I raved as we helped ourselves to some cocktails.

This was literally *everything* I'd been working towards for the last few years. I don't even know how I managed to get to this stage so quickly, but I guess luck has always been on my side. If I was going to achieve being the richest entrepreneur in Joburg, this was my way in.

When my dad and aunty taught me that to get anything in life I had to bend the rules, I finally woke up—and now I'm successful. If I'd followed my mum's way, which was to stick by the book, it would have landed me with nothing but a menial paid lab job after university, and knowing that the industry pretty much only favoured white people, I decided to finally follow my dad's advice and start bending the rules. If the police and government in South Africa barely follow the rules then why should I? They're the ones that have taught us, right?

Everyone seemed to be enjoying themselves with all the music, food and the drinks, and I finally felt much more calm and free of stress.

As I walked over to the bar to check that the cocktails were still being made, Mr Underwood approached me with nothing but glee on his face, partially because he seemed to have had a bit to drink.

"Now that you're stuck with me, Ms Khumalo, how do you feel?" he said, grinning at me from ear to ear.

"Are we ever going to call each other by our first name since now we're 'friends?'" I enquired, completely ignoring his previous question.

"Depends. Do you want me to? Casual business partners sometimes become *too* casual," Underwood replied.

"Nope, you're right. Don't call me by my first name," I remarked quickly. "Just wondering if you were still able to set up that meeting with Alexander Petrov?"

"My word is my word, Ms Khumalo. He said he can come by the Blue Panther Monday afternoon for a brief meeting. I must warn you, though, he doesn't like to waste time so make sure to have all of your business proposals written out before the meeting," he sternly advised me with slurred words.

"Already done. I wouldn't waste time with Petrov; this is like a drug dealer's X factor moment. But, remind me, what part do you want to play in this just so I'm clear?"

"Honestly, not much. I would prefer to keep my hands *mostly* clean. The main thing for me is to make sure I have enough capital to start off my business and enough to keep it going if things don't go to plan. I just know that if I got investment elsewhere, it would take me much longer and I may not even be able to convince anyone that it's a worthy start-up. Also, as you know, I used to work for Petrov so I prefer to stay within the boundaries of what I'm used to."

"Okay, sounds credible," I said, still unconvinced by Underwood's story, but convinced enough to take the opportunity to work with Petrov.

I walked over to the balcony to get some fresh air, thinking about how I was going to convince Petrov to work with me.

"I've missed you, friend," Thato said as he joined me on the balcony.

"Where have you been? I haven't seen you in weeks," I muttered firmly, now used to his regular disappearances.

"Chill, you told me to go deal with the problem so I went to deal with it, but I had to lay low for a few weeks," Thato disclosed.

"Why would you have to lay low? I told you to just make sure that those guys in the Cape Flats would stay off our area," I clarified.

"Yeah, and do you think that guys like that respond to pretty talk?" he said.

"Oh my goodness, Thato! You *did not* do what I think you did. How many times have I told you we are not in the business of hurting people; that is not what we do!"

"Oh, give me a break and wake up, Kaya. We're in the *drug* business; we don't own a dog-cleaning parlour. As I've said, if you don't want to know then don't ask. I'll deal with the dirty work; you just stay looking pretty for the clients and I'll keep sorting out the movements."

I felt like slapping him in the face for that comment. "Don't you dare talk to me like that, Thato, I'm warning you. You know what, I honestly can't deal with you right now," I hissed as I walked back inside, not at all wanting to be in his sight.

My relationship with Thato has been weird these days. It felt like I was only putting up with him because I had to. Theoretically, he was my employee so I would expect him to respect my orders, especially as I was the one that would be under the most pressure from the law, but no, Thato does whatever he wants whenever he wants to.

It has circled round and round in my mind many times as to why I never listened to Genesis all those years ago and distanced myself from him; now, it was too late. Thato is the main reason the police have recently been sniffing around my club as he tends to leave a trail behind him everywhere he goes.

About six months ago, I asked him to deliver a package to some clients I had in Pretoria. I told him to just drop it off, collect the money and not say anything to them, knowing that these particular clients could get rowdy when they're unfamiliar with someone. Instead, he demanded that they count the cash they were going to give him a few times over to make sure it was all there. Of course, his demanding attitude sparked up an argument and long story short, I lost one of my biggest clients. It was just getting tiring to keep a big baby around these days for the sake of sentiment, and I've frankly decided I'm only giving him one more chance.

I plodded back inside, feeling extremely underwhelmed at the fact that I was struggling to enjoy my own party. Everyone was having such a great time. I literally had spent a fortune on all the drinks, canapés, waiters, DJ, lights, the list goes on. Yet, I've barely had three seconds of enjoyment. I just felt so frustrated.

Mandy was usually my go-to when I wasn't enjoying myself but she looked like she was having the time of her life dancing on the rooftop with some of her friends. Ander, my accountant, was chatting up all of the women I'd invited from my Instagram circle, and Mr Underwood was…well, he was just blacked out on the sofa. I wanted everyone out.

"Guess who?" someone said as they covered my eyes.

This was the worst time for someone to come and irritate me, and if it was a client, I would have no choice but to be their entertainment for however long they wanted to bug me.

"Who?" I replied pathetically, now almost convinced it was one of the clients by the smell of strong old man cologne.

"Look up," a deep voice giggled.

I got up super slowly, really not feeling in the mood to be someone's amusement for the sake of business. I turned around as if I was being forced to stay at the table to finish some food I didn't like. As I unwillingly looked, I saw Pops looking right back at me.

"Wait, what!" I shouted at the top of my lungs. I screamed for a good few minutes, not giving him any space to breathe as I hugged him with my whole being.

"You're out already?" I raved, still in shock. "And you're in Joburg?!"

"Is this how you greet your dad when you're in front of all your cool friends?"

I was literally grinning from ear to ear, it was like so much life had just been sucked back into me.

"Oh, just come here, Dad!" I shouted with exhilaration as I squeezed him again.

"I've missed you too, Kaya," he chuckled lightly.

"Can I get you anything to drink—a glass of wine, a cocktail, Prosecco?" I asked intently whilst also being in panic-host mode, trying to make him feel as comfortable as possible in this vain Joburg social circle.

"I'll have a beer, thanks," he laughed.

"Ah, yes, of course. Good to see your taste for the finer things in life still hasn't become apparent," I mocked as I rolled my eyes.

"Get on with it, girl! I'm not here long," he smiled.

I came back with an ice-cold Carling beer, just the way he liked it; his favourite beer by far.

"Just the way I like it," he said as he sipped it refreshingly, "and to think I can have as many of these as I want now."

"You sure can, Pops. Let me know if you want anything else, and I mean *anything.*"

"Okay, okay, Kaya. Why don't you just enjoy your own party now? Enough with nagging me," Pops breathed.

I still wasn't enjoying the party even though my dad was here now—I wanted everyone to leave so Pops and I could be alone. I found that this Joburg 'elite' group was mostly annoying, self-absorbed and shallow, but I *had* to be around them because they literally made me my money. It's draining!

Every Saturday morning, I go to pilates exercise classes with some of these women who only talk about their parents' private jets and if their (cheating) boyfriends are going to propose to them (I know they cheat because I've been a target so many times). On Wednesdays, I have private poker events in my club and that's when I hear all these 'loyal' men talk about all the fun they've had on the weekend with other women and just other generally misogynistic table talk. That's only just the start; it's like I'm living my dream but sacrificing my sanity as an expense. I really don't know how much longer I can pretend. At least, I haven't turned into one of them. I don't think so anyway.

I'd completely drifted off in my toxic social-life thoughts when I realised my dad was picking up his stuff ready to leave; probably tired of all the weird and fake plastic energy around him.

"Oh, wait. No, no, Pops; don't go yet! I wanted us to talk when everyone was gone," I said as I ran over to him.

"Sweetie, it's okay. We can catch up this week on the phone," he tried to reassure me.

"Nope, no. Come, let's just quickly catch up in my room, pleaseeeee," I begged him.

"Mm. Okay. Fine, but ten minutes, because I've got to get back to my friend's house soon; we're leaving early for Cape Town in the morning and it's a long drive."

"Yes! Follow me. Now, you'll get an exclusive tour of my house," I winked.

I showed him the whole top floor—my Pulp Fiction inspired cinema room, my pretty much unused beauty room, my also *very* unused guest room (apart from Genesis' surprise appearance), my walk-in closest (which was very unnecessary as I recycle the same five to ten outfits), and, finally, my very *very* used bedroom which I spent absolutely all my time in.

"Honestly, I am blown away," Pops said. "I don't even have the words. Did I really make you, Kaya?"

"Let's look in the mirror and find out," I giggled as I dragged him over to my bathroom mirror. "Make yourself comfortable wherever you want—take the bed, the sofa, bean bags, anything."

"I'll take the bed. I think my prison body needs some five-star mattress treatment," he sang.

"Okay. I'll take the bed too," I grinned.

"So, father dearest, my first and very obvious question is, how is it possible that I'm looking at you right now?"

"Haha! I knew you were going to start there; not even a 'How's it going Dad?' or 'Have you met anyone yet?' My Kaya is straight to the point."

"Well, you said we don't have much time so I thought we'd get right to it and, of course, you're not seeing anyone, you just got out of prison," I replied sarcastically.

"Glad to see you haven't changed since 2018! Well, to put it bluntly, the records will say good behaviour, but between you and me, I knew a friend who knew a friend who knew a friend," he smirked slyly.

"Was it that lawyer I paid to help you?" I enquired.

"No, that lawyer was actually no help at all. Just some old friends from my younger days, that's all."

"Well, either way, I'm glad you're out. I could cry Pops, honestly," I said, so close to tears.

"Don't cry, my love. I'm home now and I'm not going back in."

"Promise me, Pops."

"I promise!" he smiled. As much as I wanted to believe him, I knew from his ways that that promise was pretty empty, but I really hoped that this time he would stay out of trouble.

"Pops, why don't you come and work for me this time, rather than all those people who threw you under the bus in the first place?"

"My sweet daughter, always looking out for me. It's a kind offer but I'm actually going to try and do things differently this time. I want to start something legal. I've lived more than half of my life doing stupid things and I feel that I now have a chance to make things right," he sighed.

"Oh, come on, Pops. We both know that you're not going to last a week doing that!" I teased but quickly realised I had offended him. "Just joking, Pops. Of course, you're gonna do really well. And if you need any money for setting stuff up, I'm always here to help."

"Thanks sweetie, but I've got it all sorted so don't you worry."

"How did you find where I live now by the way?" I wondered.

"Your aunt told me. She also told me you haven't picked up her calls in weeks. She's worried about you," he said.

"Yeah, I know. I'll make sure to give her a call tomorrow. Busyness is not a good excuse. I really should go over and see her; I've not been the best niece. Why don't I come over for a few days in the next couple of weeks so I can see you both and we can all cook together like old times?" I suggested.

"Good idea! But, I need to go now," my dad said as he began to get his things together.

"Okay, let me see you out downstairs," I offered.

"No, no. I can see you hate this party. Stay here and avoid everyone until they leave," he chuckled.

"How did you notice?" I replied, feeling embarrassed that he could see how out of place I was amongst these kinds of people.

"Well, you've disliked snobby people since you were a baby. I know you better than you think," he revealed.

"Oh, wow," I sighed with relief, knowing that I've had sense since birth.

"I'm glad to be back, sweetie, and thank you for hosting me. One thing though; don't change for these people because I can see you're already starting to," Pops admitted, looking me straight in the eyes.

"No, I'm not Pops. I haven't changed," I defended myself.

"Are you sure? You always told me you would never get acrylic nails done," he sighed as he raised his eyebrows at my nails and walked out of my room.

Maybe he was right. Have I started to become like one of them?

14

2012

Luke had to pull me out of the car as we reached my dad's house because I was suddenly so filled with fear, wondering if he even wanted to see me.

"Luke, maybe we should just go back home? My mum has called me like a thousand times," I said as I whimpered in fear.

"Kaya, you have got to face this fear; if not, you will never get your chance to meet him. Now, come on. I'm right here with you," Luke reassured me.

I finally agreed and managed to walk grudgingly over to my dad's front door, shaking from head to toe and sweat pulsating from every gland in my body, I could feel my whole throat drying out. Anyway, I knocked.

It was pitch black inside the house and, after knocking twice, I concluded that we'd probably come when everyone was asleep so I motioned to Luke that nobody was there and started walking back to the car.

"Kaya!" Luke whispered.

"Yeah?" I whispered back.

"Look, a light just went on," Luke murmured.

My head shot back around and I glanced at the window where the light was coming from. As I heard someone begin to unlock the door, I ran towards Luke in fear but didn't make it in time.

"Hello? Who is there?" a man with a gun in his hand said to me.

With quivering lips and a racing heart, I replied "M-m-me," feeling like I was absolutely about to wet my pants.

Luke ran beside me in full protective mode. "It's okay, Kaya, I'm here," he whispered.

"Who is me?" the man demanded.

"Roger, put the gun down! It's Kaya," I heard a voice in the background say. Recognising that it was Aunty Andrea, I felt breath return to my lungs again.

"Oh, oh my goodness. Oh my goodness," he said as he dropped the gun. He walked over to me and said, "Kaya, is that really you? Is that you my daughter?"

He embraced me slowly and held me for a while. I could feel his tears dripping onto my forehead and it just felt like a missing piece of a puzzle in my heart had been replaced. I couldn't even cry because there were no emotions that could explain how I was feeling. I didn't feel like I was truly living in this moment.

As he let go, I looked over at Luke who gave me a supportive smile, as if to say he was truly fortunate to have experienced this moment with me. That's when I decided that this was all I needed.

"Yes, it's me, Dad. It's Kaya," I replied softly.

"Please, come in and make yourself at home. I'm assuming that this is your boyfriend?" my dad asked, smiling softly.

"Yes, Sir. My name is Luke," Luke so boldly introduced.

"Great to meet you. You are both welcome."

I so vividly remembered everything about this place; it was as though I took a mental photograph of everything I saw when I came to find him the first time. The flaking wallpaper on the living room walls, the creaking wood all over the floor, the battered sofas…still, I liked being here.

My dad positioned himself opposite from where I sat on the couch and just stared at me for a good five minutes straight. No one said a word, not even Luke.

"Should I make us all some tea?" Aunty Andrea offered, finally saying something.

"Yeah, sure, I would love some. Let me come and help," Luke interjected, clearly wanting to leave my dad and I to catch up alone.

"I just…I can't believe it, my girl. I can't believe it," he said as he put his face in his hands, crying again.

"I know. Me too," I replied, still not able to comprehend my emotions.

"You look just like me, it's like I'm looking at myself in the mirror," he said tearily.

"Like twins," I confirmed.

"Hold on, does Nandi—I mean, does your mother know that you're here?" he asked with fear in his eyes.

"No, she doesn't know, and I don't plan to tell her," I said.

"Oh," he said. I couldn't quite make out what exactly his reply meant but I think it could have meant a lot of things. "Is everything okay between the two of you?"

"Oh, yes of course! Things are just fine. I just wouldn't want her to worry that I'm out so late," I lied.

"Well, how's school? You must be getting ready to leave now, right? Tell me everything; I want to know."

"School is great, Dad. I'll be going to Stellenbosch soon to study Chemical Engineering," I smiled.

"Stellenbosch, *the* Stellenbosch?" he gasped as I confirmed his question with a nod. "That's awesome my girl! Wow, I'm so proud of you. From how quickly you learnt how to speak, I knew you were a genius in the making," my dad responded.

"Haha, thanks. I guess I got it from you and Mum."

"How is your mum?" my dad asked expectantly.

"Er, yeah, fine thanks." I just about managed to get out, still burning with anger in my heart for what she had done—even the thought of her name made me feel irritated.

The next thing that came out of my mouth shocked me, especially as we had only just met but I just knew it was now or never.

"Can I move in with you?" I said abruptly, like my tongue was working faster than my mind.

"What do you mean?" he chuckled in a confused manner, opening up a can of Carling beer.

"I want to move in with you and Aunty Andrea. It will be in a few months when I move to university—I'll spend my holidays here with you guys."

"Why? What's happening at home?" my dad replied, suddenly worried.

"Nothing, really. I just want to be with you both, that's all."

"I mean, I'm not saying you're not welcome here, but don't you want to spend time getting to know us and learning about all the things we've missed out on before we discuss that kind of stuff?" he reasoned. "I'm sure your mum wouldn't want you to rush making such a huge decision like this, and I know your grandma will miss you."

"You remember Gogo?" I smiled, feeling more relaxed now that I realised he had known Gogo longer than I had.

"Of course! She was my mother-in-law, Kaya," he pointed out.

"True. I guess I'm just surprised to hear that even though it's obvious. But no, I've made up my mind. I really want to live with you after high school. Mum and Gogo will be fine."

"Well, okay, but only if you can get your mother to agree."

"She's already agreed," I lied again, not at all caring about the potential repercussions.

"Hmmm, your aunt and I will think about it and maybe we can figure out some *shared* arrangements for you once you start university between here and Gogo's house. We should be in a nicer place by then anyway."

"Oh, really? Where will you be moving to?" I asked curiously, seeing as I knew it would be my new home.

"There's a quiet suburban area we put a bid in for. We've finally saved up enough to buy it."

"Sounds nice, is there a spare bedroom for me?" I said, knowing I may have cheekily overstepped.

"Like father, like daughter," my dad laughed. "Yes, there are three bedrooms in this place so there will be space for you if that's what you want."

"It is what I want, Dad. It is what I want," I stressed.

"I'm so glad this isn't awkward between us. We're speaking as though I've been around you your whole life," my dad confessed with relief.

"Like twins," I said again.

"Do you remember anything about me at all?" he asked with great intent.

"Honestly, not really, no. I remember you getting me ready for school at times and, on the odd occasion, helping me to brush my teeth, but I couldn't remember what you looked like until Aunty Andrea showed me a picture of you."

"Wow, I guess I can't expect you to when I haven't seen you since you were four. It's been fourteen years," he said as he looked to the floor with sorrow.

And to think this was all because of my mother. How selfish is she?

"And you're sure this has nothing to do with you and your mother?" my dad attempted to verify.

"Of course not, why would it? Mum and I are all good," I lied for the third time.

2021

I just had a few last-minute touches to be made for the meeting with Alexander Petrov tomorrow. The only question I still wasn't sure how to answer was the fact that I knew he was going to ask me why he needed to come into business with *me*. I mean, I had a good track record but I'd only been doing business here in Joburg for five years, and I knew from past experience that people without years and years of experience to their name could be unreliable and flaky, especially when it comes to the police.

I guess I was just hoping he would be sold on who I was as a person, and that I was a determined, hardworking and trustworthy businesswoman. Oh, and may I add, the only 27 year old woman to have made a successful and large drug business in Johannesburg. I just hoped he would buy my selling point.

Just as I was about to shut my laptop away and put on a movie, my apartment phone started ringing. I looked at the screen and could see it was the concierge reception calling me. *I didn't order food, did I?*

"Hello?"

"Good evening Ma'am, sorry to disturb you at this time. Someone is here in the foyer asking for you. Should I send them up?"

"Um, okay. Yeah, send them up," I replied, thinking Mandy had probably lost the spare key I'd given her and had seen my text asking her to come and help me finalise some things for the meeting.

I opened the door as I heard footsteps land and strolled over ready to put myself back into business mode.

"Hi daughter."

I paused briefly, very confused.

"Mum?" I said with bafflement in my voice. "W-what's going on?"

"Can I come in?" she replied regally, scanning my living room to see if anyone was around.

"Um, y-yeah, sure," I stuttered, still in a state of shock at her sudden appearance.

She pushed a suitcase fit for a king into my apartment, and I looked at it briefly wondering what it was here for—*not to stay here*, I thought to myself.

"You've decorated it beautifully since Gogo and I came here last. I love the lighting; it captures this place well," she said as an attempt to do small talk. I nodded in response, afraid that if I opened my mouth I might bite her instead of being polite.

"How are you?" she said with a forced smile. I put a thumbs up towards her whilst pretending I was distracted with housework even though the whole place was clean and tidy.

"Any plans for the summer?" she continued, trying to force a verbal response out of me. I shook my head politely and opened the fridge to get myself a glass of water, trying to cool myself down from all the tension.

"Kaya, come and sit down please. I came here to talk to you about some things."

I pointed to the water as if to say it was a busy enough excuse to keep me away from her.

"Please," she said sternly.

It's like no matter how old I get, child instinct always kicks in. When my mum uses that stern voice, I don't even waste time obeying. My mind resorts to thinking she's going to hit me with a wooden spoon.

I walked over grudgingly, hoping to play no part in Nandi Khumalo's drama tonight seeing as I didn't want to be distracted for tomorrow.

"I came t-to apologise to you," she said hesitantly as if she was being forced to say it.

"Oh," I replied. "Thanks."

"No, seriously, Kaya. I'm sorry for the way I hit you and spoke to you on Gogo's birthday. It was…unprofessional."

"Unprofessional…?" I began.

"Exactly."

"*Unprofessional?*" I re-emphasised.

"Yes, that," she continued

"I wish for once you would stop putting on this front! It's just strange! Which mother calls themselves unprofessional, like it's a corporate job?" I said, as I moved away from her.

"What would you like me to say?" she defended.

"Oh, forget it, Mum. What did you *actually* come here for?" I scoffed.

"I told you; I came here to make amends for the way I acted on Gogo's birthday. I don't want things between us to be unhealthy," she reasoned. I thought she was out of her mind.

"Apology accepted. I'm going to bed now and I'll be leaving early in the morning for work. Make yourself at home," I exhaled.

"I'm sorry I'm not Gogo," she snapped as I was halfway up the stairs.

"Excuse me…? What does Gogo have to do with you coming unannounced to my house after almost punching me in the face?" I said sternly. I knew the peace wouldn't last long.

"I just want us to get along, Kaya. I want us to be close," she pleaded, trying to turn her snarky comment around.

"Oh, here we go, Mum. Listen, honey, that boat has sailed far far away," I laughed sarcastically as I tried to leave the argument.

"You don't even know half of what I've protected you from knowing, Kaya. How do you think I feel seeing you be best friends with every other family member but me; knowing that if I revealed what was truly going on you would see *me* as the saint. I've sacrificed so much in order to protect you!" she reasoned.

"Give it a rest. You don't even tell me anything so how can you expect me to see *you* as the saint! You're the reason my whole life has been so messy," I shouted, trying to hold myself back from exploding.

"You want me to tell you the truth? You really want me to tell you the truth?" she shouted as she started crying.

"Yes, Mum! Tell me the truth; tell me how *you* are the supposed saint," I expressed.

She sighed gently, trying to rein herself back in as she realised she was becoming all 'unprofessional' again.

"Kaya…if I tell you the truth, it will really hurt you," she said painfully. I realised that now may have been my only moment to finally get to the bottom of this Khumalo mess so I thought it best to also rein myself in.

"Look, Mum," I said, trying to be more gentle after my shouting, "I know you've been through a lot, I'm not denying that. But I've paid such a heavy price because of you and Gogo's silence—you can't blame me for trying to put all the puzzle pieces together when I was younger," I muttered.

"I know, dear, I know. Truthfully, I came here to do *more* than apologise to you. I came here to tell you the truth, from start to finish," she admitted with tears flowing.

"So tell me Mum," I said as I made my way back to the sofa. "I'm right here, and I'm not going to judge you."

"Okay," she smiled tearfully as she looked me right in the eyes, reminding me again of the beauty in them that I didn't inherit.

"When I was eleven, I started secondary school as I'm sure you are aware. On my first day, Gogo came to drop me some lunch, and back then, she *really* couldn't cook Uphuthu," she said as we both laughed.

"Who said she can cook it now?" I cackled.

"Well, someone had to say it! But, trust me, it's *much* better now than it was back then," Mum teased. "Anyway, she came by the school gates when we were all playing at lunch time, and, because we had just moved into a new town, the town which we live in now, no one knew me there. As soon as they saw Gogo, they began to ask me questions everyday as to how my mother was dark-skinned and I was so fair. I guess they'd assumed I was coloured until they saw Gogo. I always ignored them, thinking they were all out of their minds. Eventually, I'd had enough of their bullying and teasing and decided to ask Gogo about it, thinking I would be able to go back to school the next day and prove them wrong about the fact that I was also white."

"So, until then, you had no clue that you were mixed race?" I asked.

"Nope. I just thought I came out a little different, that's all. Sometimes, the police would stop and ask my mum and I why we were so many shades apart, but I always told them I was black. Gogo would just tell them that I came out a bit funny."

"What would they have done if they knew you were mixed?" I gasped.

"It wouldn't have been good news. I could have been sent to an orphanage or something. They did all sorts to mixed-race children during apartheid. I just thank God my features are not very European, so it was much easier for me to pass as a light-skinned black woman.

"Anyway, so, when I asked her, she told me to come and join her on the sofa so that she could tell me a story, and one thing about my mother is that she doesn't sugarcoat *anything*, no matter how young you are. It's either she says nothing, or she tells you how it is, plainly. Nonetheless, she began by telling me the story she told you about Benjamin Dlamini and Uncle Henry, which I thought was a sweet love story," she smiled.

"It was…." I trailed off as I grimaced.

"Yes, it was. But then she also told me how it ended, *and* how I was conceived. At first, I was really confused because I hadn't once heard the word 'rape' and was limited in any sexual education knowledge. I don't think I fully grasped it until I lost my virginity in my teenage years," she said.

"Mum!" I screamed as I covered my ears.

"Well, yes. I too had a past Kaya—I still don't know why you think I'm a robot."

"Jeez," I gulped.

"As I was saying, when I reached my teenage years, I finally understood what rape was, and I was traumatised to think that I was conceived out of hatred instead of love. I so desperately wished that Benjamin could have been my father instead of that pig."

"Me too, Mum. Me too. But which part of this don't I already know?" I asked impatiently.

"Yes well, it was the trauma of this discovery that led me to make many terrible decisions—one of which was marrying your dad when I was seventeen."

"*Seventeen?*" I interrupted.

"Yes, dear. I was seventeen when I married him and I had you when I was twenty-three.

"I met him at a party in 1986, when I was fifteen years old, and these were the days that many of us girls started to fall for the 'bad boys' because of all these American movies. He stared at me for literally the whole party but I was trying to play hard to get even though I thought he was the most handsome guy I'd ever seen in my life. However, my few flirtatious bouts of eye contact led to an exchange of details, and after that, he harassed me almost everyday until I stupidly agreed to be his girlfriend.

"Gogo *hated* him and always told me that I was far too intelligent to be with someone like him seeing as he was always getting in trouble with the police. Gogo wanted me to get on with my career pursuit of being a lawyer—it was a dream she never got to accomplish but wanted me to live out for her. But, one thing about Gogo's parenting style is that she always allows you to learn from your mistakes, so she didn't force me to break up with him."

"But Pops is a good man on the inside, she must've seen that eventually right?" I blabbered on.

"Kaya, be patient, I'm getting to it; but yes, your dad was very sweet at first. We ran off to get married—I was seventeen and your dad was twenty two. It was a stupid decision, really, because we were broke. He was selling drugs on the corner and I was still in high school. Eventually when the money ran out, I had to beg my mother to let us live with her."

"How old were you at this point?" I asked.

"I was nineteen. I'd just graduated from high school and was making plans to do Law at university if I could find a way to get a scholarship. We moved in and, at first, things were okay, but Gogo just couldn't stand him and made it known every two seconds. I felt bad because I was caught between my mother and my husband, not knowing how to please either of them.

"However, one day, Gogo and your dad had a really bad argument and he pushed her to the ground. I ran into the room and almost tackled him for touching my mother like that. That was when things started to go downhill for me and your dad. He began to hurt me…badly…" she admitted.

"He what?" I thundered.

"Give me a moment, Kaya, I'm nearly there. So he began to hurt me whenever he felt like I wasn't listening to him, or if I would answer back to him. I was trapped in a hellhole marriage and didn't have the guts to divorce him for a long time. However, back to the part of me being the product of rape, I remember being scared that what happened to Gogo would happen to me also; so, on my wedding day I celebrated, thinking there was no chance such a thing could happen to me because, now, I had a husband. But history always repeats itself."

"I don't understand," I sympathised, burning with anger and stricken with pain.

"Have you ever heard of marital rape?" she uttered.

I felt like I was about to be sick; I could literally feel the vomit rising as I realised what she was alluding to. I didn't want to answer her question because I knew that, as soon as the truth was thrown out, all the lies would be revealed.

"No, Mum, no!" I sobbed. "Please, don't tell me it was Dad who raped you."

"I-I'm sorry, darling," she cried. I could tell all the air had left her lungs because of the truth she had kept from me all these years.

"Am I the product of Dad's abuse to you?" I screamed with fear. "Am I? Mum, please tell me. Just tell me."

"Yes, Kaya, I'm sorry. You're the only one he didn't succeed in punching out of me."

"OH MY GOODNESS!" I wailed. I didn't even have the words to describe how broken I was feeling in this moment; I just wanted it to be a lie.

"I was just trying to protect you from the truth, Kaya. I knew how much pain it would cause you. I'm so sorry," she wept.

I walked over to the corner of the room and stayed crouched there for a few minutes. There were just no words that managed to come out. My dad was an abuser and a rapist and I had built a close friendship with him over the past nine years. What was wrong with me? How did I not see it? I was so disgusted with myself.

"Mama," I whispered.

"Yes, dear," she replied softly.

"I'm so sorry," I cried.

"What are you sorry for? There's nothing to be sorry for."

"I went to mend a relationship with Dad and I betrayed you. I'm so sorry, I didn't know what I was doing," I said, so ashamed of myself.

"It's not your fault, Kaya. Trauma led me to the wrong person and you shouldn't feel guilty about it. I should have known you needed a father figure and I'm sorry for not being able to be that for you. I just need you to know how much I love you and how much I've loved you being in my life. You were not an accident or a mistake. God wanted you to be here," she disclosed.

"How can you believe in God after all of this, Ma? If God was real, he would have stopped all of these bad things that happened to us," I said cynically.

"Some people are just bad people, Kaya. God can't stop that," she croaked.

"I love you so much, Mama. I'm sorry this happened to us," I said as I walked back over to her and curled myself in her arms, desperate to make up for all of the years I'd ruined.

"Ma," I said again as the emotions died down.

"Mmhmm," she said softly.

"Why is it that you stayed with Dad until I was four if he did all that to you? How did you forgive him?" I questioned.

"I didn't forgive him. I still haven't forgiven him. I was just too much of a coward to make him leave my life."

"So, what changed when I was four?"

"He…laid his hands on you. That's when I finally came to my senses and made the police take him out of our house. There was no *way* I was ever going to let him lay a finger on you."

"He would beat his own daughter too? He really is a pig!" I exclaimed. "You're so brave, Mama. I'm so proud of you and I promise that we will move forward from this. For starters, I'm going to get Dad out of my life."

"Take your time, my love. Don't make any swift decisions just yet because, from the sound of it, he's changed," she tried to convince me.

"No way, Ma. I'm done with him. The thought of him right now is repulsive."

"He's still your dad, Kaya, and I know that, deep down, he loves you," she began to rationalise.

"I don't have a dad," I answered.

15

2012

I was drooling like a puppy with excitement when I saw Luke from my dorm window. It just felt so good to see a familiar face after moving to the university. I ran down the stairs to meet him outside.

"Hey babe. You look beautiful as always. Here, these are for you," he said as he brought roses out from behind his back.

"Aww, Luke, you didn't have to. You don't look too bad yourself," I said, smiling as I kissed him on the cheek. "Woah! You smell *good*; so, is this what you're spending your professional rugby money on now?"

"I wish they were paying me that much, haha. No, this is one of my dad's old colognes that he gave me because he said I'm a 'man' now, whatever that means. Can I just say though, your campus is so beautiful. You're making me jealous for not going to university," he raved.

"Isn't it?!" I agreed. "Scrubs up well compared to our high school, right?"

"No disputes there," he emphasised. "I was thinking we could get something to eat in town? There's a really nice coffee shop I drove past on my way up here."

"Sounds good. Can I quickly introduce you to my friend Mandy? I met her a few days ago and she's *awesome*," I said excitedly.

Mandy is a friend I met on campus not long ago. She's also on my course but we're not in all of the same classes. When I met her, I was captivated by her unique style—she has this perfectly straight-cut jet black hair that comes to her shoulders, piercing green eyes that are rounded off by her gorgeously thick black eyelashes, and *her clothes*. She's like a hippy-rockstar-bohemian South African queen—I was literally blown away. I couldn't help but stare at her all morning as I studied on an outside bench.

Eventually she came up to me saying, "Is everything okay?"

"Y-yeah, of course," I stuttered, feeling embarrassed that she'd caught me admiring her.

"Alright, cool. Just that you've been staring at me whilst I've been reading my newspaper," she continued.

"Oh, no, no. I just thought you looked nice, that's all," I half admitted, not wanting to tell her I thought she was the coolest person I'd ever seen.

"Cool, you look nice too. I'm Mandy," she said as she reached out her hand for me to shake it.

"Thanks!" I beamed with excitement, feeling thankful that I'd made a friend. "I'm Kaya."

"I was just about to go shopping to get some new shoes, wanna come with me?" she asked.

"YES! I mean, yes," I coughed.

It was such a simple friendship, but I was sure it was going to last a lifetime.

Luke and I walked over to find Mandy in her dorm room. Something I'd come to realise about Mandy was that she literally always had her music on the loudest volume possible—she didn't care if she was disturbing anyone. I knocked twice but didn't hear an answer; *understandably so* from all of the head-banging drum and bass music.

I peeped through the door to see if she was inside and there she was, smiling back at me on her bed, reading another newspaper.

She turned off the music. "Did you know that it's illegal to sit in the car without a seatbelt?" she asked, as I poked my head through the doorway.

"Yes, Mandy, I did know," I laughed gently. I pushed the door open a little wider to make it obvious I had a guest. "Mandy, this is my boyfriend, Luke, that I was telling you about—I wanted to introduce you to each other."

"Hey soldier!" Mandy continued, "I can tell you're a keeper."

"Nice to meet you, Mandy. I've heard some good things about you," Luke added.

"*Some* good things? So the other things haven't been so good…" Mandy joked. "Just kidding. I don't want to take up too much of your time though; let me leave you both to it. You should come down again soon, Luke, so we can all plan to do some fun stuff? Like a double date.

"You have a boyfriend?!" I exclaimed, quite surprised.

"No, of course not," Mandy sniggered, "but I like to date freely—I can always hit someone up for a double date and they'd be down."

"Oh…nice," Luke commented, seeming slightly disturbed by Mandy's forwardness.

"Yeah, that would be cool," I said, nudging Luke firmly in the ribs. "Anyway, I'll catch you later, Mandy. We're making sushi tonight right?"

"Right," Mandy confirmed.

As Luke and I made our way to his car, I could see how puzzled he felt about our interaction with Mandy. It made me feel slightly uncomfortable because I desperately wanted him to like her.

"What is it, Luke?" I asked.

"No, nothing," he said unconvincingly.

"Come on, spit it out," I nagged.

"No, seriously nothing. I just think she's an interesting character."

"Okay…but interesting in a good way?" I said, hoping for a good answer.

"Mmm, not necessarily," he replied.

"Then, what?" I pestered.

"I just think she's going to land you in some trouble, that's all," he admitted.

"What? Why would you say that? Mandy is fabulous!"

"Fabulously *high*," Luke revealed.

"Huh? What do you mean? I didn't smell any weed from her room."

"Yeah, well, Mandy was on mandy," Luke sighed.

"What's mandy? And how did you know?" I asked innocently.

"Ecstasy. And I know because I've taken it with the rugby boys a few times. Not anymore though."

"Oh, woah. Well, I know I won't be influenced by that kind of thing so you don't need to be worried about me," I tried to reassure him.

"1 Corinthians 15:33, *bad company corrupts good character*," he whispered under his breath as he reversed out of the car park.

"Did you just quote a Bible scripture on me?" I laughed.

"What? Why's it funny?" he said defensively.

"It's funny, because you don't believe in God but you're pulling out a scripture to reason your case!" I teased.

"Oh. Well, I do believe in God now," Luke murmured with an embarrassed look on his face.

"Yeah, and I believe I'll grow wings in five minutes. What's the coffee shop called?" I continued.

"It's called Coffee 505 and, I'm serious, I believe in God now," he pressed on.

"Are you serious?" I said, focusing completely on our conversation now. "You mean like, you're a Christian now?"

"Yes," he said, focusing on the road and clearly trying not to look over in my direction.

"Well, that's new. When did this happen?"

"A few weeks ago," he confessed.

"*A few weeks ago?* We've spoken almost everyday on the phone since I came to Stellenbosch, so why didn't you tell me this?"

"I'm telling you now," Luke said egotistically.

"So, what does that mean for us because you know I don't believe in God and I'm certainly not going to listen to you breathe the Bible down my neck."

"Nothing between us has to change; we have our separate beliefs and that's fine."

Our coffee shop lunch was almost completely silent the whole hour. I could tell that Luke was in his own thoughts and was disappointed at my reaction. As for me, I felt let down that he had all that time to tell me and he didn't. As in, if I hadn't heard him quote a Bible scripture, he would've said nothing to me.

However, the thing about Mandy was still playing in my mind. Was she really on drugs or did he just get her personality confused? I guess she's an open book so there's nothing she would really hide from me if I asked her when I got back but, if she was on drugs and did them regularly, is she really someone I should hang out with?

Yes, I should, I thought to myself. I shouldn't judge a book by its cover and I didn't believe in Luke's preacher mode message anyway. She's a good person and that's all that matters. I didn't really know where this was going to leave Luke and I—there was friction there because he wasn't so fond of the way Mandy behaved and there was even *more* friction because he hadn't been truthful about his rediscovery of faith. I honestly wasn't sure of where this was going to take us…clearly not the Kaya and Luke happily-ever-after dream I'd thought of.

"You okay?" Luke asked, leaning out of his car window as I began to walk back into my dorm.

"I don't know, Luke. Let's just take some time to think about all this. Are you okay?"

"I don't know, K, I don't know," he sighed. "I'll call you tomorrow?"

"Yeah, okay," I agreed, hoping there was some way we were going to be able to solve this issue.

The first thing I did as I walked back into my dorm was to go straight back to Mandy, hoping she would be truthful with me about her recreational habits as that would be one less hurdle Luke and I would have to get over. I took my time making my way to her room as I knew that if there was news I didn't want to hear, it could be the destroyer of me and Luke's very healthy relationship. Well, it was healthy up until today anyway.

I knocked lightly as I couldn't hear any head banging music anymore.

"Mandy?" I said quietly, just in case she was asleep. I didn't hear a response so I crept in to see if she had her headphones on or something. Just in case, I decided to check every corner of her room in case she was hiding anywhere but she seemed to be out.

Something came to my mind. *Perhaps I should just check to see if I could find anything.* After all, Luke and I's relationship partially depended on this; I know he won't let this Mandy thing go if I didn't prove him wrong.

I checked everywhere I could in her room for any trace or evidence of drugs but I literally couldn't find anything. In fact, her room seemed completely PG—there were teddies *everywhere*, perfumes, make-up and all things rockstar-girlyish. Luke must've been wrong—she just has a bubbly personality, she wasn't high.

I decided to go back to my dorm feeling satisfied and excited to clear it up with Luke tomorrow.

"Hey, are you Mandy?" A short guy with an afro and glasses said to me as I shut her door.

"Er…no, I'm her friend. Are you looking for her?" I asked sceptically, assuming it may have been one of the swarms of guys that chased her around.

"Yeah, I came to pick-up," he said quietly as he looked around the hallway suspiciously.

"Pick up what?" I replied innocently.

"Is that a joke?" he laughed under his breath. "Come on, be serious now. We're talking about the same Mandy right? The one who sells the…*drugs*," he said as he mouthed the word 'drugs'.

"Mandy s-sells w-what?" I stuttered as my throat closed up and went dry.

"Oh, this must be a prank; you're funny!" he said sarcastically. "I'll just call Mandy myself. Catch you later."

Oh my gosh! Did I just hear that Mandy sells drugs? What is it with me and becoming friends with drug dealers? Not only Thato, but Mandy too.

Argh.

16

2021

Johannesburg is really beautiful at the crack of dawn. The hustle and bustle usually starts by then and I find it comforting to watch the sunrise as South Africans begin to appear for work in the morning. I love looking down from the balcony and guessing each person's life story—what their go-to Nando's order is, what they bought for their niece's first birthday, whether they wanted to be a rapper or singer when they were younger, the list goes on.

The sunrises still can't beat those on Gogo's veranda though. Joburg is a completely different feeling as you see different faces all the time coming from every single direction. With mornings in my little hometown, I knew every single face passing by our house in the morning, and they knew mine. Nowadays, there's still comfort in the sunrise but absolutely no comfort in the unfamiliar faces.

As I sat and made myself a morning coffee, I remembered the university open-day I went to at Stellenbosch. It was a strange memory because some parts of me felt like I achieved what I needed to achieve, yet some other parts felt like I completely let myself down. I'm a self-made businesswoman, and that's all I ever wanted, so I could say that I achieved my ultimate goal—*that's what I tell myself to keep my conscience clear anyway.*

To the majority of Africa, the fact that I'm complaining about my life makes me look like a spoiled little girl, but I wish they understood that escaping poverty doesn't lead to immediate happiness or sanity of mind.

When Gogo and Mama came to visit my penthouse in Sandton earlier this year, they were literally in shock at how I'd managed to buy something like this at such a young age. I mustn't lie to you, I'm not at all complaining about the area I live in or my house; both of these are an immense privilege. When the interior designers completed this place late last year, I was nearly in tears because I felt I was on MTV cribs which was once only a distant fantasy in my teenage years. Yet, after about a month, that feeling departed from me and I felt like I didn't deserve it.

At least, I was happy that this morning, I would get a break from work and get to catch up with an old friend, one I hadn't seen in nearly ten years. The thought of seeing someone for friendship's sake rather than only for business is the only thing that has put an honest smile on my face in months.

I put my coffee right back down. For once, I had a natural kick to start my day and that was a feeling of excitement; something I literally never feel anymore. I couldn't stop smiling! I tried to hide my smile when Blessing walked in as I knew she would start asking me questions.

Within the first week of moving into my current home, I met Blessing in the corridor. My old neighbour was shouting at her for putting a red sock in the washing machine with the whites. *Typically*, I'd never seen a housemaid fight back but, at that moment, Blessing took off her left slipper and began threatening to hit my old neighbour with it. She was fired on the spot but hired right away by me and I quadrupled her previous salary. I knew Gogo would absolutely love her so I could not waste the opportunity to be around someone like her all the time.

"Eh, my daughter, don't even try to hide that smile from me this morning. I can see your eyes are sparkling like fizzy water!" Blessing shouted as she entered my house this morning. I immediately burst out laughing because who even says something like that? That's another thing about Blessing; she makes the most random jokes and has absolutely no inside voice—even when she's whispering, she's literally just shouting in a husky voice.

"Buh-lessing! I'm just happy to be alive this morning. 'Grateful to God' as you say," I said, beaming.

"You've already started being cheeky, and it's not even 7am. Please, just don't come back pregnant." After she made that comment, I ran away from her and into my room.

I decided to put on a white poplin shirt, some blue jeans and some white trainers. It was the first time I would wear something other than a suit in ages. I even decided against my regular strong oud and put on the light, floral perfume that Mama got for me. I didn't stop there; I let my curls out, put on some makeup and danced and sang in front of the mirror. I was actually happy for once.

"Kaya! Your phone is ringing like crazy from here. Come and take your phone!" Blessing screamed.

"Coming!" I said as I ran into the living room. Blessing was basically like a second mum to me so when she shouted at me to come and do something, I didn't even hesitate…for fear of the wooden spoon.

"It's your mama," she smiled. "I'm so glad you've both worked things out because I was this close to twisting your ear and forcing both of you to talk it out."

Mama and I talked *everyday* now; it actually seemed like we were inseparable, especially after all that lost time. As we were both busy, we worked out a routine that worked well for both of us—she called me in the mornings and I called her in the evenings.

During the day though, we texted non-stop about the silliest of things—what kind of eyeshadow we were wearing, funny baby pictures, and mostly showered our chats with memes. To think that three months ago we were enemies and now, we're best friends—it was just insane. I myself could hardly believe it, but we actually had a lot in common. I've loved every second of it.

"Hey Mama," I sang.

"Hey gorgeous. How are you?"

"I'm feeling positive today. How are you?" I replied.

"I'm feeling positive today too, dear. It just feels like it's going to be a good day—mostly because my boss is on holiday. How are you feeling about today?" she asked.

"I feel good; slightly nervous but good, I think," I admitted.

"You'll be fine; it'll be just like old times," she reassured me.

"How are *you* feeling about yesterday Mama?" I said, making sure to turn the attention onto her.

"Urgh, Indodakazi, why are you nagging me with these kinds of questions so early in the morning?"

"Tell me!" I badgered.

"It was good…very nice actually. He took me to a very, *very* fancy restaurant—there was live music and we danced all night," she said. I could hear her trying to hide her smile on the other side.

"Look at you getting all shy, Ma! I'm so happy for you. I hope this works out for both of you," I sympathised.

"Kaya Imka Khumalo, it's just been one date; stop being so dramatic! He's a nice man and I like what I'm seeing so far, but I'm not going to rush it. One step at a time."

"Uh-huh, you'd *better* take it one step at a time, Ma."

"Okay, dear. I'm going to head to work now. Call me later and tell me how it goes?" she said.

"Will do, Ma. See you."

I was so proud of Mama—she had finally started getting herself out there and getting to know someone again, something she hadn't done since my dad. She deserved this and I hoped and wished all the best for her so that she could truly be happy again.

My dad and aunty have been calling me for months and I haven't given them the slightest inclination as to what the problem is. I don't plan to talk to them until the stress of my business reorganisation is complete. Now that Alexander Petrov and I are working together, it's a business deal of a lifetime.

After I presented my business proposal to Petrov three months ago during our initial in-person business meeting, he had agreed to do business with me.

"Why should I go into business with a rookie 27-year old female drug dealer?" he sniggered as he looked at his men and then looked at me condescendingly on that day. It was the one question I'd dreaded him asking.

I looked at Mandy with much fear in my eyes knowing that, as misogynistic and offensive as the question was, it was the deal-breaker. Mandy squeezed my hand under the table, giving me that support to know that I could do it.

"Good question, Mr Petrov," I began carefully, sweating under every inch of my skin. "Well, to begin with, I'm the only drug dealer in Johannesburg to have taken over this many territories in such a short space of time…with no deaths to my name." I looked over at Thato in the corner of the room and saw him shaking his head at me in indignation. It was true that I didn't have any deaths to my name so why was he shaking his head at me? Any murders were on Thato's hands, not mine. My orders are never to kill.

I continued, ignoring his contempt. "Also, I may be a woman, but which woman have you seen in this business that has this many *men* under their control? Not to talk of how young I am. Mr Petrov, I'm talented and you know that. I can make us a lot of money and you would barely even have to lift a finger," I said, clearing my throat as I felt like I was about to pass out.

There was silence in the room for about 45 seconds. I could see because I couldn't stop staring at the clock, wishing for the moment to be over.

"I will let you know my decision soon," he said as he stood up and left the room with his men; they literally followed him like silent minions.

I was checking my phone every second after the meeting wondering when and if he would call. After a week, when he still didn't call, I reached out to Daniel Underwood hoping that he would know the verdict, but even he wasn't aware of what Petrov wanted to do.

Eventually, after three weeks, I heard back from Petrov when he came to my *doorstep* at 3am in the morning. I thought it was completely inappropriate and I was embarrassed when he saw me with no makeup on, my hair in a bonnet and in my pyjamas.

"We have a deal. I'll be at your office at 9am," he said bluntly.

"O-oh okay," I replied, feeling completely out of it and understandably afraid. Nothing else was said—as soon as I agreed he just walked away and into the lift.

Strange man, I thought.

***

When I leave my house, I always have to look left and right to make sure I don't bump into my creepy neighbour who lives by the elevator. The first day I moved in, Mr Fourie sat outside his apartment and watched me bring each of my boxes up to my apartment one by one, catcalling me each time I came up. I was so angry that I actually went to sit in a park for a few hours to cool off. I wasn't even thinking about my stuff or the fact that it could've been stolen.

When I came back into my new home, I found Mr Fourie sitting on my couch—he had even helped himself to a glass of wine! Trying not to get angry again, I calmly said, "Mr Fourie, please leave my property before I call the police."

He replied, "Hey, hey beautiful; no need to act like that. Come, sit and have a drink with me and please, call me Greg."

I immediately lost it again and screamed, "Get out. NOW!"

"Okay, okay. No need to get angry, it doesn't suit your pretty face," he chuckled. That was just the *first* encounter I had with him, not to talk of all the other times he's been inappropriate. I've complained so many times to the company about his harassment but, of course, when he's a white middle-aged millionaire in South Africa, they're not going to do much.

With my swift and successful escape this morning from Mr Fourie's creepiness, I continued in my excitement. Pangs of nervousness came over me again when I got into my car because I realised I didn't even check to see if he had cancelled on me because of sickness or cold feet.

Phew. No cancellations, we're still good to go.

One thing I love about Johannesburg (which everyone else tends to hate for understandable reasons) is driving in this city. I feel like I'm in Fast & Furious on these roads every day and I love that no day is the same—it's literally like stepping into a movie every time you decide to go anywhere. I get it, it's dangerous; but I can't help but find it super exciting, just like the day Thato took me on his bike 20 years ago.

As I parked and walked up to the coffee shop for my arranged morning catch-up, I felt another overwhelming wave of panic but this one was stronger than those I had earlier this morning. *What was I going to say? How will he react to seeing me after all this time? Maybe I should go back home*—my thoughts were cut short immediately.

"Kaya, wow! It's so great to see you," he said. All the fear left me as I remembered he was quite literally the only person who ever made me feel safe. "I still can't believe I'm looking at you in the flesh!" he continued.

"Hey Luke," I replied. "It's great to see you too."

***

Luke looked different; the same but different. His face looked almost the same with an expected increase of manhood in his eyes, nose, and lips. However, there was just something about him that made me feel I was looking at a different person—a glow of some kind.

I could tell he had matured a lot based on his Chelsea boots, his brown overcoat, and his leather man bag; it was certainly different from the Luke I remembered in a jumper, beanie and trainers. He seemed to have lost his earrings too; that's a pity because I thought they really suited him.

When we were younger, he would refuse to wear anything that made him look 'grown' as he would call it, but I think it suited him—it made him look like Luke. I wasn't sure how I felt about the Luke that was standing in front of me; it just felt like everything about him had changed. I wondered if he was thinking the same about me.

He pulled my chair out for me as we found a quiet table in the corner, away from all the banging and clashing of the coffee shop kitchen.

"Here, let me get that for you. Ladies first…" he said with a twinkle in his eyes.

"Oh, thank you," I smiled. "Very kind of you."

We sat down facing each other but looked around for a while wondering who was going to start the conversation.

"Let's be honest—this is awkward, isn't it?" Luke laughed. For a second, I wondered why he had to make it more awkward by saying it but then we looked at each other, dead in the eyes, and burst out laughing.

"Yes, it really is," I admitted with more laughter. "Your personality hasn't really changed, has it Luke? Still saying things you know you're not supposed to say," I chuckled.

"What can I say? You can take the boy out of the hood but you can't take the hood out of the boy! I just can't help it; I had to relieve us of our thoughts."

All of the tension and awkwardness went away at this point; it felt like we were teenagers again at Mr and Mrs Singh's restaurant laughing over food and revision. Now, I was feeling excited to catch Luke up about my life in the last decade—how university was, my failed relationships, my newfound love for guitar and how I've settled in Johannesburg.

There was so much going through my mind that I didn't even know how or where I was going to start, especially the part about how I graduated top of my class at Stellenbosch; it was always his prayer for me. However, Mama taught me to ask someone how they've been first so you don't pile all your news on first, in case they haven't at all been in the same place. Good advice, Ma.

"So, how are you Luke? What have you been getting up to?" I asked enthusiastically. He seemed really excited about the question which indicated that we were going to have so much to talk about.

"Good question. I've been getting up to a lot; things have been busy, especially since I moved to Joburg. But, honestly, I've been enjoying every second of adulthood for the most part. There are many goals I've started to see being accomplished in my life such as buying my own house, becoming a rugby coach and writing my own music. It's been dope; what about you?" he grinned.

"That sounds exciting. Congrats on all of that by the way; I'm so glad you've managed to accomplish all of that so quickly. I agree with you on the adulthood part, I've enjoyed it so far. I've also managed to buy a house and I've got my own business running; it's going great. Although a question I've actually been wanting to ask you since I reached out to you is why you've moved down to Joburg?" I asked.

"Ooo, not necessarily my choice I must admit!" he huffed jokingly. "It's actually because my…wife is from here so I decided to make the move for her."

I could feel my heart sinking every millisecond deeper and deeper, wondering how I was going to respond to this without showing my discomfort of this discovery. I looked down briefly at his hands and noticed the wedding ring on his finger. How did I not realise this at first? He smiled broadly and lifted up his left hand.

I didn't really know how to react; it's like I was so happy for him but so sad for myself simultaneously. I quickly brushed the disappointment off my face and said, "Luke, that's…incredible. I'm so happy for you. When did you get married?"

"Thank you, I'm happy for me too. Cindy and I got married about a year ago now. However, we met about three years ago or so," he explained. "What about you, are you planning to get married?"

"Ha, er…no, that's definitely out of the question," I stressed.

"Why's that?" he asked.

"There's just no time, and I don't want to have kids or cook or clean for anyone—if you can tell me one South African man who would be okay with that *and* would be a good husband, you can let me know."

"Oh, Kaya," he laughed.

Changing the subject, I decided to find out what married life has been like for him. "How have you found being married then?"

"Honestly, married life is amazing. I'm not saying it's perfect, but it's like you can do everything with more support."

"And how did you meet?" I asked lightly, trying not to make it seem like an interrogation but innocent interest.

"I came to Joburg for a year in 2018 to study in Bible College and Cindy was also in my cohort. We began as close friends but things just naturally became more than that," he said.

Hmm, sounds familiar.

"I prayed about it and spoke to my mentor and pastor and I felt the confirmation from God that she was the right one for me to be with. That's basically our story. Actually, Cindy and I have just started up a new church."

Church. That was the worst thing that could have happened to Luke and I.

"Look, here she is," Luke said as he flipped his phone towards me and showed me a picture of them on their wedding day. She looked absolutely stunning—a beautiful dark-skinned woman, huge glimmering brown eyes and the most gorgeous smile; from the look of things, she seemed like the perfect wife.

"Enough about me though, K; what else have you been up to?"

He used to love calling me 'K' and I used to love him calling me that too, but I felt that now he was married and we were far from young-and-in-love teenagers, we should keep our friendship purely professional.

"Honestly, not much…just swinging it with Thato and Mandy—we're all in business together. Also, I go by Kaya now."

His face changed twice in one sentence; I guess the fact that he hated me being friends with Thato and Mandy still hadn't changed. The second time his face changed was when I corrected him about my name—I felt majorly awkward.

"Oh, okay," Luke said, taken aback and raising his eyebrows in what seemed like disapproval. "What exactly is this business?" he said, immediately looking at my Birkin bag and Cartier watch.

I *knew* I shouldn't have mentioned Thato and Mandy, but I just wasn't thinking straight after he dropped his wife bomb on me. I wanted to leave at this point because I knew I couldn't lie to Luke about what I did for work, but I also wanted to protect him from the truth.

If I lied, Luke would do that thing he always used to do where he mutters a prayer to God and tells me if I'm telling the truth or not. It felt like that day in 2013 all over again; it was one of the top three worst moments of my whole life. This was the first time we had spoken since then and I was suddenly afraid that if I admitted the truth, we would pick up exactly where we bitterly left off.

"Does it really matter what I do?" I asked hesitantly.

"Yes, because the fact that you feel you have to hide it from me shows you may be doing something you shouldn't be doing," Luke defended, quite rightly to be honest.

I took a deep breath in, sighing and not knowing where to start. He was going to be so ashamed of me as he would see me as the woman he always dreamed I wouldn't become. I knew he would tell me that I'm worth so much more than this and that I should never have led this kind of life; that I was too smart for this.

"Okay, let me ask the question like this: how comfortable would you feel sharing your 'business model' in a courtroom?" he asked.

"Um, I guess not very," I admitted, feeling ashamed.

"Right. And what's the sentence that court might give you for this 'business model?'" he continued carefully.

"Maybe…twenty five years or more," I sighed deeply. "Luke, I'm sorry, I know this is all wrong. I've come to realise this more recently but I'm in too deep and there's no way out now; I've got to finish what I started."

"Woah, woah, Kaya, there's no need to apologise. I am not here to judge you. Seriously. When you sent me a text last week, you'd already been on my heart for a while because I just felt that something was wrong. You don't need to lie to me, it's me. And I know things have changed now but I'm still the same Luke. You know, the Bible says in Romans chapter 2 verse 1 that—"

"Luke, no. I don't want to hear your crazy Bible talk right now. This is exactly what drove us apart in the first place. I'm not interested and I have my own life now. I *don't* need you judging me. I want us to be friends but I don't want to hear you preach down my ears."

I could immediately see the hurt in his eyes from all that I'd just blurted out. I wondered if he'd at all healed from anything in the past or if he was upset for another reason—I couldn't tell. I just wanted the subject to change but then, I realised that Christianity literally *was* him. He didn't have anything else to talk about. I figured I could at least give him the truth; after all, I trusted him.

"I'm sorry, I really didn't mean it like that. I'm happy for you and your church and your wife. I was just trying to say that I live my own life and I just wanted you to understand that we're quite different. I'll tell you the truth."

It took me a minute to even think about how to phrase it so it didn't sound so bad.

"I run a few clubs; you've probably heard of one called the Blue Panther…but I'm also one of the biggest drug dealers in Joburg. There, I said it."

He did something straight after this that I didn't expect—he came over and hugged me for a really long time. At first, I wanted to push him off because the hug was going on for a while but then, I just allowed it and the strangest feeling came over me—peace. I literally had not ever felt this sort of peace before. It was bizarre and weirdly supernatural. I didn't want him to let go.

As he let go of me and sat down, my phone began to ring.

Thato, what now?

"Sorry, Luke, I have to take this. It may be important."

"Go ahead," he said.

"Kaya, you have to get to the station now. The police just took Alexander Petrov. I'm sending you the location. Get here as soon as you can!" Thato exclaimed.

Yep, that peace certainly didn't last long.

2012

I sat on my bed kicking my heels and waiting for Mandy to come over for our sushi dinner so I could ask her about whether any of this drug stuff was even true. I wondered what this would mean for Luke and I if any of it turned out to be true. Would I be able to convince him to let it go?

Mandy is my closest friend here and I value the fact that she's never judged me like all the other girls from my classes who are stuck up and horrible. If I lose Mandy then I would be all alone; therefore, I couldn't afford to lose her—I needed her for my sanity and peace of mind.

I waited and kept my eyes on the courtyard, hoping I would see Mandy come back soon, but it was getting dark and I was really tired after all the drama that had happened with Luke. I wanted to call him and apologise so we could sort everything out, then I realised there was nothing to apologise for—it just seemed like we were becoming two different people and growing apart.

I mean…if I even decided to try out this whole God thing for him surely it wouldn't even be genuine because I'd be doing it all for him. I just couldn't see how this was going to work for both of us because I had made up my mind about what I thought about God. It's not that I didn't think he was real, I just couldn't see how he was subject to a religion or a book or a faith. I also didn't want to hear Luke try to convert me 24/7 so this whole thing just seemed wrong.

My eyes were beginning to shut as the expectation of Mandy coming over for dinner grew dim—I guess I would catch her at another point.

"Kaya!" a voice that sounded like Mandy shouted. "Wake up! I just spent a good hour running around the shops to find us some nori to wrap our sushi in. We gotta eat—I'm starving."

"Huh?" I muttered quietly as I rubbed my eyes and cleared the nap drool from my mouth. "Oh, right, yeah. Give me a few minutes to get up and I'll meet you in the kitchen."

I could hear Mandy banging every pot and pan and, from the way it sounded, she probably hadn't ever cooked before.

"What kind of knife can we use to chop salmon?" Mandy asked me as I walked in, dumbfounded.

"Er…the same knife you'd use to chop anything?" I laughed.

"Yeah, but surely vegetables get chopped with a different kind of knife from meat? Does salmon even count as meat?" she continued, believing she was getting somewhere with her points.

"Don't worry, Mandy. I'll do the cooking," I suggested, so that we didn't end up with runny stomachs in the morning. "Have you ever cooked before?"

"If cheese sandwiches and oven pizza count, then yes," she smiled proudly.

"Oh gosh," I said, grabbing the knife out of her hand.

The only thing on my mind as I began to chop up the salmon for our sushi was asking Mandy about this thing—I watched her every inch but nothing really seemed strange about her mannerisms… nothing that screamed 'drug dealer'.

Also, after hanging out with Thato all of my life, the one thing I noticed when he began dealing drugs was that he would get phone calls every two seconds and he was always checking his phone suspiciously. With Mandy, absolutely none of that was happening. I wanted to ask but I just didn't know how to without offending her.

"Mandy…" I began, still thinking about what I was going to say.

"Uh-huh," she said as she stared into space on a bean bag.

"I was just wondering if—well, basically, there was a guy that came by your room earlier when I came to look for you and—"

"Jason? Yeah, he told me that you guys bumped into each other," she said.

"Well, yes. I guess that may have been him. I was just wondering if you…you know," I hinted.

"If I?" Mandy said with eyebrows raised. "If you're wondering if we're together then certainly not! He's tried it a couple of times but he's really not my type."

"No, that's not what I was hinting at. It's just that he said that he came to 'pick-up' so I just wondered what for?" I speculated.

"Oh, you're wondering about the drugs?" Mandy laughed, looking relieved.

"Yes! That's it. That's what I was wondering about."

"What is there to wonder about, friend?" she giggled, seeming clueless.

"Well, why would he be trying to pick up from you?" I carried on.

"Why wouldn't he? Everyone comes to me for drugs on campus," she said.

"Wait, what?" I expressed anxiously.

"Kaya, how didn't you know…? I thought that's why you were staring at me the day we met?"

My heart felt like it was breaking into a million pieces. I felt like Mandy had lied to me but, in essence, she had done absolutely nothing wrong. It was my own naïvety that had landed me in this position and that made me angry with myself. Why was I so oblivious and unaware that my friend was dealing drugs on campus? What was I going to say to Luke?

"Wait, so you're a drug dealer? Like a proper drug dealer?" I whimpered.

"Girl, are you upset? How didn't you know this? I've literally been such an open book with you. I thought I told you that I do some illegal things to make money?" she explained.

"I thought you were joking!" I huffed quietly.

I sat there quietly for a few moments trying to gather my thoughts. I really didn't want to respond negatively but I'm pretty sure my face said it all.

"So, you're like a…criminal?" I tried to clarify.

"If that's the term you want to use, but I prefer the term 'rule-breaker'," she chimed.

"And you're okay with that?" I debated, not understanding her lack of remorse for what she was doing.

"Are you *judging* me?" Mandy said, sounding confused.

"No. Actually…yes, I am. This isn't right. I don't know how to feel about it, Mandy; you could go to prison."

"I could, but don't you know that all the police here are dirty? As long as you give them a little something, they won't do anything, especially not to a *sweet* and *innocent* university student," she said childishly.

"Mandy, this is why we're still fighting for women's rights. You can't just abuse your womanhood because you want to break the law!"

"You're so innocent, Kaya, and I love it. Don't worry, I know you'll come around soon," Mandy jeered.

"What do you mean by that?" I snapped.

"You'll see," she said, beaming. "Can we just have a good time and eat sushi together in peace? I don't want us to argue. Look, if you have such a problem with what I do, I can agree not to bring it up and not to do any drugs or deals around you. Does that sound good?" Mandy reasoned.

"Fine," I agreed. "But I'm telling you, I won't ever deal drugs with you or take them; I'm not like that."

"Kaya Khumalo, take it from me, you and I are more alike than you think."

17

2021

I didn't waste any time at all. I ran straight out of the coffee shop and frantically tried to find my car keys in my bag—this was far more important than the reconciliation of myself and Luke's friendship right now.

"I'm coming with you," Luke said as he ran after me to my car.

"What? No! Thank you for the offer but you can't follow me where I'm going," I panted, still looking around for where I parked my car.

"Kaya, I know what you're like when you start to panic—your vision goes all fuzzy and you have panic attacks. Let me drive you to wherever you need to go so that you get there safely and then I'll leave you to it. Please, it's the least I could do," Luke insisted.

With a few seconds of hesitation, I decided it was a good idea in case I had a serious panic attack in the car.

"Okay," I agreed.

My mind was spinning with thoughts all over the place, but the main thought that came to my mind was that this may be it for my life. I knew this moment was coming for me at some point but I didn't think it would be this soon. If the police had caught Alexander Petrov then they were definitely coming for me next. After all, Petrov and I are now in business together and if they had Petrov (who literally had every aspect of law enforcement under his control in Johannesburg), then I was certainly not protected. How could this be happening? Was there a rat in all of this?

"What are you thinking?" Luke asked. I could see the panic rising through him too.

"I don't even know what I'm thinking, Luke. I just know I'm in serious trouble."

He paused for a moment and then seemed to relax a little. "It'll be alright. God has told me everything will be fine," Luke tried to reassure me.

"How do you know that, Luke? When did God tell you this?" I asked, hoping for any kind of peace right now.

"He told me this just now. Don't worry, He's got you in his hands. We'll talk about it later."

For once, I just decided to listen and trust Luke because that was the only thing I could hold onto at that moment. The fear of a lifelong prison sentence over my head was just too much for me to bear.

How did I become this? I'm a good person. I suddenly remembered the days Luke used to pray for me when I was about to write an exam.

"Luke, can we pray?" I whispered, trying to hold back my tears of fear.

"Of course. Should I pull over?" he suggested.

"Yes, please," I replied.

I knew that deep down in my heart I still didn't believe in God but I needed to take every chance I could take; I just needed reassurance.

Luke pulled over at the nearest petrol station and took my hands, allowing us to have a few seconds of silence before he began.

"Dear heavenly Father, thank you for the precious life of Kaya. I know you love her so much and I know you've been calling out to her since the day she was born—she's a miracle. Lord God, I know I heard you a few minutes ago when you said that everything will be alright; I pray that you are able to show her this today. I pray for peace over her heart and over her mind and I just pray that you will help her come to you so that she can walk in your true will and purpose. Thank you Jesus for going ahead of her. In Jesus' name, amen," Luke prayed.

I felt that peace come over me again and I suddenly felt assured that what Luke was saying was sure to happen.

"Thank you Luke, I really needed that," I said with hope in my tone. "Luke, can we just talk before I get to the station? Because I don't know if this is going to be my only opportunity to tell you everything that has been on my mind over these years. I know I would regret not saying anything if I don't tell you."

"I'm all ears. I also think I have a few things to get off of my chest," Luke confessed.

"Thanks," I breathed.

"I guess I'll just start with everything happening right now because I don't really know how I got myself into this mess. Well, I do, but I didn't ever realise I was going to become this monster of a person," I sighed.

"You're not a monster. I know you've made some bad decisions but you this isn't really who you are," Luke said, trying to correct me.

"In a way, but they were still my decisions," I contended. "I really didn't want to be like this, Luke. At first, I just thought it would guarantee a lifelong friendship between Mandy and I; but then, we started craving power and money and my dad really encouraged it all. That was another person I just wanted to make proud and I thought the best way of doing so was to be more like him. I knew I had the brains and the personality to make this into a successful business, not just on a small scale like my dad but on a huge scale with Mandy. But then, Thato started misbehaving and disobeying my orders, which I guess I knew he was going to do but…Luke, he's killed people. A lot of them," I muttered as tears began to fall from my eyes.

"Oh my goodness," Luke gasped. I could see his heart breaking as he looked into his windscreen mirror and away from me.

"Luke, it's that bad. He doesn't just kill the people involved as well, he's also gone crazy at times and killed whole families, women and children included. I'm a monster, Luke, I told you. I deserve everything that's coming to me today," I continued as my eyes were balling with tears.

"As hard as this is for me to hear, and I'm not by any means excusing the things you've done because it's true, you've done some bad things, Kaya. However, God is giving you a second chance today—I just know it. God has forgiven you," Luke whimpered.

"How can God forgive me when I can't even forgive myself?" I said.

"Because he loves you that much, Kaya; he always has. We're going to get you out of this mess, I promise you," Luke comforted me.

"Okay," I said quietly. "The other thing I wanted to say was that I'm really proud of you, Luke. I'm proud that you decided to be a good man and live a good life and I wish I could have been wiser to join you on that journey you took. It's one of my biggest regrets. I'm sorry for everything and the way we ended."

Luke looked away and put his hands on the wheel, taking some time to process everything I'd just said. I could see that he was thinking of a way to wisely frame his reply because I had just dropped something huge.

"I appreciate your apology, and I, too, apologise for the fact that I didn't fight for you to stay away from Mandy. I blamed myself for that for such a long time. For the next thing I want to say, I just want to be careful in the way I say it because I have the utmost respect for both you *and* my wife. I believe that yes, things may have been different if you had been interested in getting to know God with me all those years ago.

"But, perhaps they also may not have been; maybe we both would have realised it wasn't meant to be at all. However, I don't want you to hold onto the past or onto what we once had because Kaya, once we come to know our identity in God, we realise that he turns everything around for our good. So, don't hold onto the idea that I was the only one that you could have been with; there are more people out there that would be suited to you," Luke explained.

I wasn't sure if I completely understood his apology or his explanation but I knew that he cared about me which is all I really needed to know.

"Thank you, Luke. I'm ready to go now," I announced.

"*Bro*, you're acting like you're about to die or something," Luke laughed hysterically.

"Luke, this is serious," I said, trying to keep in my laughter, but he just wouldn't stop laughing, and then I just couldn't stop laughing. We laughed all the way to the police station.

He always had a way of turning the most serious situation into laughter.

2012

It's nearly the end of my first term here at Stellenbosch and I've become really lonely. Luke barely picks up my calls anymore because he's either at church or he's hosting his new Christian fellowship. Genesis and I have drifted a lot because I don't want to put her in the middle of what Luke and I are going through.

I haven't been home in months to see Mum and Gogo because whenever I get a chance to visit family, I go to see Pops and my aunty. Thato's pretty much become a complete ghost—I don't even know if he's dead or alive because it's been that long since I've heard from him. And Mandy? Well, Mandy and I have had so many arguments about the drugs that it just seems easier if we stay apart.

I can't be alone anymore though—all I do is watch movies and cry. On most days, I don't even have the energy to eat and you could see that in my body weight; I'm about half the size that I was when I came to university. I can't do it anymore; my only option is to make up with Mandy. What other choice did I have?

I opened my curtains to see if Mandy was perched on her regular bench in the courtyard, reading her newspaper. My eyes felt like they were burning with fire because I hadn't seen daylight since Tuesday, and today was Friday. Yep, loneliness had driven me to stay in my room and not go to class. I needed to do something about this, because I felt like I was wasting away my life and becoming depressed as the days went on. I looked out, eyes burning, and saw her in her regular spot.

I finally mustered up the energy to get out of my bed, brush my teeth and take a shower—things that were once so simple but now seemed like heavy-loaded tasks. I wasn't sure what I was going to say because Mandy told me she didn't want to talk to me until I'd come to my senses and stopped being so judgemental towards her. I still didn't think what she was doing was right but this time, I was going to really try to find a way to maintain our friendship.

I walked down to the courtyard—or dragged myself I should say, and practised what I was going to say in my head again and again. Even if we didn't make up, I was just hoping we wouldn't have a massive fight and give everyone something to talk about.

"Hey," I said to her as I tapped her on the shoulder.

"Oh. Hey," she said grudgingly, turning back to her newspaper again.

"How are you?" I asked.

"Never been better," she replied, still refusing to look at me.

"Can we squash this? I really haven't been okay since we stopped being friends," I pleaded.

"I'm not the problem; *you* are."

"Um, yeah, sure. I am. Whatever…" I said to try to get her to stop ignoring me.

"So you accept that you're the problem?" she said pridefully.

"Yes, I promise not to judge you anymore," I settled with her politely.

"Great stuff," she smiled, finally looking at me. "Woah! Kaya, you've lost so much weight! Are you down that bad?"

"I'm okay now," I lied. "Just glad that we're friends again."

"This will make you feel better," Mandy said, pulling out something from her bag. I looked at it more closely and saw that it was from her stash.

"I don't take drugs, Mandy," I exclaimed quickly.

"Here we go again," she said, rolling her eyes.

"Okay, okay! I'll hear you out," I replied, not wanting her to turn around again.

"Better," she said, grinning. "You're in a *really* bad place and this is a quick fix. Trust me, just try it once and if you don't like it then you don't have to try it again. Do you want to stay depressed?" she pressured.

"No," I admitted. "Okay, fine. If you think it will make me feel better then I'll try it. Just this once."

18

2021

I wanted to be sick. I don't know who I was more afraid of facing—Petrov or the police. I paced up and down the car park five or six times, worrying that this may be the last time I was in fresh air that wasn't in a prison yard.

"Okay, I'm ready," I exhaled as I closed my eyes.

"You sure? I'll be right outside waiting for you," Luke reassured me.

"I'm sure. What will you be doing whilst you wait for me? It might be a while until I'm out."

"I need to call Cindy—my wife. Is it okay if I update her on what's going on?" he asked.

"Yeah, sure. I mean, at this point, there's nothing to hide right? The police already know," I laughed darkly. "Okay, see you," I said, trying to be positive.

I had to forcibly put one foot in front of another as I walked towards the police station. The place looked about a hundred years old and was so dingy from the outside. It didn't help that birds were crowing everywhere too—it looked like a horror movie, and it certainly felt like I was living out one.

I called Thato as I waited by the side of the entrance, not wanting to be too hasty in going inside.

"Hey friend. Are you here yet?" Thato whispered as he picked up.

"Yeah, I'm here. Where are you?" I replied, also whispering.

"I've been waiting in my car, watching to see if Petrov comes out, but I still haven't heard anything."

"Hmm, I wish we knew more. I think I'm going to go in and see if I can speak to Petrov," I suggested.

"What? No way. If they recognise you, they'll arrest you!" Thato shrieked, forgetting he was supposed to be quiet.

"Thato, they probably have tons of evidence on me by now; there's nothing to hide. If I don't speak to Petrov and sort this out then his men will most likely be on their way to kill me tonight. I need to just clear this up with him so he doesn't think I have anything to do with this," I urged gently.

Thato was silent for a while, clearly realising that we were all in danger if I didn't find a way of making peace.

"You're right," he said. "But I don't understand who did this?"

"Let's talk later, Thato; we don't know if anyone may be listening in on this call. I'll text you when I'm out."

"Okay. Stay safe, love you."

"Yeah…you too," I said forcibly.

I turned and walked into the entrance, keeping my head down in case I was being looked for. I just needed to find where they were keeping Petrov and find a way of speaking to him. I quickly checked if I'd brought my purse and had cash because I knew it would come in handy in case I needed to bribe anyone.

I crept all the way down the main hall until I found the holding cells. The guards didn't even seem to notice me; they were just sitting around eating and laughing.

Finally, I found where I thought they may be holding Petrov, but first, I needed to put on my best behaviour for the guard on duty outside his cell.

"Good afternoon, Sir," I beamed heartily. "I was just wondering if you know where they may be keeping someone called Alexander Petrov? It's just that I'm his girlfriend and he hasn't called me since yesterday. I've been *so* worried," I said as I pretended to get close to tears.

"How much do you miss him?" the guard responded, looking for a bribe.

"This much," I replied, rolling my eyes and handing him some cash.

"Follow me, sugar," he said, licking his lips over the fresh cash I had just handed him. It made me feel queasy.

He unlocked the holding cell and signalled to me that I could go in. I anxiously stepped in slowly, scared that Petrov may scream at me as soon as I crossed the border of his cell.

"Hello," Petrov greeted me, winking at me at the same time.

"A-a-afternoon, Mr Petrov," I stuttered uncontrollably.

"Why are you nervous? Sit down," he chuckled obscurely.

"Is this part of the trick?" I said, shaking from top to bottom.

"Trick? Why would I be tricking you?"

I sat down slowly beside him keeping my eyes on him the entire time in case he pulled out something from behind him. Seeing how these guards didn't even notice me when I crept down the hall, I knew if anything happened, no one would be able to rescue me in time. To calm me down a bit, I decided to think of the prayer Luke and I had prayed when we stopped on the road.

"Why are you here, Mr Petrov? Why have they arrested you?" I whispered, looking around for cameras.

"Don't worry, darling; there aren't any cameras here." He winked at me again. "However, in answer to your question, I don't know why I'm here. Well, actually, I have a strong *inclination* as to why I'm here, but I was hoping you would be the one to confirm that for me."

"So you think *I'm* the reason you are here?" I panicked.

"I never go into business with a snake. Never. I've had over 40 years of experience in this industry so I know when I can smell a rat."

"Oh, so you *don't* think I'm the snake?" I asked, fear beginning to leave my voice.

"As I said, I never go into business with a snake."

"So…who do you think told the police? Because it seems that they know our business operations inside and out," I exclaimed.

"Hmm, it's a good question and it's one that I've had the last 24 hours to think about. I don't know if you would want to hear what I'm suspecting though," he delivered gently.

"I *do* want to know, Mr Petrov; this is serious."

"How well do you think you know your friend Mandy?" he began.

"Very well, she's my best friend. A sister to me actually."

"Well then, *I smell a cat fight*," Petrov sang whilst he smirked.

"What do you mean? Why would you smell a cat fight? Mandy wouldn't rat on us, Mr Petrov; she's basically my business partner," I started to clarify.

"She hates you, Kaya. I can see it all over her."

"No, she doesn't! Why would you say that?" I hissed, all fear seeming to leave me now.

"Women hate other women when they feel they have to compete in elegance, beauty, brains and talent. In every one of these things, you are far more superior to her. Why wouldn't she want what you have? The easiest way for her to do that would be to take you down."

"*What….?*" I murmured.

"So, here's what I suggest. I've already made some calls so I will be out of here tonight—everything is cleared up from my end. However, you need to get your side of the business tidy and in order so we can continue smoothly in all of this."

"And how do you suggest I do that?"

"Oh, isn't that clear by now? Get rid of her."

"Mr Petrov, I don't even know if she's done anything wrong and she's my friend—even if she's betrayed me I would never kill her. Murder is wrong!"

"Are you seriously in this business and telling me that murder is wrong? Ms Khumalo, if you want to remain in business with me, then you know what to do. But just know that if you don't follow my orders, we'll do the job and I will know where you stand in your loyalty to me."

"But Mr Pe—" I tried.

"That's it, Ms Khumalo. I'll give you 24 hours starting from now and if not, I will be making some more calls."

"But—" I continued.

"That's it, Ms Khumalo," he said as he lay down on his bed and turned away from me.

I felt sick to my stomach for many reasons, but the only image I had in my mind was Mandy's funeral, all because I would be the one to put her in a ditch. What was I going to do? If I betrayed Petrov then he would get rid of Mandy and potentially get rid of me too. But I could never do that to Mandy, even if this scandal *was* true.

2012

I really didn't want to ask Mandy if I could eat dinner at hers again tonight but I was broke, like *broke broke*. I'd been eating noodles for the past three weeks and my box had just about run out—how I was going to feed myself over these next few weeks until I saw my dad again, I didn't know. I knew my pride was too high to go to Luke or Gogo for some money so I'd just been surviving day-to-day with literally no money to my name. I had no clue how I was going to get out of this mess; I'd literally spent all of my bursary money on a new laptop which I *needed*—it was a university essential.

"Can I eat at yours again tonight Mandy?" I asked her on our favourite library table. We loved sitting right in the middle of the library so we could see every single person that walked past and make up stories about their lives. Every time a good looking guy walked past, Mandy always slipped her phone number into their pocket. She had a collection of small pieces of paper with her number on ready for those moments.

"At mine, *again*?! I was going to ask if you could make me that chicken stew your mum taught you to make," she whined.

"Erm, yeah, sure. Maybe next week? Just been enjoying your food recently, that's all," I lied, almost gritting my teeth at the half-cooked burger she made us last night.

"You're lying," she said, eyebrows raised.

"No, I'm not," I lied again.

"Ah!" she gasped. "You're broke aren't you?"

"Why are you shouting it out loud for everyone in this library to hear?!" I cautioned her quietly.

"*Tell me the truth*," she mouthed gleefully.

"*I'm not broke*," I mouthed back with an attitude, cocking my head to the side like Brandy used to do in her music videos. "I prefer to say that my bank account has taken a short advert break," I then said confidently.

"This is so funny! Can you imagine, you used to whine at me all day long for dealing yet I'm far from broke and you're struggling to put food on the table. Who's in trouble now, huh?" Mandy teased.

"Oh, give me a break Mandy. I still wouldn't ever do what you're doing."

"Is that so?" she said, pulling out a ton of cash from her bra.

"Where. Did. You. Get. That. From?" I stammered as I quickly calculated the 15,000 Rand in her hand. My whole body was stuck on the money, drooling at the thought of how many chicken stews I could make with that, how many new shoes I could buy for Luke, new books for Gogo and new bags for Genesis! It was tempting, but no. *No, Kaya, no!* I thought to myself, but I knew that wishful thinking had started to get the better of me.

"Easy money, sis. You can join me anytime; we could do this together and make even more money from it," Mandy tried to convince me.

"No, I can't. It goes against all of my morals," I said, but I could hear how unconvinced I was beginning to sound in my voice. It's like the money could speak and it was seducing me.

2021

How did Petrov expect me to process what he'd said in such a short space of time and come to a decision? Was he even *right*? Had Mandy betrayed me because, deep down, she hated me, or was this a stunt that Petrov was pulling to test my loyalty? I couldn't tell if he was lying or if I'd been blinded to the truth this entire time because of my love for her. I never noticed Mandy doing anything strange or acting suspiciously in any way so how could this be true?

Surely, she never would have got me into business with Underwood or Petrov if, the whole time, she wanted to take me down—it just didn't make sense. Mandy has always been rooting for my good from the beginning, even though to some people she may have had a strange way of showing that; I was *sure* that I knew her heart.

I really didn't know what I was going to do or what to believe, but what I did know was that if Mandy had done this, it was over for her—she was a dead woman walking. It also meant that I would be losing my closest friend in the whole world.

I slipped out of the station discreetly, taking deep breaths in and out at every step so that I didn't fall on the floor and have a panic attack—I had had way too many near-panic attacks today; I just wanted to get home in one piece.

I could see Thato waiting in his car with eyes peeled in every direction in case of a sudden surprise. As soon as he spotted me coming out of the station, his eyes glimmered with relief knowing that we were probably safe from prison or death. He smiled, saluted me and then drove out of the car park slowly—if I went to speak to him in his car, it would look suspicious. This was not the time for us to spark up conversation either; all he needed to know was that we were safe.

However, instead of me feeling relief for Thato, I felt a sadness rising up in my heart for him because it suddenly dawned on me that he's spent half his life looking over his shoulder. After a whole morning of reflecting on my life and regretting the decisions I'd made, I feel like I could have done more to stop him from entering this way of life.

He's become so used to being a criminal that I don't think he's ever stopped to ask himself what he *really* wants in life—a wife, kids, to move abroad? He doesn't seem to think he has any choice in the matter. His life's motto is 'kill or be killed', which saddens me greatly. I had hoped for a lot better for him, but what can I say? I'd hoped for a lot better for myself.

Luke was nervously pacing up and down when I came back to the car. I could see him biting his fingernails whilst trying to distract himself on his phone.

"Thank God!" he exclaimed as he saw me. "Thank you Jesus, thank you Jesus. You are so good, God," he said hysterically as he fell on his knees and lifted his hands to the sky.

"I'm okay, Luke. I'm safe," I said cheerfully, placing my hand on his shoulder as he stayed kneeling on the ground. "I'm not going to prison."

"Amen. I'm so glad to know that all is well. Cindy and I were praying for you over the phone; we knew it would all be fine but I could feel the worry rising up in me the more time you spent in there. This is another moment that reminds me to always trust in God's word."

I smiled at him gently and said, "I don't even know how to begin thanking you for today, Luke. It's like I got off so easily."

"Come on in the car. This time, *you* can drive and you can tell me everything that happened in there!" he said, seeming enthralled.

"Yes, of course. There's definitely good news and…bad news," I exhaled.

"Okay, let's be positive and start with the good news," he suggested as we got into the car. It was wise to start considering that this journey was probably going to be more dramatic than the first one. "So, tell me what happened," he said.

I began carefully and slowly so that I didn't become a ball of emotions. "The good news is that I'm not going to prison because Mr Petrov, who is the man I've been working with and is currently being held in jail, said he's going to make some quick calls and get us out of this shambles. The other part of the good news is that I think you're right…I need to find a way out of this illegal rubbish and get my life back on track."

"Hmm…okay," Luke murmured.

"What?" I asked as I began driving.

"Well, I know I said God would get you out of this, but he doesn't mix good with evil, so he wouldn't get you out of this by Mr Petrov making some illegal phone calls."

I hesitated. "I don't understand?"

"He's going to get you out of this, Kaya, but not like this. Let's just keep watching and praying, I know he'll make it more clear to us soon. What's the bad news?"

"Well…" I huffed, "Mr Petrov believes that Mandy is a snake in my business."

"Mandy? Why would he think that?"

"I mean, it does make sense in some ways. Mandy and Thato are the only ones who know the business in enough detail to put Petrov in a jail cell," I sighed.

"Interesting…and Mandy hasn't contacted you yet, has she?" Luke remarked.

"No…she hasn't. Oh my goodness, why hasn't she said anything yet?" I stressed, beginning to realise that Petrov may have not been talking nonsense.

"Okay, calm down for a second. It doesn't sound like Mandy would do this to you because, even though she's wild, betrayal doesn't seem to be in her nature. But I guess you never know until an opportunity presents itself. What else did Mr Petrov say about this?"

"He believes she went to the police because she wants to take over my business, which I don't understand because I treat her as if we're practically equal business partners. What more could she want?" I reiterated. "And, it gets even worse. Petrov says I have to 'get rid of her' otherwise *he* will do it…alongside me and everyone else that works with me. So I'm not sure if there really *was* any good news," I delivered numbly.

Luke was quiet for a few minutes, closing his eyes and thinking deeply. As he did this, I began to think deeply as well; if I could just come out of this situation alive, I would turn my life around. I really would.

"Do you want out of this, Kaya?" Luke asked assertively, as though reading my current thoughts.

"Yes, I do. I think I do. I don't know, Luke; what if I don't?"

"The reason I'm asking you this is because I felt God saying to me just now that he has provided a way out for you but you must be willing to take it."

"Then yes, I'll take it. Whatever it is," I agreed. "But, Luke, is God angry with me? Does he hate me? I've been such a terrible person."

"No, Kaya, not at all. God is love. Therefore, he can never hate you because his nature is just not that. He's forgiven you."

Luke sighed and looked out of his window so I knew that something was bothering him in his mind. Looking out of the window and into a car mirror was always how I knew that he was thinking of something really deep.

"What is it?" I asked, bracing myself for the response.

"Honestly, I really do think Mandy betrayed you, K," he articulated sadly.

"Is that what you felt God said?"

"Yes, I think he's confirmed that," he croaked.

"Right," I said, refraining myself from the slightest emotion. I didn't want us to crash because of any kind of outburst I may have. "So what does this mean for my way out?"

"It means that God is saving you from the calamity that Mandy has just brought about—you may be the only survivor," Luke replied dimly.

"I don't understand," I said.

"Put it this way, God hates evil but people have free will to do whatever they want to do. Mandy has had free will to basically cause a blood bath between you and Petrov's business, but God is warning you to get out. If you have time to warn anyone else, try your best."

"Are you saying that you think people are going to die? And I may be the only one that survives what's coming next?" I panicked.

"Potentially," Luke speculated.

"Then we have to stop it!" I argued.

"Kaya, we can't. It's already started," Luke expressed.

Interlude 2

I found a room. It's a white room.

There's no music, but I just feel like dancing; I'm filled with so much light and joy.

The only way for the light to beam out of me is for me to move my body. So, I move my body.

I'm in white garments. I'm moving more and more, and I feel a smile start lifting my face up and up. I'm dancing faster now; I'm running and dancing.

My movements aren't making sense, but I'm free.

I don't care if anyone laughs at me, I'm so free. I've never felt so free. I'm so happy, so overwhelmed.

What is this thing inside of me that won't stop me dancing?

I need an answer.

I felt like I was in a maze—I didn't know what I was looking for but I was trapped and I needed to find this thing that would launch me into destiny.

I found it. I won.

This is joy.

This is light.

This is love.

19

2013

I felt quite discombobulated and uneasy here at Pops and Aunty's new place because everything felt unfamiliar and new. The house still smelt of paint, new carpeting and cigarettes that the workers were probably smoking when they were doing the refurbishing. Nonetheless, I was glad to be able to spend Christmas and New Year's here and away from my mum.

It was different from every other festive season I'd celebrated with Gogo and Mum—Pops and Aunty Andrea had *a lot* of friends and family so they were in and out throughout the holiday. It was very loud, boozy and extravagant compared to my usually quiet Christmas dinner and New Year's toast between just us three Khumalo ladies but, nonetheless, I was up for a change.

I still hadn't spoken to my mum since I'd left for university and, deep down, I was hoping she would have reached out to me or come to visit me on campus, but she was just as stubborn as I was and she was clearly very hurt that I'd mended mine and Pops' relationship. From the way it was going between my mum and I, we were probably going to remain in bad communication for the rest of our lives. However, I really missed my mum's food—Aunty Andrea's food was nice, don't get me wrong, but it was just different and it didn't come with the memories I'd attached to my mum's food.

Gogo calls me at least every other day because she misses me so much. She complains and says the house is so boring and lonely now, which isn't much of a surprise to me because my mum is not very entertaining company. I do worry for her a lot, especially as her blood pressure was getting quite high just before I left for university, but I still don't have the strength to go back home and explain to them why I'd decided to move out; it was much easier to just focus on my current reality.

I was waiting all day for my dad to return home so I could have an in-depth conversation with him about something I wanted to begin doing; however, I knew I needed to seek advice and get approval from him before I decided to make such a huge step.

As soon as it was 8pm, I heard the front door swing open and my dad's steps on the doormat. *Finally*…. However, the nervous anticipation began to take effect and I could feel the script I'd laid out in my head beginning to crumble. I decided that, instead of overthinking it, I was just going to jump right in and have the conversation I'd finally built up the courage over the past month to have with him.

"Evening, Pops," I greeted.

"Evening, beautiful," he said, kissing me on the forehead and giving me a big hug.

"Studied hard today? Your exams are coming soon."

"Yes, Pops, of course," I could feel the nervous flutters in my stomach as I began thinking of when the moment would be right for me to have this conversation with him.

"That's my girl. Do you want anything from the shops? I'm going to run out and get a few beers because it looks like we're all out," he said as he opened the fridge.

"I'm fine, thank you. I was just wondering if we can have a quick chat before you go out? I need to ask you for some advice about something," I added quickly.

"Can it wait until I grab the beers?"

"I mean, it could, but I would prefer if we could talk about it before you head out," I expressed.

"Okay, let's have a seat. Should I ask your aunt to join us?"

"Umm…actually, yes please. I value your joint opinions," I emphasised.

As my dad went to go and get my aunty, I brought out my laptop as I had written up a business plan on there (the same laptop that made me broke and close to starvation). I needed to ensure they knew I was serious about this and had a logical approach to what I was about to propose because I didn't want to be laughed at. If they gave me the answer I was hoping for, my whole life was about to change.

"Hey my love, I've been told that I've been invited to a discussion with the 'cool kids'," Aunty Andrea joked.

"Indeed, you have, sister, probably for the first time in your life," Pops teased.

"So, why have I been summoned by my darling niece?" Aunty Andrea said as she plopped herself on the couch right beside me, ignoring Pops' insult. I stood up because I knew how nosey my aunty could be and I didn't want her observing my business plan. I wanted to make it seem very professional and so I thought if I stood up in front of them then it would perhaps do the job.

"This seems serious!" Pops bellowed.

"It is," I asserted, bringing out the poshest and most wise woman voice I possibly could.

"Ready whenever you are," Aunty Andrea said delicately. She was always so delicate.

"Okay," I exhaled. "I think it's best if I started by asking both of you a question."

"Mm-hmm. Go on," Pops said, urging me on impatiently.

"Patience, Pops, patience. What do you think about university students earning their way through their degree by selling drugs?" I asked.

"Erm," Aunty Andrea began as she started laughing, "I mean, it depends what for. Why are you asking?"

"Answer first," I said.

"From my perspective, kid, you do whatever you have to do to gain respect and pay your way through life. We're an open house here, and we all know I pay the bills by selling drugs. For starters, it took us out of the Cape Flats and bought us this house we're living in now. So, if someone wants to do it and they have the brains to carry it out, then why not?" Pops concluded.

"True," Aunty Andrea added. "I feel that, as coloured people, we've been given a disadvantage in life from the very beginning, so you've got to take anything you can get to put yourself back into the advantage."

"Interesting perspectives," I continued, "but how would you feel if it was *me* doing it?"

Their faces suddenly moved from deep thought, to shock, and then to disbelief at what I was alluding to.

"*You?*" my dad cackled. "Kaya, honey, come on. You wouldn't last two seconds amongst those wolves."

"Exactly!" Aunty Andrea exclaimed hysterically. "And we were speaking about the sorts of people that didn't have any other choice but to be in that hustle. You're going to get a great job after university."

"You'd be surprised, Aunty. There's no job opportunities even if you have a great degree," I said.

"Even so, if you work your way up, you'll eventually have a really good income," she defended.

"That's exactly the problem; I will *eventually* have a really good income. That could be in 20 years from now—why would I wait if I could have that now and more?" I argued.

"Slow down. This doesn't really sound like you doing the talking; it sounds more like someone has been speaking to you about this. Since when did you even care about money? I think you should take some time to reconsider what you're asking us. This is a dangerous business, my girl," Pops expressed.

"I appreciate your concerns, but I want you to know that I have the brains to pull this off. If you don't believe me then just take some time to look over my business plan," I said whilst handing them my laptop.

I knew it would take a while for them to read over it so I took a short break and headed over to the kitchen to get a glass of water before we reconvened. I was sure that once they saw how strategic my plan was, they would stop underestimating me, and, ultimately, I knew it would make them proud. I was basically following in Pops' footsteps but my plan was to turn it into an empire. I could be one of the *biggest* and most successful drug dealers in South Africa; maybe even one of the biggest in the world if my plan went in the direction that I wanted it to go in.

"Have you finished reading over it?" I asked confidently as I walked back into the living room.

"We have…" Aunty Andrea said.

"I'm quite blown away to be honest. This is…really good," Pops admitted.

"Thank you. I spent a long time on the plan. I don't think anyone in the market has thought of anything like this yet," I said excitedly.

"It's insanely intelligent. How did you come up with this?" Pops enquired with much confusion in his voice. "I've been doing this for 30 odd years and I've never had an idea like this."

"I told you both, I have a real plan for this. This isn't just low-level drug dealing, this is a whole network and empire that I could build if I do it right and plan everything accordingly. The point is to get people so involved that they don't even know they're part of a drug network; it's money laundering drug money but through people who don't even know they're transacting with drug money. Eventually, some of the top businesses and firms will be part of it too, but I plan to just start with smaller businesses like cafes, barber shops, florists, etcetera."

"I agree with your dad; this is really brilliant, Kaya. But have you thought of what the consequences of this may be?" my aunt considered.

"Yes, I am aware but that won't happen. As soon as I branch out of university, one of my first plans is to get the district police involved so that there are no secrets. As long as money continues to flood their pockets, they will be happy to work alongside me. There are always some obvious risks but I plan to keep them to a minimum," I explained.

"I'm not sure how I feel about this, but I'm here to support any decision you make," Aunty Andrea concluded.

"I'm really proud of you and this idea. It's amazing to see someone following in my footsteps but going at it one hundred times better. I'm with you all the way," Pops beamed excitedly.

"Thank you, guys," I smiled as I jumped on them for a group hug.

"Just one more question, though, sweetie. I read on the plan that you want a friend called 'Mandy' to assist you. Who is she?" my aunt asked curiously.

"She's my closest friend at the university. Actually, she's been selling for a few years now and has her own business on our campus."

"Interesting. So you've both agreed on the plans and she's agreed to be your assistant?" Pops questioned.

"Erm…no, she hasn't yet agreed to be my assistant. I haven't even told her that I plan to sell drugs yet, but I was planning to ask her as long as I got your approval."

"Hmm, only because, from my own experience, it's quite a jump for someone to go from running their own business to becoming the assistant of someone else's," Pops continued.

"Yeah, it's a fair point, and I've thought about it. However, Mandy's personality is quite…erratic to say the least. Therefore, I think I'd need to establish my position as the one in charge. But as long as money is involved then Mandy doesn't mind."

"Okay, I'll take your word for it. I just hope this doesn't ruin your friendship—make sure to watch your back with her. When will this start?" Pops finalised.

"Well, now that the both of you are in support, I plan to start tomorrow."

"Tomorrow?" Aunty Andrea shrieked.

"Indeed," I winked. "And, don't worry, Mandy would never betray me."

2021

"Thank you for everything today, Luke; you truly are God sent. I'll call you in the next few days as soon as this all blows over," I said kindly, pulling over to his car that was parked at the cafe we'd met up many hours earlier.

"It's my absolute honour. Please, do keep me updated—my wife and I will be praying fervently for you, and for Mandy and Thato to be safe in all of this," he acknowledged.

"Can I ask why your wife is so comfortable with you and I meeting, especially with all the unspoken tension from our past?" I asked carefully.

"Yeah, sure. Cindy and I don't hide anything from each other," Luke affirmed.

"Why?" I asked. "I'm not saying it as if it's not a good thing, but how do you manage to stay so open?"

Luke started laughing at my curiosity, "I'm married, Kaya. I have no choice. Once you make the decision to become one with someone, you have to have the integrity to uphold your promise."

"Right…so, as soon as I reached out to you, she knew?" I continued.

"Yep, immediately. We spoke about it that same evening you sent me a message. It was actually her suggestion that we meet up and clear the air, because she knew how much healing I had to do from our relationship," Luke admitted.

"Wow. She must be wonderful. I'm genuinely glad that you're blessed with a marriage with so much trust," I supported. "And…I'm sorry to have been the reason for your healing process."

"It's okay…I'm sorry also. But yes, I'm very blessed with Cindy. We trust each other because God's love is in our hearts. We wouldn't just be hurting each other if we abused each other's trust, we'd be hurting God." He paused for another moment, humming and thinking to himself. "Can I recommend that you do something this evening?" he said.

"Sure. What?" I replied.

"Try just speaking to God tonight before you sleep. Tell him how you're feeling and what you're going through. He wants you to have a relationship with him."

"Is that what he's just told you?" I wanted to know.

"With that one, I don't need to hear a direct word from him. It's simply knowing his nature that lets me know that he wants a relationship with you. It's a fact. It's who he is," Luke reaffirmed.

"Right. Okay, I'll try," I accepted wilfully. I actually wanted to understand this whole faith thing a lot more.

"See you soon," Luke said as he smiled warmly and shut the door.

I felt a flinch in my heart as he walked away because I realised I was by myself again and I had to deal with my reality in the present. I just wanted to get home so I could understand what Mandy may have done to the business and our friendship.

***

When I entered my apartment, the first thing I did was run upstairs to my bedroom to check if all of our business records were still in the safe. I frantically put the code into the number dial and opened the safe. *Phew, everything is here.* But then how was it possible for Mandy to get her hands on any of the records that could've been handed over to the police? Everything in this safe was the only way the police could put any charges on us. I realised that I wouldn't get any answers by pondering on the potential of things; I had to just call Mandy and find out what was going on. I was still unconvinced that she could've done this.

I called her, and it went straight to her voicemail: "Hiiiiii. Yeah, it's Mandy here. I can't hear you bro! Just kidding, I'm not actually here. See ya, wouldn't wanna be ya. Why would I wanna be ya when I could be the most amazing person ever, which is me!"

I rolled my eyes at the very annoying voicemail I'd listened to about a thousand times in the past and put my phone down in frustration. If she'd done this, she might have been halfway across the world right now having the time of her life on an unknown island. She'd literally left me in her mess. The only thing that I could think to do was follow Luke's advice and pray to a God I still didn't really have a clue about. I was on my last hope, so even if he didn't exist, it would still be better than nothing, right?

I got on my knees beside my bed and tried to get in a comfortable kneeling position. I stayed there for a while thinking about how I was supposed to do it but it just felt weird and odd. I thought that, perhaps, if I got onto my bed, crossed my legs and lifted my hands towards the ceiling, it might feel less awkward. So I got up and did just that but it didn't feel any less weird.

"Dear the almighty God," I started, but I just cracked up in laughter thinking about how funny Mandy would find it if she was watching me right now. Then it suddenly dawned on me that Mandy may never be able to witness such a moment with me ever again. I breathed out deeply but held myself back from the tears because I still didn't know what was going on.

I remembered that Luke's words were 'speak to God' not 'pray to God' so it was probably better for me to do just that and not force something I didn't know how to do. *Okay, here goes.*

"Hi God. I could be speaking to thin air right now, but I thought it was worth giving this a go because, from today, you seem pretty real. But that could just be a coincidence. If there's anything I really want to say, it's just that I'm in such a pickle right now…more than a pickle actually, I'm in a mess. I might not come out of this alive because, from the looks of things, this is bad news. I may look like a pretty, nice-smelling, put-together woman on the outside, but on the inside, I just feel so rotten. I need your help, if you *can* help.

"I want to be a better person. I want to leave all of this behind and be more true to who I feel I was created to be, and that's certainly not a murdering, money-hungry drug dealer. I'm really sorry for…everything. Basically, I just want a fresh start. Can I have a fresh start? That's kinda all I wanted to say. I hope this message reaches you wherever you are."

I didn't know what was supposed to happen after this—was a God-like ghost going to come out of the wall? Or was there going to be a huge thunderous voice speaking to me in the next few minutes? I wasn't sure so I thought I would just wait and see what would happen.

I sat there waiting in silence for a few minutes; still, nothing happened. Had I prayed or talked to God wrong? Or maybe I was supposed to ask for permission before I prayed to God so that he would hear me. *Whatever. I probably did it all wrong*, I thought to myself.

Just as I was about to get up, my phone began ringing on the other side of the room. Maybe God was calling me on the phone? I turned it over so I could see my screen. *Mandy*. How is this an answer to my prayer?

I didn't even bother with small talk. I had to know immediately if Mandy had done what Petrov had said she'd done. "Was it really you, Mandy?" I asked frightfully.

"Hello to you too, friend," Mandy laughed unemotionally.

"Can you answer the question please?" I said assertively.

"Was *what* me? Be more specific."

"Did you sell me out to the police?"

"I did what I needed to do," Mandy voiced.

Those words felt like a bullet that pierced through all of my vital organs; it felt like time had literally stopped.

"What does that even mean? Don't get me angry, friend," I said painfully.

"I was looking out for myself and my future. Please don't take it personally," Mandy snarked.

"*Don't take it personally*? Are you out of your mind, Mandy? You've basically been a sister to me for the past decade and you're telling me that I shouldn't take it personally for destroying my whole life?"

"Which sister makes the other do all her dirty work for the business they're supposed to be equals in? I did us a favour and just made official the state of what our friendship *really* was," Mandy continued bitterly.

"I never said we were equals, Mandy. I told you from the beginning that I would be in charge, but I told you you'd still get a huge cut of the money. I just wanted to make sure the business didn't end up being a reflection of your unpredictable behaviour but I've always valued you in this business. I couldn't have done it without you," I communicated passionately.

"You *couldn't* have done it without me—you're right. I literally made you into what you are today, Kaya Khumalo; therefore, I have the power to take it away as and when I see fit. Your time is up. It's my turn to run what was rightfully mine," Mandy declared.

"You…you—" I stuttered pathetically.

"I what?" Mandy cackled. "You're pathetic, Kaya, and without me, you're nothing. Listen, I don't want things to be awkward between us. I genuinely wish you the best and I hope you don't dwell on this too long. You're smart; you'll get a great job in the city and you'll still do well. It's time to let the adults do the work now," she scoffed.

"Mandy, you've just ruined ten years of friendship for the sake of money? If it's more money you wanted I would have given it to you. I've always valued you more than the money, Mandy. Why would you do this?" I said as I began tearing up.

"The same reason you made me your assistant—you always cared more about power than our friendship. I'm simply finishing off what you started," she snarled.

"How long have you been planning to do this, Mandy?" I said as the tears began falling.

"Mmm, I'd say the initial thought came in around a year ago now," she admitted unapologetically.

"So you're telling me that you got me into business with Daniel Underwood and Alexander Petrov so that you could tear my business apart?"

"You got me!" Mandy laughed.

I paused in silence for a few seconds, trying not to let anger drive me to my next response. I still had to remember that her life was in complete danger and the main thing I cared about was keeping her safe.

"P-Petrov is after you, Mandy. He doesn't want you to get away with this. Please get away and find somewhere safe until I can get this under control," I pleaded with her.

"Nice try, Kaya," she said comically as she hung up the phone.

My heart sunk to the bottom of my chest in grief. What more could I have done? She was dripping with hatred for me. She had absolutely no remorse for what she had done. I didn't know what I was going to do in the midst of all of this, especially as I now knew that Petrov was really serious about getting rid of her.

20

2013

"Friend, this place is *far!*" Mandy exclaimed dramatically as she entered our new house. "I had to get like three buses and walk about an hour. I need some water."

"Okay, Mrs Drama Queen," I giggled as I took her bags from her. "Anyway, at least my dad will be taking us back to campus on the weekend so you can rest your beloved body until then."

"Indeed, it is my beloved body, I can't believe I just put it through so much without tending to it," she continued theatrically.

"Alright, alright. The Mandy Show is over now. Whenever you're done *tending to your body*, we can talk about that thing I wanted to tell you about," I replied excitedly.

"Give me a few minutes to just rejuvenate my mind," she said. "This house is dope though; your dad and aunty have done a spectacular job."

"Thank you kid," Pops sang as he came into the living room. "I'm guessing you're Mandy, Kaya's *only* friend at university *even though she pretends she has more*," he said as he whispered the last part. I gave him a good elbow in the belly.

"Yes Sir!" Mandy beamed with a twinkle in her eyes. "She's more than a friend, she's my sister."

As those words came out of her mouth, I felt such a deep acceptance. *I'm her sister, wow*. I was even more sure now that I wanted to carry out this plan with her because I realised I could really trust her.

"Make yourself at home; no guest that stays with us should feel awkward in any way. Anyone who is a friend of my daughter is family to us," Pops smiled.

"Aww, I love you guys," Mandy said as she ran over to hug me and Pops. I always admired how comfortable Mandy was to be herself regardless of the circumstance. It made me feel like I could also be myself.

"I'll be back on the weekend to take both of you girls back to university. I've got to go on a short business trip but I'll see you soon. Be good and stay safe, okay? It was lovely meeting you, Mandy."

"It was lovely meeting you too, Pops," Mandy grinned.

"See you Dad," I said.

"He's great," Mandy stated. "I wish my dad could be a lot less boring and strict and way more like your dad. I can tell he was one of the cool ones growing up," Mandy vented.

"Yeah, he's amazing, and he really likes you as well. I can just tell. So, what are your parents like? I've never really asked."

"I mean, there's nothing much to say about them. Boring, stuck-up, middle-class…nothing exciting," Mandy voiced. "My mum's favourite hobby is gardening and my dad loves fishing. From that, you can tell exactly what kind of people they are."

"Oh. Well, it would still be nice to meet them one day," I said wishfully.

"Enough about my boring parents. Tell me this exciting news you have," Mandy asked. "Wait! Are you and Luke getting married or something?"

"Huh? No girl. Luke and I are *far* from getting married right now," I sighed.

"Hmm, then I'm not sure what you've brought me here to talk about. The only two things you talk about are school and Luke; you know I'd be on my way out if you start talking about our exams," she proclaimed.

"Whoops! I wanted you to come so you could explain the thermodynamics module to me…" I tricked her.

"Girl, you've *got* to be kidding me. I travelled all the way here to study when I could be partying and having fun? I'm out!" she huffed as she began picking up her stuff.

"No, no. Wait, Mandy!" I giggled. "I'm just kidding, friend. That's not actually why I asked you to come."

"That was *not* a funny joke, Kaya; I was this close to revoking my 'sister' statement about you," she said as she put her thumb and index finger in the 'this close' position. "So, what am I here for?"

"Well…I thought about what you said all those weeks ago about the 'food' market and stuff," I started.

"Am I in some sort of friend-rehab?" she asked.

"Far from it, friend. Quite the opposite actually," I said, grinning cunningly.

"I don't get it…" Mandy whispered as she thought to herself.

"What I mean…is that I want you and I to be in this together," I revealed.

"Wait, are you trying to say that innocent old Kaya Khumalo wants to come over to the dark side and join me in my fatal affairs?" Mandy said with eyes wide open.

"Well, on certain conditions," I announced.

"Oh, here we go. What are these 'certain conditions'?" Mandy questioned.

"The conditions are that things are run *my* way. So I will be in charge of admin and all of that but we will have a pretty equal pay. All you would have to do is bring the clients in and I'll do the rest," I proposed.

"Hmm…so you basically do all the boring stuff and I do the fun stuff and get the same pay?" Mandy asked.

"Exactly. However, I think that if I had an extra five percent it would be more fair," I suggested.

"Hold on; why would I do business with you, for *you* to be in charge, when I can keep running my own business and take 100% of the pay once I've paid my supplier?" Mandy snapped back.

"Fair point, but take a look at my business plan and you'll see why my way is better," I replied, smiling proudly.

Similarly to when I showed Pops and Aunty Andrea, I knew it would take her a while to read over it but, this time, I wanted to watch her react to the plan right before my eyes. I needed to see her face of approval towards my thoughts; in fact, I realised that I really enjoyed this feeling of approval suddenly—it gave me an adrenaline rush. *Finally*, I had the limelight in some way because of my brain, not because of my body or beauty. This felt great.

"Woah, I'm gonna be *so* rich!" Mandy exclaimed as she started twerking and dancing ecstatically all over the living room. "Also, yeah, count me out of being in charge. I don't wanna deal with all that admin stuff you'll have to deal with. I'm good with 45% and to party with clients all day for the rest of my life."

"I knew you'd like the deal. So you're on board with it then?" I made sure to clarify.

"On board? Girl, I'm like in the middle of the ocean right now; we boarded weeks ago," she laughed.

"Whoop, whoop!" I exclaimed. "But we have *a lot* to do; we need to start bringing the clients in immediately so we can get this lifted off of the ground."

"I already have clients so that's no problem at all," she proposed.

"Ah, no, Mandy. Read the business plan again. Our clients are of a much higher calibre than university students," I snorted.

"Huh? So how do you expect me to bring them in?" she asked worriedly.

"Well…that's up to you; that's your job in all of this," I winked.

"Goodness me," Mandy exhaled with a daunting realisation of what she would be involved in. She continued, "That's why they say, *money doesn't come easy*."

2013

"These packages look good, friend!" Mandy said as she high-fived me. "I love the way we've decorated them; they're so pretty that *no one* will ever suspect what we've put in them."

"I agree. We did a great job with these. We should do these summer packages every year. If we can get all of these sold by the end of this week, we will make a huge profit," I said blissfully.

Summer had finally come, and Mandy and I were in our final week of our first year at university. We'd spent the last six months growing our client base both on campus and within Cape Town. Things were taking off and beginning to pick up pace even quicker than we'd expected. Our credibility on campus was undoubtedly better than anyone else who tried to sell here. What was even better was that people here didn't make it obvious that this business was running—so many people were buying from us, even some of the students' parents.

The summer packages Mandy and I made was an idea that came to us a few weeks ago. The plan was to make a package that would last our customers for the weeks we were all away from school. We also had a payment option which allowed clients to pay in instalments as long as they gave us their address and phone number. It was exactly these sorts of ideas that were bringing in major income.

However, when we decided to do these packages, I knew we'd need help from someone who could drive so that they could go around to people's houses and collect the money as and when necessary. So, I called Thato a few weeks ago to join us in the business. At first, Thato was understandably shocked that I could be running something like this, especially as it was hard enough for him to get me to smoke pot, but as soon as I explained why I'd decided to do this, it finally convinced him.

The job description I set out for Thato was to handle the affairs that required travelling to various places to collect and drop off packages, which was already much of what he did with his current 'gang'. My aim was that, hopefully, at some point, I would have enough money to pay him full-time so he could leave those dangerous people he was around all the time.

As Mandy and I were on the last package, there was a loud and thunderous knock at my door. Mandy and I suddenly stopped what we were doing and turned to each other slowly wondering if we were about to be busted for something.

"Are you expecting anyone, Khumalo?" Mandy asked with fear in her voice.

"No," I said, trembling. I motioned at her to begin hiding all the packages whilst I crept towards the door. "Who is it?" I said shakily.

"Open up and find out," they said, but the voice seemed so familiar that I immediately became more calm.

I opened the door slowly and peaked my head through so that I didn't show Mandy frantically putting all of the packages into my wardrobe.

"Hey babe," Luke chirped at me. "Have you missed me?"

"Oh…Luke? Wow, um, I wasn't expecting you at all," I squeaked.

His smile turned upside down as I had seemingly offended him by my lack of excitement. "Is that the welcome I get when I surprise you after not seeing you for nearly three months? You don't sound excited at all."

"Oh, no! Of course I'm excited to see you, I've really missed you," I lied as I looked back at Mandy to see if she was finished. Seeing that she was still hiding the packages, I stepped outside of my room. "Let's…um…take a walk out in the courtyard."

"I was actually hoping we could just chill out in your room for a little bit; I'm quite tired from the journey up here," he breathed.

"Okay. No problem. We can go to one of the benches and lay out on the grass," I suggested, trying to ensure he didn't come into my room.

"It's so hot outside, can't I just lay down in your room for a bit?" he asked, moving closer to the door.

"I don't really want to be in my room right now," I said as I blocked him from trying to reach for the door handle.

"Is there something wrong, K?"

"No, why?" I pretended.

"You just seem really nervous and agitated right now," he suspected.

"Nope, I'm all good. I just don't want to be inside, that's all," I lied again.

"Well, you were just inside a second ago before I knocked on the door."

"I was actually just about to head out," I stressed. Why wasn't he taking the bait?

"You're hiding something," he said, forcing eye contact with me to see if there was something I was hiding.

"No, I'm not!" I defended myself.

"Wait. Is there another guy in there or something? Is this why you've not been picking up my calls?" he questioned forcefully.

"N-no, Luke. Chill out," I stuttered.

"Move out of the way, K," he said as he forcefully moved me aside and barged into my room.

"Hey Luke," Mandy said casually, pretending to be reading a magazine on my bed. I sighed in relief, reminding myself peacefully that Mandy was the best actress I knew.

"I don't understand…why wouldn't you want me to see Mandy in your room? There's nothing to hide?" Luke asked with much confusion.

"As I said, I just wanted to be outside."

"Okay…so can I relax for a bit then?" he asked.

"Sure. Mandy, I'll catch you later, yeah?" I eyed her, implying that she should leave the room.

"Yep. See you later, friend!" she bellowed dramatically as she ran out of the room.

"Something just seems really strange and off with you guys," Luke muttered as he shook his head. "I can't figure out what's going on yet but I know I'm not crazy."

"Here we go again," I complained. "You're always finding a reason to make our relationship more complicated than it needs to be!"

"You know what? I don't want to fight right now. I'm probably just tired. Sorry, babe," he apologised.

"It's okay," I said, feeling really guilty.

I tucked myself into his arms as we both began to fall asleep; it was the most close I'd felt to Luke in months. It felt like we'd been going through a storm because of his surprise on me about his faith and the fact that he still didn't like that I was close with Mandy, but at least things were a bit less rocky now. We'd started talking things through about his faith—how things changed for him so suddenly and how it was going to affect our relationship, which, according to Luke, wouldn't affect much. However, I knew that it was only a matter of time.

Still, I hadn't asked him how it all started and I'm not really sure I wanted to know because I didn't want his faith to influence my thoughts. I was happy seeing the world the way I was currently seeing it. All I knew was that he'd woken up one day and suddenly "felt the love of God overwhelm him" or something like that; not that I really believed it, but it's his life. I was just glad to be back in his arms, feeling peace for the first time in a long time.

"What is this?" I heard Luke say as I was woken from my nap.

"What's what, babe?" I said as I rubbed my eyes open. I could only see faintly through the gunk in my eyes that he was standing near my wardrobe with something in his hands, but the disorientation I was feeling from a disturbed nap completely made me miss what was happening.

"These packages!" he shouted angrily.

I was suddenly awake and I could feel the panic set into my heart as I was exposed in front of the one I loved so much.

"Luke, let me explain," I said as calmly as possible. "It's not what it looks like…just give me a minute to explain."

"Explain what? That my girlfriend came to university to get a highly respected degree but is instead leaving with a degree in drug dealing? Are you crazy, Kaya?" Luke screamed hysterically.

"Please, calm down, babe. Please, just give me a chance to explain it all to you," I whimpered in fear.

"Kaya, I'm about to leave this room and when I walk out, we are *done*. I'm giving you less than 60 seconds to explain," Luke professed.

"Okay, okay! Look, M-Mandy and I have this all under control, and it's not like I personally do the drugs—*well*, I've only tried them once or twice. I'm still going to graduate and everything, but this is just such a huge opportunity of success for me," I tried, knowing full well that I'd failed to make the explanation sound worthy in any way.

I could see silent tears streaming down his face as he looked at the Kaya he couldn't recognise; it was the look of utter disappointment and betrayal. As he turned away from me and let out a small wail, I didn't even bother to stop him; I just knew it was totally over. I felt sick to my stomach when the door closed. I'd traded the love of my life for money and status. I'd literally sold my soul.

Who even was I?

21

2021

The only thing I could think to do was to head to the club to see if any of Petrov's partners would be there; perhaps, to reason with them in saving Mandy's life. She'd really messed up.

Out of all people, I would have expected Mandy to know how something like this ends. I mean, even if she wanted to betray me, why would she be so foolish to leave so many trails behind her? Surely, she would know that Petrov would be after her. *Oh, Mandy, why?*

I looked absolutely chaotic and, for once, I was completely unafraid to show it. In some ways, I realised how much Mama had rubbed off on me. I'd been putting up a front all these years to show the Kaya Khumalo I'd wanted them to see. I'd been the clean-cut, put-together businesswoman with not a single flaw in her except that she worked too hard. I was like a perfect porcelain doll in these people's eyes so I wasn't surprised to see the shock on people's faces when I turned up to my club in a soup-stained jumper, tracksuit bottoms and Crocs.

"Good evening, Ms Khumalo. Is everything okay?" one of my security guards asked me as I walked through the back entrance.

"All good, thanks," I said without a smile, removing myself from any kind of conversation.

I ran straight upstairs to the private area to see if I could find anyone there. I searched every corner high and low but couldn't find anyone. Why hadn't Thato called me yet? He was the only person I could think of that could help me figure out what to do next about this Mandy situation. I knew Thato cared about her too so he'd want to do everything possible to keep her safe regardless of how she'd betrayed us. Well, I hoped he would want to do that anyway.

I called Thato four times; each time, it went straight to voicemail. I just couldn't understand what was happening.

"Hey Thato, please call me back when you get this. It's an emergency. Come to the club right away, if not, I might go mad."

I ran back downstairs to the security guard. "Hey, just wondering if anybody has come by to look for me this evening?" I asked him.

"Not that I know of. You're the only one that has come from this side tonight. Let me radio the front to see if they've had anyone come for you," he replied.

"Thanks," I muttered under my breath.

"Boys, has anyone come for Ms Khumalo tonight?"

"Nope," one of them replied on the radio.

"Sorry, Ms Khumalo," he said.

"Thanks, anyway," I sighed.

My last call option was Daniel Underwood; he was the only other person who knew in part some of the operations Petrov and I were involved in. After all, he was also a mutual friend of Mandy so I guessed he'd have her best interest at heart.

The phone barely rang for a second when he picked up, "Good evening, Ms Khumalo," he said charmingly. He never seemed to drop his charm for a moment.

"Hey Daniel," I breathed, trying not to let the stress of the situation get to me.

"You're calling me Daniel…? What's up…?" he replied with confusion.

"Have you seen or spoken to Mandy?" I asked.

"Not since a few days ago. Why? Is everything alright?" he questioned.

"Yes, everything is fine," I bluffed, but I remembered that this was a matter of life or death and I really needed all the help I could get. "Actually, no, everything isn't alright, Underwood. Mandy's made a mess of things and she's in danger. I'm only telling you this because it's urgent. Please, don't tell Petrov I told you this. *Please*," I urged him.

"You have my word, your secret is safe with me. To tell you the truth, I never really liked Petrov anyway. Sorry; back to the important bit—how is Mandy in danger?" he said worriedly.

"Mmmhh," I exhaled, not wanting to tell him the whole truth but knowing I had to. "Long story short, she ratted out Petrov and I to the police so that she could take over my business. She clearly hasn't thought this through but, either way, Petrov found out and wants her dead by tomorrow. He told me that if I don't kill her then *he'll* kill her and probably me and my employees. I don't know what to do," I cried quietly.

"Oh, no. I'm sorry to hear that," Underwood groaned. He paused for a while and then finally continued, "Do you want me to be honest?"

"No," I continued to cry. I knew exactly what him being honest meant but I certainly didn't want to hear it.

"Well then, you already know what I'm going to say. Promise me you'll try and keep yourself safe?"

"I'll try. Thank you for everything, Underwood. It was a pleasure working with you."

"You, too, Kaya. Truly, you're one of a kind. All the best," he murmured softly as he ended the call.

I had two options at this point—I could go home to my apartment and wake up with a gun to my face because I hadn't followed through with Petrov's orders, or I could go back home to Gogo and Mama where they probably wouldn't be able to find me for a week or two.

I think I'll go with option two.

22

2021

It would be too dangerous to be in Johannesburg after tonight. I needed to think fast and my only option was to go back to Gogo and Mama and lay low for as long as possible, maybe even forever if Petrov was after me. My plan was to drive as quickly as I could back to my apartment, pack a bag and then leave. I couldn't even withdraw money from an ATM because I wasn't sure what was tied to my name at the moment; it was best to figure that out in the next few days, when I could get through to Thato.

I walked through the back of my apartment complex with my hood up and glasses on so that no one at the concierge would be able to know if I'd come in. I also made sure to leave my car at a supermarket nearby. One of the main things running through my mind was that I was leaving without saying goodbye to Blessing, my housemaid. How could I just disappear on her like that? And I knew I wouldn't be able to take any of her phone calls for now. How was she going to be able to pay her bills or find someone who would pay her as much as me? *I'll figure it out*. I could never leave her hanging like that.

My mind was everywhere—I knew I just needed to get my stuff and go but I felt like I needed to linger around a little bit so I could say my final goodbyes to this place. I was really going to miss it.

After a few minutes of procrastinating, I went into my room and packed a bag, essentials only—tops, jeans, tracksuits and a few pairs of shoes. It wasn't like anyone in my town cared about any of these materialistic things anyway. I'd be silly to strut around with a Chanel bag on my town streets; I think they'd all think I'm deranged.

After thinking about how I was going to say goodbye to Blessing, I began writing up a letter for her. When I was finished, I hid it in the cleaning cupboard above the bathroom sink. I knew no one would think to look there for anything anyway. It read:

Dearest Blessing,

I'm going away, I think for a very long time, if not forever. Firstly, I just want to say thank you for pressing on the importance of a relationship with my mother because, if it hadn't been for you, I'm not sure I ever would have heard her out. Secondly, I think I believe in God now, but I'm not sure if I will ever go to church so maybe you'll have to keep praying on that one for me. Thirdly, I've just paid your salary for the next three years so I hope this will be okay with you for the time being. If I'm still alive in the next few months, I will ensure to find you another role if you don't already have one by then. Lastly, if you didn't already know, I used to be a drug dealer. I say 'used to' but I've actually only just quit today. I also need you to know that the money I paid you for your salary was actually every bit of legal money I've earned since I was 18 but never used—it was from my 'legal' account. I'm done with drug money and I'm sorry that I ever paid your salary with it. I hope you can forgive me.

I want you to know that you truly are a blessing, Blessing. I love you forever and ever.

Kaya.

I placed it in the cupboard with a tear droplet from my eyes falling onto the paper, sealing it with my sorrow. I can't believe that I'd managed to make a mess out of Blessing's life too. I never realised how damaging my selfishness could be.

I did one final scan of my apartment just to check that I hadn't left anything that could be used to find me. I decided to leave my cinema room until last because it was the room I was the most sad to leave behind. I could hear the echoes of laughter, tears, and shouting Mandy and I had had from all of the movies and series we'd watched together. It's like I was leaving her behind also.

I walked in slowly, switching the light on and smiling at every corner of the room. However, I felt like I could see something sticking out from behind my giant beanbag on the other side of the room. *Was that a leg?*

I crept towards it and as I walked even closer, I saw a pool of thick red liquid encircling the area and realised it was a dead body. I jumped back in shock and covered my mouth with both hands in case I let out a scream. I wanted to run but I knew I needed to see who it was lying dead in my apartment.

As I came around the bean bag, the face of Thato was staring back at me completely unmoving and still.

"Thato?" I whispered. He didn't even flinch; it was like every drop of life in him had been sucked out. "Thato, please wake up. No, no, no, you can't leave me. You can't leave me, friend."

I shook him and shook him with every bit of might as my tears fell all over his lifeless looking face hoping that the Thato that once fell off his bike at eight years old was going to get up, dust it off and carry on. I just wanted to take back every horrible thing I'd said to him in the recent months. I'd basically traded my friendship with him for Mandy; yet, he'd stayed loyal to me until the very end.

I wanted to mourn and grieve over him but I realised that whoever killed Thato had probably come looking for me. I also didn't need any kind of evidence to know that Thato died in my place in order to protect me. How could I have allowed him to die instead of me?

I couldn't be here a single second longer—I had to get out of here. Someone was literally trying to end my life and they'd succeeded with Thato's. The safest place for me to be right now was with Mama and Gogo.

"Bye, friend," I wept as I let Thato go, just about managing to gather the strength to get up and walk.

I cried the entire journey to the airport, not even knowing how I was going to explain any of this to my family. How was I going to explain this to *Thato's* family? I didn't know how I was going to look them in the eyes without guilt knowing that I was the reason that they would never be able to see their son again.

"Everything okay?" the taxi man asked me as he peered at me through his rearview mirror.

"Yes," I said, sniffling unconvincingly.

"Whoever it is, I'm sure you deserve better," he criticised.

"Thanks," I lamented.

I mean, he was right. Although this had nothing to do with a bad dating experience, Mandy had basically been my 'boyfriend' all these years. I'd put all my trust in her and I *did* deserve better.

***

Arriving at Gogo's at close to 4am, I just hoped that with a good night's rest, I'd be able to process my thoughts much easier by the morning time. I collapsed on the floor as I got to the doorstep probably due to a mixture of a lack of sleep, an empty stomach and oh, wait…seeing the corpse of my dead best friend just a few hours before.

As I thumped on the floor, Mama, who has always been a light sleeper, ran to find who it was on the doorstep at this time of the night. The smell of Mama's hair when she found me weeping on the doorstep brought strength back to my knees as I was reminded that I'm still loved regardless of all of these terrible mistakes and crimes I'd committed over nearly the past decade.

"Ingane! Oh my goodness!" she shrieked. "How did you get here?" She looked around frightfully on the streets and around the porch to see if someone had done this to me.

"I'm okay, Mama," I whimpered. "I just need some rest."

"No, don't get up, let me carry you sweetheart," she said empathetically.

"We'll talk about it in the morning, Ma."

I once again remembered Luke's words about speaking to God as Mama tucked me into bed. I couldn't explain the feeling, but I just felt like God had been with me after that phone call with Mandy. I wasn't sure how Mandy calling me and trash talking our whole friendship was him answering my prayer but I was just so sure that he had heard me.

As Mama left my room, I began to pray. "Dear God, I can barely get the words out right now; I feel so weak and fragile on both the inside and the outside, but I feel as if I need to pray again before I go to sleep. First of all, I just want to say thank you for giving me Mama and Gogo. I know my relationship with Ma has been rocky, but I'm so glad that I finally understand her after all of these years. All I so desperately wanted was to understand her so that I could truly know if she loved me or if she just felt forced to pretend; I know it sounds silly but I really wasn't sure for a long time.

"To tell you the truth, God, I'm not sure if I've ever truly known what love is. I've been running around everywhere trying to find it all of my life but I only managed to get snippets and segments of it. I guess that's why I didn't even notice that someone I called my sister would end up betraying me. I just wanted her to love me. How can I accept or understand love when I'm not even sure of what it is? I just want to be truly loved, and if you're what love is, in the way Luke described it to me, then I really want that. I'm so broken on the inside, in a way I don't even know if you would be able to understand even if you are the 'almighty God'. The brokenness inside of me is so complex that I'm not sure it can be fixed.

"Thato dying on me today just reminded me of all the complexities within me. I feel sick even thinking about the fact that he's dead. I feel unworthy of love, so much so that him dying for me for the sake of love feels so wrong. Of course, I don't think I've fully grasped that Thato is gone yet; I don't know if I ever want to grasp it. But I think that, deep down, I've always known that Thato wasn't always going to be around. The way he was living was too reckless; he just about dodged a bullet every single time. I just wished his death wasn't for *me*. It makes me feel so ashamed. Thato could've been so much more; he was always such a selfless person and sometimes, I feel that he cared more about me than he did his own life—I guess that proved to be true in the end. I hate this. Truthfully, I hate myself right now.

"I really need to be honest with you about something, God; something I've never told anyone. I'm tired of pretending it didn't happen because so much of my life has been navigated by this one trauma. It's a trauma I just can't seem to get rid of. I've been extra triggered by it recently because of Mama and Gogo's stories. Although what my dad did was utterly vile, I think I was so deeply affected by it because I realised that there's been an even deeper problem for all of us Khumalo women. It's like wherever we go and whatever we do, there's this curse of rape and abusive men that follow us around everywhere. It's almost like it gets passed on as a baton from generation to generation, like a family heirloom.

"You're probably wondering why I'm saying all this, and I know I've been taught my whole life that you're an all-knowing God but, just in case you aren't, I'm saying all this because…I too was nearly raped once. Yeah, I know…it's deep, right? It happened the day Luke walked out of my life. I was heartbroken and Mandy's suggestion was to numb the pain—I got so hammered that I was practically paralysed. I didn't even know who this guy was but he found me in the bathroom and used it as an opportunity to try to do as he liked with me. I remember that even though I'd lost control over my body, my mind was still functioning. I wanted to scream out for Luke but I knew he was never coming back. Never. I didn't know what to do; all I knew was that I felt unbelievably worthless.

"Admittedly, I prayed to you that night, God. I prayed that you would get me out of there with the same rights over my body that I'd stepped in with. I was desperate. I guess…you must have heard me because I can't describe to you how I got out of there but someone came to save me. I don't know how to describe it but the person who saved me seemed…heaven-sent. All I know is that I woke up in one piece in my bed.

"I don't know why I didn't pray to you after that—you saved my life and I selfishly continued to seek life for my own gain, but you've humbled me and reminded me that when we do things for our own selfish desires, we may end up with much but we lose our soul in the process.

"What I do know is that, deep down, that's why I've always feared being around men or being in a relationship. It's like I feel that a curse is hovering over my head just waiting to be fulfilled. Everyone thinks it's because Luke and I broke up that I'm afraid of men, but no. Deep down, it's because I've always known there's something wrong with the women in this family. I don't want the same story as Ma and Gogo. I can't live out the life that I know so bitterly disappointed them.

"God, if I survive this, will you take this curse away from me and my family?"

2021

I woke up forgetting the reality I was in. Instead, a feeling of peace and tranquillity came upon me as the sunlight peeked through my blinds and rested on my face. I could hear birds flying through the air and Gogo and Ma cooking in the kitchen. I sensed the beginning of a fresh start dawning on me.

It was strange because the only thing I couldn't hear was the light bustle of cars driving around because of the morning rush to work. It wasn't like the sound of Joburg in the morning, but there was still the slightest atmosphere of a 9-5 work culture in my small town.

I checked my phone thinking it was around 7 or 8am but saw that it was afternoon. I jumped straight out of bed because I hated being up this late, but I also had grace on myself because I suddenly remembered why I was even here in the first place—my best friend was shot dead and killed in my apartment last night.

"Afternoon, sweetie," Gogo said to me as I walked into the kitchen. Kissing me on the cheek lightly, she handed me some tea and oatmeal.

"Thank you, Gogo. I've missed you so much," I said in truth. I was so glad to be able to mourn the events of the past few days with Gogo and Mama by my side.

"I've missed you too, darling," she smiled, but she seemed like she was hiding something. I knew this because Gogo is someone who never struggles to make eye contact with people so there must have been a reason why she was avoiding my face now.

"Morning Ma," I murmured softly, giving her a hug.

"Hey baby," she said sadly.

"Is everyone okay? You both seem a bit sad," I asked.

They exchanged looks with one another still keeping quiet about what was going through their minds which made me anxious. Could they have already known about Thato?

"Ma, please tell me what's happening," I enquired in a tone of desperation.

"Tell her, Nandi," Gogo hesitated.

Mama walked over to the living room area and picked up the remote, turning back to me with a face of dismay.

"Have you seen the news this morning, Kaya?" Mama asked me quietly.

"No…what's on the news?" I replied in fear.

"Um, I think it's best if you watch it for yourself," she said, handing the remote over to me.

I walked over to her and took the remote from her hands wearily. Gripped with the trauma of the night before and knowing that whatever it was wasn't good news made that nauseous feeling come right back.

I turned on the news channel and sat there, waiting in anticipation for whatever Gogo and Mama were upset about. I looked back to them after a few minutes as I hadn't seen anything of relevance to me, but Mama prompted me with her head to watch on.

"Breaking news from Sandton, Johannesburg. In the early hours of this morning, around 5 members of what seems to be rival drug gangs have been found dead in various areas of Sandton. Three people who have been identified under the names of Alexander Petrov, Mandy Roberts and Thato Kyleson were found dead in two locations, one of which was at a club called the 'Blue Panther' and the other location at an apartment located in the Sandton area. The other two remain unidentified for now, but are assumed to be connected to a Russian gang run by Alexander Petrov.

"The police are currently investigating the links between the drug dealers but, for now, this is being ruled as a bloody war sparked between the two of them. At the moment, there are no suspects as it seems the victims were involved in each other's murders. However, more information should be released in the coming days." I switched off the TV as soon as she finished saying these things.

"I'm so sorry, sweetheart," Mama interjected before I could even process these happenings.

"I-I-I d-don't know w-what to s-say," I stuttered profusely. "E-everyone is d-dead. They're all dead. They're all dead," I sobbed.

"It's okay, honey," Gogo said as she ran over to comfort me in her arms.

"Gogo, it's all my fault!" I wailed loudly. "How am I deserving of a second chance and they are all dead?"

I could barely breathe as I felt the pain of grief seeping itself into my body. I wanted this to be over. I wanted to take it all back so I could reset the fate of their lives.

"This was never your story, Kaya," Gogo began. "You are one who is to turn the history of the Khumalo's around. You are a child of light, one who trail-blazes in everything. You were brought forth on this earth to laugh in the face of darkness. The devil used your gifts for evil but now, it is time to use them for good. You will not be like the rest of us. Do you hear me, Ingane?"

Even though I was wailing in pain at every word Gogo spoke, I felt everything she said so heavily in my heart. I realised that actually, I *don't* deserve it, but something was still giving me the chance to live out what I didn't deserve. I *was* unworthy, but I was being offered the opportunity to walk in someone else's worthiness. I *should* have died, but I know I've been handed life instead.

"How did I get this so wrong, Gogo?" I asked sorrowfully.

"My dearest child of light, when you came into this world, your mother and I knew that history would change for the Khumalo legacy—once a history of trauma and abuse to be transformed into hope and prosperity. I just knew as soon as my eyes fell upon you.

"When you ran away from home and started up this 'business' of yours, I hoped that loving you through it would encourage you to see that this was never your calling. I had to have faith in the bottom of my heart that you would see that this treasure box that seemed full of gold and jewels was really a pit of destruction and terror.

"I know that your mother and I have been terrible examples at times to look to, especially when it comes to faith. We never spoke about God in this household or even talked about any relationship we might have with a higher power but I want you to know that he is real and he cares. In fact, this moment is a testament to prayer. I never stopped praying for you—praying that you would stop this nonsense and experience and encounter the love of God in your heart.

"When you were born, there was a local missionary that happened to be in our town for a few weeks and I asked him to come and pray for you and dedicate you. Inasmuch as I thought he was a bit crazy and dogmatic about God at first, there is something that he said about you that I will never forget. He said, "Do you know that this child is going to change the course of events for this family? She's going to be one that breaks free."

"I can't forget, Ingane. He looked at you with such hope and faith and that is the only thing that kept me believing that you were going to stop this. Now, it may have taken the loss of your two friends to make you realise this, but sometimes, we have to get things so wrong to recognise what's truly right. You veered off-path, very off-path, but had it not been for that, maybe you wouldn't have desired to get your life truly right and live out those prophetic words. You are *not* this person, Kaya Imka Khumalo; you never have been.

"In fact, none of these people you were around were truly those people, but you must thank God for his mercy over you. Mercy that was over you because someone was praying for you; *I* was praying for you. You don't deserve this, but there is a God that is altogether the definition of love. He keeps no record of wrongs. The question you should be asking yourself now is not 'How did I get this so wrong?' but rather, 'How can I allow God to make me right?'"

I was lost for words at Gogo's speech. She walked off with Mama into the back of the house to allow me some space to process everything. It was the most powerful thing anyone had ever said to me; it felt like the words were piercing right into me. Gogo and Mama had been praying for me all this while that I had been acting as a tyrant.

I can't even imagine how it would feel to see your child destroying the world for nearly ten years when you knew she should have been saving it. Knowing me, I would've given up on that person by now, but they continued to have faith that things wouldn't remain the same. I'm meant to be the one to change the fate of my lineage for good. Wasn't this what I prayed for yesterday?

23

2021

It's been a few weeks since I received the dreadful news. I've been trying to take each day as it comes. I continued in my routine of waking up early, eating meals at set times and exercising, but I know that I need a friend around to just help me get through this season.

Then I remembered that I hadn't even updated Luke or his wife yet on anything that had happened over the past few weeks, and I respected the fact they'd given me space to reach out to them in my own time.

"Hey Luke," I said as he picked up the phone.

"Hey Kaya. It's great to hear your voice," he responded cheerfully. "Just to let you know, you're on speaker phone as I'm with Cindy."

"Hey Kaya! Great to finally talk to you," Cindy's melodic voice said on the other end of the line. Her voice was so beautiful and clear like a Disney princess.

"Lovely speaking to you too, Cindy," I said happily.

"How are things?" she asked with concern.

"Um, er, things are things I guess," I began carefully, so I wouldn't cry. "I'm just taking each day as it comes."

"Bless you," Cindy sympathised. "We've not stopped praying for you; you're constantly on our minds."

"I'll take every prayer I can get!" I laughed gloomily. "But anyway, I actually called to express my gratitude to both of you. I just want to say thank you so much for your prayers and care towards me. I mean, Luke, you were right; I seem to have been the only one to have come out of this alive but I'm so grateful to have the opportunity for a fresh start."

"I'm so blessed to hear that you're safe," Luke began, "and, look, I'm truly sorry about Mandy and Thato. It's not what anyone wanted to happen. I know how much you loved them. Just know that if it's painful for you, it's painful for God as well. We're always here for you."

"Always here for you, Kaya. I'm going to save your number if that's okay?" Cindy offered.

"That'd be great," I answered.

"We're actually driving home to see my parents, so would we be able to call you and have a proper conversation tomorrow? I just want to make sure we can properly find out how you're doing and understand how we can help you going forward," Luke suggested.

"Oh, you're coming back to town?" I raved.

"Are you back in town?" Luke chuckled lightly.

"Yes, potentially for a really long time," I complained with an eye-roll.

"Oh, wow. Fabulous!" Cindy exclaimed. "We can all meet up this week."

"I guess we can. Are you driving all the way from Joburg?" I asked.

"Yep. It seemed like a fun and spontaneous idea when we decided to do it but now that we still have another 10 hours to go, it's possibly a very regretted decision," Luke grumbled loudly.

"Ah, well, you'll learn next time," I scolded playfully.

"Yeah, yeah. We'll see you soon then, Kaya," Luke said.

"See you soon," I smiled as I cut the call. I was actually really excited to meet Cindy.

I felt a weight lift off my shoulders after that conversation knowing that I would have some comfort around me other than Gogo and Mama. Family love is amazing but sometimes, you just need friends around to help you get your mind off it all.

But how could I have forgotten that Luke's family lived here? *Genesis* lived here. It was like my memory had just been thrown out of the window. That was the best news I'd heard all day; it would be like old times where I would tell Gen about all my problems and she'd give me wise counsel.

Except this time, my problems were two dead friends, a busted drug business and a life full of regret.

2021

I'd seen Genesis a couple of months back when she came to visit me in Johannesburg but we hadn't kept in regular contact because I'd been so distracted with solidifying my relationship with Alexander Petrov.

I still can't figure out how I feel about knowing that Petrov is dead. I mean, if Petrov is dead then surely no one is after me, right? They probably all think I'm dead anyway. The only person who knows I'm still alive is Daniel Underwood; can you imagine? The one I didn't trust all along was the one who helped save my life.

I just kept staring at myself in the mirror every time I walked past one because I wanted to make sure that I wasn't a ghost. Imagine if they'd killed me and I'm in hell right now? How could I be sure that I came out of there alive? Honestly, I needed to stop overthinking and just try to love myself after all the pain I'd caused everyone.

As much as I wanted to go and have fun with Genesis today, I knew that I first and foremost owed it to Thato's family to explain what had happened. I needed them to know that he'd protected me until the very end, even if it meant they hated me forever. It was the right thing to do.

I'd barely brought anything along with me from Johannesburg, and I'm glad I didn't because I wanted to leave behind the vanity and narcissism of the past and stay true to the reserved Kaya on the inside of me. Although, in doing so, I'd literally been living out of Mama and Gogo's wardrobe for the past few weeks; therefore, I looked like a mixture of a vintage store and a businesswoman—it was a very confusing look. Either way, I'd finally plucked up the courage to get ready and go to see Thato's family, regardless of how interesting I looked.

"Going somewhere?" Gogo asked me just as I opened the front door to leave.

"Yeah, Gogo. I'm going to see Thato's family."

"Very brave of you, Ingane. Whatever their reaction, you just hold onto what I told you," she reassured me with a gentle hug.

"I'll try Gogo."

I walked out onto the pavement and started on the journey I knew too well to Thato's house. It was so lovely to be outside again here. The trees were thick and full of life, nearing their harvest season. My favourite was the apricot tree because of the beautiful orange colour that bursts forth from its apricots. The fruits that grew here were always so sweet and delicious, free from pesticides and chemicals.

Another thing I loved about being at home was how the streets were pollution-free in comparison to the contaminated air in Johannesburg. Most people here worked and did everything locally so the main mode of transport was on foot or on a bike; cars were secondary here.

My heart started beating faster as I approached the road where Thato and I shared our very treasured memory. It was the road that we'd ridden on twenty years before when Thato was given his brand new bike. It was like my imagination was being superimposed on my current reality of seeing young Thato and I trying to take on the world. It's like our two worlds collided.

I guess Thato had always protected me; he always had an instinct of brotherly love for me and it just upset me that I began to resent that about him.

Sitting down at the very place that we had stumbled over the pothole, I looked up at the sky and began to pray in my heart. I prayed that God would forgive Thato for the bad things he'd done and would see that Thato didn't know any better. He was just a lost soul, and so was I.

I began to cry as it occurred to me that I would never be able to create any memories with Thato again—I could only look back and reflect on the memories we'd once had. He was gone for good. How would eight year old Thato take it if he found out he was going to die for me twenty years later? Maybe he would have saved himself from it from the very beginning.

I needed to get to his family before I talked myself out of going due to a spiralling of thoughts. I was nearly there; in fact, just a few steps away, but I was so afraid. I hadn't seen his family in years, maybe even since I'd left for Stellenbosch, so to turn up on their doorstep and deliver this truth to them just felt wrong. But, I don't know if I would be able to live with myself if I didn't do it.

As I got to Thato's doorway, I remembered the cinnamon buns his stepmum would make for us in return for babysitting his baby brother on the weekends. She would beg us for a few moments of solitude, and baking was one of those precious moments for her. Now that I'm an adult, I know exactly how she must have felt having a child that depends on you at all moments of the day; even if you don't feel like looking after them, you have to anyway. She always tried her best to be a great mum to both Charlie and Thato, and even though Thato always gave her a hard time, that never stopped her from treating him like her son.

I knocked at the door and waited in extreme anticipation for what would come next. I wasn't even sure if I would be able to speak in the moment.

"Who are you?" a young teenage boy with gamer headphones said to me rudely.

"*Excuse me?*" I said. "Who are *you*?" I defended, almost forgetting I was speaking to a child.

"Not telling you," he hissed back at me and stuck out his tongue. "What are you doing here?"

Suddenly remembering that I was at least twice this boy's age, I honed in my tone, put on a more gentle face and tried to smile.

"Does anyone called Jennifer or Ryan live here?" I asked, pretending to be sweet.

"Yes they do, they're my parents. What do you want with them?"

"Wait, *Charlie?*" I shrieked.

"How do you know me? STRANGER DANGER!" he shouted naughtily.

"Shush!" I demanded. "Do you not remember me?"

"Stranger danger!" he continued.

"Oh, Charlie, would you be quiet! It's Kaya you naughty little boy," I urged him, twisting his ear.

"I don't know a Kaya," he whimpered as I continued to twist his ear. It felt like a reflex response as it was something Thato and I always used to do to him when he misbehaved.

"Where are your parents?" I queried.

"They're in the back garden having a drink," he finally revealed.

"Thank you," I smiled. "Now, come here!" I shouted as I gave him a huge hug and almost squeezed him to death.

"Get off of me!" he whined.

Charlie was so grown up, I couldn't believe it. The last time I'd seen him he would have still been a toddler, so to see him on the brink of puberty and having a non-babble conversation was absolutely astonishing. I can't believe it flew over my head seeing as he looked *just* like Thato when we were that age—shaggy blonde-brown curly hair, light brown eyes, caramel skin, gap teeth. He was also *just* as rude. Thato was the sort to start trouble with anyone in the neighbourhood, even if they were a pensioner; it was just his way of expressing all that pent up energy inside of him. At least, I was glad that Charlie was using it to play games inside instead of running around and causing mayhem on the streets—it was much better that way.

I walked around to the back of the house where the side gate was so that Charlie didn't start screaming and calling me a weirdo again. I peeped through the gate cut-outs to see if Jenny and Ryan were hanging out in the back like Charlie had said. There they were. They looked so relaxed and happy that I felt that wave of guilt cross my mind again to know that I was possibly about to ruin their evening, or maybe even their life.

I pushed slowly through the gate so that I didn't alarm them too much; I immediately lost my sense for words and ended up just standing there at a distance hoping it wouldn't take them too long to notice that I was there.

"Mum, Dad, there's this weird woman that came to the door looking for you," Charlie began accusing me. "Oh, look, she's right there!" he screeched, pointing his finger at me and sticking out his tongue again.

"Would you behave yourself young man and stop speaking about this young lady in such a manner!" Jenny shouted. "To your room right now, and I'm coming to take your PlayStation off you too until you learn how to behave yourself."

Jenny began shooing him to his room as she smiled at me gently, clearly remembering that it was me. *Phew, at least that saves me an explanation.*

Ryan got up from his chair and began walking towards me with a tremendous smile on his face."Wow, Kaya, it's great to see you. It's been…"

"Ten years," I said, finishing off his sentence.

"Ten years? Are you sure?" he asked, furrowing his eyebrows and seeming puzzled.

"Yes, ten years," I affirmed.

"Come on in then, give us a hug!" he blurted out gleefully, wrapping his arms around me. I can never forget how when I was young I used to find Ryan's beer belly absolutely hilarious when he would hug me. Sometimes I would prod it with a fork when he was taking a nap or I would draw faces around his belly button with a marker pen.

"Honey, come and see Kaya!" Ryan shouted for Jenny.

"Yes, yes. Coming sweetie," I heard her voice echo quietly from inside the house.

Jenny came back out with some of her famous homemade lemonade and ginger biscuits. Jenny was always able to bring out food and drinks in a second which was something I'd always admired about her. She was just innately such a mother and homemaker; something I've never quite felt comes so naturally to me.

"Nice to see you, Kaya," Jenny said timidly, seeming to avoid eye contact with me. "Come and take a seat, and help yourself to some lemonade and biscuits," she offered kindly.

"Oh, thank you very much," I replied awkwardly.

There was some silence for a while. Everyone was looking around the garden munching on their biscuits trying to think of how to start the conversation. I looked over and saw Jenny nudge Ryan to start off the conversation, but I decided I needed to be bold about the reason I came and not leave everyone in this suspense. After all, *I* was the one who suddenly appeared in their back garden after ten years.

"I came because of Thato," I said abruptly, staring down at the floor.

They both sighed deeply and stayed quiet waiting for what I would say next. I was hoping that Ryan would have something to say but he didn't. I mean, why would they when this news was still so fresh?

"I just felt like you both deserved to know so much more than what the news or police would have told you because you're his parents." I began to get really nervous at this point because I realised they were not going to speak until I had finished my explanation. "I'm not sure how much you know about what Thato was involved in or which career path he chose but, he was involved with the wrong people," I looked back up and made eye contact with them because I wanted them to know how much responsibility I was taking for my actions.

"And…one of those wrong people was me. *I* employed Thato when I *stupidly*, stupidly decided to become a drug dealer; and, in my quest and hunger for more wealth and power, I collaborated with one of the biggest drug dealers in South African history. I didn't realise it until it was too late but it all went so wrong, and before I could stop anything from happening, Thato died in order to protect me. I'm so sorry…" I admitted regretfully.

It was yet again another awkward moment of silence. Jenny and Ryan still hesitated in case I had more to say, or maybe they just didn't know what to say. Either way, I felt uncomfortable on another level.

Eventually, Ryan lifted his head and began to speak.

"Thank you for um…coming, Kaya," he said as he looked at Jenny for her approval so that he could continue. When she nodded, he carried on, "We appreciate your honesty immensely and we're glad you had the boldness and respect for us to come and tell us face to face. However, I think it would be terrible for us to pretend that we weren't already aware of all the circumstances that took place."

"Wait, I don't understand. You already knew?" I asked.

"Of course, we knew," Jenny laughed sadly. "Thato was our son. He made some reckless decisions but, ultimately, we told him how it would end—either in prison or…killed."

"But aren't you *devastated?*" I replied with shock at their lack of emotion.

"Of course, we're devastated, Kaya. We feel like we're walking around with a gaping hole in our hearts," Ryan began. "However, as soon as Thato made his decision to join the gangs a decade ago, it felt like that was the very day we lost our son. It feels like he died ten years ago. So, don't be fooled by the way myself and Jenny have learnt to deal with our grief; both of us struggle to show emotion in general, but there's an emptiness that we've been feeling for years."

"Oh, I see," I muttered. "But how did you know that Thato died for me?"

Jenny looked back at Ryan and sighed in annoyance as I said this. I could tell there was so much going on in her head; I knew she was angry at me for some reason.

"You have *no idea* how much he admired you, do you?" Jenny articulated.

"Easy Jenny," Ryan smiled nervously as he tapped her on the leg gently.

"No, no, Ryan, let me speak my mind," Jenny said frustratedly. "Thato absolutely adored and worshipped you, Kaya, and you never noticed that. In fact, shortly before he died, he began to tell me that you'd started ignoring him and looking down on him and he couldn't understand why. How couldn't you see how much he loved you? Honestly, I always told him that you didn't deserve him by the way you treated him."

I didn't even know how I was going to respond to that; if I'd defended myself I would be gaslighting her. I was glad that she was being honest with her emotions but it left me in such a humiliating position.

"Jenny, I'm so sorry. I know I was a rubbish friend to Thato in our later years; I really regret it. I think, on the inside, I was really just angry at myself and the decisions I'd made, and I took that out on him. I wanted better for both of us."

"I'm not going to sit here and pretend it's okay, Kaya. I will always care for you because, at some point, you were like a daughter to me and I'm sure that looking back on it, you regret the decisions you made, but I lost my son for a friend who barely cared. I know he made some bad decisions but so did you, and *you* got a second chance but he didn't," she said as she began to cry.

Ryan started comforting her and shaking his head in disappointment. I wasn't sure who he was disappointed in, but I felt like it was me.

"I understand where both of you are coming from," Ryan said, "but Kaya, there's a lot of truth in what Jenny has said. Thato mended his relationship with us all a few years ago and we've known about your business all this time. I have to say, I was distraught to find out that someone with your intelligence and capability had wasted it all away on such a life; we were always rooting for you to end world hunger or find the cure for cancer or something.

"Just before he died, he told us that he was heading to your apartment to sort some things out with people that were after you. As soon as he said that, I just had a gut feeling that he was never going to come back out alive. I warned him; but if anything involves you, Kaya, Thato cannot hear whatever anyone tries to tell him—it was Kaya Khumalo and Thato Hans until the end for him. So, we knew he died to protect you. I don't want you to feel guilt or shame about it. Jenny and I want you to move on—she doesn't mean everything she's just said, she's just very hurt. But you got out easy girl, I'll tell you that much."

"I know, Ryan; *easy* isn't even the word. I know I don't deserve this, but I'm really going to turn my life around for good. Truly," I expressed.

"I hope so, Kaya," Jenny responded. "And, yes, I reiterate what Ryan has said; I may not have said everything in the way I should have had I been more calm, but you must remember this moment and use it for real change in your life. You and Thato were so much better than this."

"I understand. Thank you, Jenny. I'm sorry again," I voiced. "And, I really want you to know that I love you both even if you're disappointed in me. I'll let myself out."

"We love you too, Kaya. I'm sorry for getting so upset," Jenny smiled softly.

"See you around," Ryan said as I left.

I walked home with agony in my heart. I think it's at this point that I fully came to realise that Thato was gone for good. Not only that, I *had* hurt people. This didn't come without collateral damage. I was silly to think that I would walk away without any scars to show for it.

Another thing that had been playing on my mind was why the police hadn't yet arrested me or contacted me. Surely, they must've known that I was the one who ran the business, and, after finding Thato in my apartment, they *must* have known that I had some involvement. I couldn't keep walking on eggshells in my mind not knowing if I was going to be in prison or killed tomorrow; someone had to have some answers.

Underwood.

Thankfully, I hadn't cleared my phone numbers yet as I thought I'd wait another few weeks in case I needed to reach out to someone in Joburg. Underwood had pretty much saved my life so I knew that, underneath his fake persona, there was truly some goodness in his heart.

I rang a few times and there was no answer, but he was the only person I could reach out to so I really hoped that he would call me back. Maybe he was in prison or something? What if I was next?

As my thoughts started spiralling again on my walk home, my phone began to ring. It was Underwood.

"Afternoon, Ms Khumalo. Glad to know you're safe."

"Hey Underwood…glad to know that you're safe too. How are you?" I questioned.

"I'm wonderful, actually never been better. How can I help you?"

"Um, well, a few things," I confessed.

"Mhmm, I'm listening," he said suspiciously.

"Actually, just one thing," I clarified.

"Go ahead."

"Why aren't the police coming after me? Surely they must know I was behind it all."

"Ah, yes, I wondered when you'd ask," he chuckled.

"What is it now, Underwood? You love suspense, don't you? Like you're James Bond or something."

"Haha. You've always made me laugh, Kaya."

"So, *we are* doing first names?" I chortled.

"Yes…I think we are," Underwood decided. "Anyway, you wanted to know why no one is after you even though you really should be locked away in prison for life somewhere."

"Exactly," I said in anticipation.

"It sorted itself out," Underwood stated.

"How can a *lifelong* prison sentence just sort itself out?" I asked.

"I've been asking the same thing for myself also. I know my sentence wouldn't have been half as long as yours—"

"Thanks," I interrupted sarcastically.

"Anytime. As I was saying, I spoke to my lawyer about all of the affairs and, for some reason, the police have no interest in either you or me; all they seemed to have wanted was Petrov," he explained.

"How is that even possible?" I gasped.

"I know…it's strange. But I guess you know what these SA police are like—there's probably some money they're interested in. And, trust me, I've checked and checked, asked, pestered and prodded, and absolutely no one is coming after us. It's like you and I didn't exist in this investigation."

"Daniel, are you serious? You mean *no one* is coming after me?"

"Perhaps only me, if you let me finally take you out for dinner properly," he giggled to himself. "But yes, no one is coming after you."

"Oh, give it a rest, Daniel. We've both barely come out of this alive and all you can think about is a date?"

"Yes, yes, Ms Khumalo, I know. I'm just playing. It's been a horrible few weeks," he sighed deeply. "Do you believe in God?" he asked gently.

"I do now, yes," I said, hesitating on my answer.

"Which God?" he questioned further.

"Um, I suppose Jesus," I replied. "I'm still figuring it out, but, from what I understand, he's the one who saved me from this mess."

"So why are you living like this if you believe in God?" he prodded.

"I didn't believe in God until last week," I clarified. "Wait, do *you* believe in God?"

"I do. I always have," Underwood confessed.

"So why are *you* living like this if you believe in God?" I responded.

"Deep one. It's funny because I feel like you and I are like two survivors on a desert island, so I'll get it out in the open," he began. "The true answer is, I don't know why I've been living like this even though I've always believed in God. I was raised in a Christian household. My dad and mum are both pastors, and my siblings are Christians too, but I just wanted to be bad for some reason. I knew I was smart, good-looking and could do almost anything I wanted to do, so I left.

"That was fifteen years ago now. I was stupid and I know it but, for some reason, when all this stuff with Petrov started happening a few weeks ago, I just felt like God was speaking to me and telling me he was giving me another chance for all the years I'd run away from him. So now, it's my chance to turn things around, maybe even mend things with my family again."

"Woah…Daniel this is literally what happened to me too!" I exclaimed.

"Seriously?"

"Seriously," I replied.

"What happened?" he asked.

"It's a bit of a long story, but to shorten it in the best way I can, the day that Petrov was arrested, I went to have coffee with an old friend of mine in the morning. Well, I say an old friend, but he was my ex-boyfriend. He's really strong in his Christian faith and so he felt the need to be by my side when I went to the police station to speak to Petrov. We prayed and he began just telling me what he heard God was saying and he told me what was coming but he told me I would be safe through it all. Lo and behold, I was safe through it all. When I came back home, my grandmother told me she'd always been praying for me. It was then that I realised that someone's prayers had kept me alive."

"Wow, I'm blown away," Underwood said in a surprised tone, a tone I hadn't once heard from him.

"I know. But, is there a ritual I have to do now to become a Christian? How does this work? I know it sounds stupid but I'm not sure how to do any of this," I admitted.

"You're funny, Khumalo. It's not a stupid question at all, and I hope you don't get used to asking me questions on this Christian stuff because I'm very rusty! However, what I do know is that it's simple. I can help you right now over the phone?"

"Um, y-yes please. That would be great," I stuttered nervously, not knowing what would happen after I did this.

"Okay, no need to be nervous. Repeat after me: *Dear Lord Jesus*," he said.

I took a deep breath in so that I wouldn't rush my words and ensure that I was thinking this decision through properly and carefully. I was so comforted to know that Underwood was right there doing this with me. I don't think he understood how much this meant to me.

"D-dear Lord Jesus," I repeated.

"Thank you for dying for my sins," Underwood continued.

"Thank you for dying for my sins."

"I believe that you are my Lord and Saviour."

"I believe that you are my Lord and Saviour."

"I ask that you come into my heart so that I can have eternal life."

"I ask that you come into my heart so that I can have eternal life."

"Amen," he closed.

"Amen," I said.

"That's it," he concluded.

"That's it?"

"Yes," he confirmed. "Simple right?"

"Yeah," I laughed. "I feel…peaceful too," I said, feeling surprised. "Thank you so much, Daniel. I appreciate this more than you'll ever know. And I guess I'll never forget that I did this with you."

"Of course. It's an honour to know you, Ms Khumalo—"

"Kaya," I clarified adamantly. "We're friends now."

"It's an honour to be your friend, *Kaya*. I believe you're going to flourish into a very wonderful woman. And, one day, I also hope you won't pass me off on that dinner offer," he laughed.

"Hmm. Well, I'm not not saying yes, but let's recover from this first."

"Couldn't agree with you more. Lovely speaking to you," he sang.

"You too, Daniel," I said as I put the phone down.

Who would've thought that the man who assisted me in drug dealing would one day help me become a Christian.

24

2021

"Ahhhh! Kaya!" Genesis screamed as she opened her front door. "What a surprise! What are you doing here?"

"What do you think?" I laughed. "Coming to see you and your beautiful face." It was lovely to see her.

"Come in, sis! We've got a party going on today because Luke is home," she grinned at me.

"A party?" I asked.

"Yeah! Sorry, I realise I didn't pre-warn you. Let me know if you feel too overwhelmed at any point."

"Oh no, I'll be fine," I reassured her. "I need to be around people right now; it'll help me get my mind off things."

"Some things like what?" she questioned suspiciously.

"Just…a lot, girl. We'll catch up later today, hopefully," I sighed.

"Phfff, I feel you. Life has been life-ing lately. We *need* to catch up," she said in quiet excitement.

The smell of their house was still exactly the same as it was ten years ago. Their mother's sea-breeze diffusers with a hint of vanilla dotted all over the house and the smell of fresh linen wafting in from the laundry room hadn't changed at all. I started chuckling to myself as I realised that their family photo had *finally* changed. It was the first thing you saw as you entered the house. Their last picture was a goofy braced-faced Genesis and pre-pubescent Luke, which was just hilarious. Now, it was a much more recent Luke and Genesis with their now grey-haired parents.

"Oh, wait. This was so silly of me, I should have told you…" Genesis said as she caught me staring at their updated family photo.

"Told me what?" I said, a bit shaken up.

"Luke and his…wife are here."

"Oh, yeah, I know," I laughed, knowing that Genesis *thought* she was giving me some breaking news.

"Oh…" Gen said, surprised, "and you're okay with that?"

"Of course! Girl, I need to catch up with you."

Just as I said that Cindy came running over to me with such a look of excitement and joy on her face.

"Kaya! Ah, I feel like I'm fan-girling right now. I'm so excited to see you. I've been asking Luke all day whether you'll be coming and what time you'd be here! Can I just say, you are *so* stunning," Cindy exclaimed, not seeming to catch a breath.

"Good to see you, Cindy," I said as I hugged her gently. "But, if *I'm* stunning then *you* must be stunning with a capital S," I complimented.

"Oh, stop!" she giggled.

"No, but seriously, you look amazing," I reaffirmed.

Cindy was exactly how I'd expected her to be in person; she was quite small, very curvy, beautiful glowing skin, perfect teeth and just all round beautiful. Her beauty perfectly complimented her personality too—she was the sort of person who made everyone around her feel comfortable. Her presence just felt like a radiant light.

"Come in and join us at the party! Luke's parents have cooked up a storm and everyone has started dancing because Luke's DJ cousin has jumped onto the decks. Come on!" Cindy pleaded with me.

"Um, okay, sure," I said nervously.

How was I going to act around Luke now that Cindy was around? I didn't want to make either of them feel awkward, but the more I thought about how weird this actually was—the fact I was friends with my ex and his wife—the weirder it made me feel. Regardless, I was going to be brave and stick this one out.

In Cindy's defence, the atmosphere was really buzzing and everyone seemed like they were having a good time: there were uncles and aunties in every corner sipping beer and eating barbecued meat, some of the younger people were dancing to the amapiano music, Luke's cousin was playing and taking selfies, little kids ran all over the garden zapping each other with fake guns, and some of the oldies shared stories and laughed as they fanned the smoke from the barbecue. I wanted to say hello to Luke's parents but I couldn't see them anywhere. I spotted Luke quickly by his cousin who was DJing, probably giving him some music tips that were far too outdated for his cousin's generation.

"You look a little overwhelmed," Cindy acknowledged. "How are you feeling?"

"Do I seem that out of it?" I asked, feeling self-conscious.

"Erm, yes. A little," she laughed. "But that's normal, don't worry. I felt exactly the same."

"I guess I'm just trying to get used to it all. This is just like a whole new world to me again. I don't even remember how to interact with people outside of Joburg," I confessed.

"Understandable. Can I be real with you?" she asked.

"Yes, for sure," I reassured her.

"I haven't come to visit your town until now because I was afraid that the people here wouldn't like me, maybe they'd think I was stuck up or something," she sighed.

"Really? Why would you think that? You're so sweet Cindy," I said.

"I guess maybe I was just overthinking it. When you're newly married, you kind of have this thing at the back of your mind that you need to be the perfect wife and well-liked by everybody, but I just want to let go and be myself," she said.

Inasmuch as I wasn't sure why Cindy trusted me enough to tell me these things, I was relieved to know that she was just as human as me. She wasn't as perfect as I'd made her out to be; she'd probably struggled with the same insecurities as any other woman; I'm not sure why I'd thought any differently.

"I think you should be yourself, Cindy; you're wonderful. If people don't love you then it's a *them* problem. The more you try to put up a front, the harder it'll be to be yourself as time goes on," I advised her.

"I know, I know. You're right. I've really been praying for courage to do so, and I think I'm just going to be bold and try to do it. I need to remind myself that I am fully accepted by God and not by people."

"Exactly that. Who cares what they think? Just be you," I returned.

"Thanks, Kaya. You're amazing too, really. Also, I know this may seem weird because you and Luke were together in the past, but I want you to feel fully comfortable speaking to him and speaking to me. The past is the past. I trust Luke completely and I trust you too. I would love us to be friends," she said, holding my hand gently.

"At least, someone said it," I laughed awkwardly. "Thank you for clearing the air about that because I really didn't want to make anybody feel uncomfortable. So yeah, it'd be nice if we could all be friends," I smiled.

"Me too. Oh, I think Luke is calling you over," she said, pointing me over to a waving Luke.

"Pretty hard to miss him," I replied, sighing comically.

"Good to see you," Luke said with the biggest smile on his face as I made my way over to him.

"It's so weird to think about how different the situation was just a few weeks ago," I breathed.

"I told you God would do it," Luke chuckled as he nudged me.

"I know. He worked it all out," I accepted.

"And you feel okay?" he asked in a concerned voice.

"I feel okay, yeah. I do feel quite strange, especially trying to process the grief and the 360 turnaround my life has taken all at once, but I know I'll get through."

"'That's the spirit. God is always there for you," he continued.

"I believe he is. I…actually gave my life to Christ," I told him.

"WHAT!" Luke screamed, making everyone look at us.

"Luke, shush! Don't embarrass me, please," I urged him firmly.

"Sorry, sorry. This is just great news, Kaya. When? Where? How?"

"Yesterday, actually. I was on the phone with a…friend and he guided me through the process. I was sure I wanted to do it so I did it."

"Wow, K. Just wow. I'm so proud of you, but I know God is even prouder. Heaven is rejoicing on your behalf right now," he beamed, shaking me by the arms in excitement.

"Thanks, Luke. I'm hoping Genesis will be able to help me make the next steps into this transition as well, as I think I'm going to stay back home for a while," I sighed.

"She'd be happy to help, I'm sure. She's probably going to be even more excited than me. Actually, you've reminded me to share something with you that God spoke to me about," Luke said.

"Sure thing. Happy for you to share it," I agreed.

"Give me a sec; let me just get it out from my notes on my phone. Okay, he said:

Don't be discouraged in this season because, although it may be hard for you to make this transition, your testimony is going to be sent forth into the nations for all to see and hear. In fact, your story is going to be one of the most known stories for women in this generation around the whole world. It may take some time for you to heal and to understand who you are, but once you get through this dark season, you will have the confidence and boldness to start changing people's lives. You're going to do great things, Kaya," Luke smiled widely.

"Oh, wow. That's a lot to take in. I'm not saying I don't believe you, but I don't understand how God could use *me* with my credentials," I exhaled heavily.

"God uses people who don't think they could ever be used, it shows how equally he loves us all. He also never condemns anyone, so try not to condemn yourself for the past."

"One step at a time," I said.

"Also, one more thing. God knows your dad has been far from a perfect example; probably actually a *terrible* example of a dad from what I heard in prayer last night, but don't use that to define the Father that God is to you," Luke reassured me.

I tried not to cry thinking about what my dad had done to Mama and I. I was still so disgusted with his behaviour and I wanted nothing more to do with him.

"I know you may not want to hear this, Kaya, but your dad loves you. I know he's done *a lot* of wrong things, but trust me, he loves you. Some people just have so much hurt and pain that they mess up big time when they have a chance to show love."

"How can he love me, Luke, with everything he's done?" I said, trying to hold back a breakdown.

"I can't give you all the answers to that, but I know that God can give you the peace you're looking for. I'm guessing that you've probably stopped talking to him; maybe you should speak to him one last time to see if you can get some closure. Even if you end up shouting and screaming at him, just let him know how you feel," Luke advised.

"I'll think about it," I said more bluntly than I had intended. "I appreciate your prayers and words, Luke. Thank you," I smiled, trying to soften the blunt blow.

My mood and energy had suddenly run extra low after Luke's words and all I wanted to do was be alone. I needed to really process everything so I could decide what I wanted to do next. It would be easy enough to call my dad but even the sound of his voice could push me to do something I would live to regret. Honestly, I was sure that I hated him.

Finding Genesis by the drinks cooler, I said my goodbyes so I could go home and think.

"Thank you for having me, Gen. Can I come by tomorrow so we can catch up?" I asked, trying to hide my bad mood.

"Yep, I'm in and I should be free."

"Great. I'll probably swing by early evening," I said.

"Oh, wait…no. We have fellowship tomorrow evening. Maybe the day after?" she reconsidered.

"Hmm…maybe I can actually come by for the fellowship and we can catch up after?" I suggested.

"Are you serious?" she giggled.

"Yeah. Why not?" I said.

"I just didn't think you'd be interested, that's all," she admitted.

"Oh, yeah, you don't know yet. I'm a Christian now," I smiled shyly.

"YOU WHAT?!" she shrieked.

"You and Luke are so alike," I huffed. "Listen, I'm heading home now. Ask Luke to catch you up with all the details," I said, edging onto the porch so I could go home.

"But—" Gen began.

"See you tomorrow, Genesis!" I asserted.

"Okay, okay, fine. Be here at 7pm sharp," she stated.

"Yes, miss ma'am," I replied sarcastically.

I headed home sulkily thinking about how I was going to reach out to my dad because, as much as I didn't want to, I knew how wrong it was to have blocked him out like that without any warning. Also, I was definitely feeling calmer than a few months ago when I first found out the shocking news. However, I still didn't want him to be in my life, and what if Luke was just saying that because he felt bad for me?

I'm not saying that God didn't speak to him about my dad but who is to say that he didn't just add on that part about the fact that my dad loved me because he just *thought* that was the case? It's hard to think of a parent not loving their child because it doesn't really make sense, but *it is* possible. From my own personal experience of living with my dad, it did truly feel like he was a different man now and that he loved me, but I can't say that was truly how he felt towards me. Maybe it was just to spite Mama for keeping me from him all those years. From my work with men, I *know* how much ego and pride can take over their actions. I guess the only way I'd really be able to find out would be to speak to him. I just *really* didn't want to.

As I arrived back home, I was in perfect time for the sunset, which was my favourite thing ever, and I knew I desperately needed it to think.

I took a breath, sat down on the veranda and just looked into the distance, doing what I normally do—thinking about the lives of people who didn't make it to see the sun go down; Thato and Mandy being two of them. It still felt so unfair how different my life had been just three weeks ago and how privileged I was to be watching another sunset go down.

"Hey baby," Mama said as she walked towards me on the veranda.

"Hey Ma. Come sit," I said as I summoned her over.

I turned around to look at her before she sat down; she looked absolutely beautiful. There was something so different about her face since we made up a few months ago; she just looked so much happier and you could see it in every detail of her appearance. It was like her face was glowing more and her eyes were even brighter than usual. She seemed like a totally new person.

"How was your day?" she asked.

"It was alright," I replied, placing my head on her shoulder.

"What's on your mind, hun?" she enquired, seeming a little worried.

"A lot," I sighed.

"Mhmm, like what?"

"I think I need to speak to Dad," I revealed.

"Why'd you say that?"

"I kind of just blocked him and Aunty Andrea out without any warning and I can only imagine how worried they are. At first, I wanted them to feel stressed out and worried but now, I realise I've been harsh. I'm sure Dad has no idea that I know as well," I said.

"I support you in that. I think it's better for him to know why you haven't been speaking to him; but why did the thought suddenly spring up on you like this?" she asked.

"It wasn't really sudden. I spoke to Luke and he was just letting me know what he thinks God wants me to do," I said.

"Oh, I see…so you listened carefully to Gogo's words about God?" she questioned.

"I did, I really did. I think my whole life is finally starting to make sense now. But I think this thing he's asking me to do just seems like a huge jump seeing as I'm only just starting my journey of faith," I huffed.

"I hear you, darling, but maybe he's asking you to do this because without speaking to your dad, *you won't* even be able to start your journey of faith," she suggested.

"Why wouldn't I be able to start my journey of faith without speaking to Dad? Isn't it better if I just forget him?" I groaned.

"Well, perhaps moving around with unforgiveness and bitterness will prevent you from receiving God's love into your heart fully. I know that it certainly hindered me."

"Yeah…I think that deep down, I know it's true," I sighed. "This has really affected me. I just don't know where I would start with him, Ma."

"Why don't you just tell him the truth?" she said.

"What is my truth though?" I asked, feeling irritated.

"How do you feel?" she continued.

"Angry. Really angry," I confessed.

"Then tell him that," she urged me. "Give him a call."

"What? When?"

"Now," she said. "I'll be in the kitchen if you need me. Dinner is in an hour."

When Mama went back inside and I heard the front door close, I was left alone again; just me and the sunset.

I opened my phone and looked at Pops' contact, and my heart literally felt like it had sunk into my chest. *I can't do this*. I thought to myself.

"Yes, you can," I heard a voice from behind me say.

"Huh?!" I gasped. "Who said that?"

I looked around in shock and saw no one. Did I just make it up? I couldn't have made it up; I heard it so clearly.

I looked back at my phone and put it on the floor, questioning whether to go through with the call.

"I am with you, Kaya. You can do this," the voice said again.

"Who is there?" I said standing up, even more frightened this time. I ran around frantically for a few minutes trying to figure out who could have been hiding in the bushes or shouting out from their window.

Then it dawned on me. *God.*

I didn't even waste any time thinking through the supernatural experience that had just occurred for me because the last few weeks had been like this. I picked up my phone and unblocked his number, calling him immediately. I had no idea what I was going to say but I just knew that God was with me.

"Hello?" I said quietly.

"Oh my goodness. Is it Kaya?" I heard Aunty Andrea whisper in the background.

"Honey, is that you?" my dad said.

"Yes, it's me," I muttered.

"We've been worried sick about you. Why haven't you been picking up our calls? We thought you may have been arrested…or worse," Pops disclosed.

"Oh, right," I replied bluntly.

"You sound upset; is everything okay?" he continued.

"Not really, no. Can we talk alone Dad?" I asked. I felt sick to my stomach even calling him 'Dad' as he felt like a stranger to me now.

"Sure, sweetheart. Andrea, do you mind if I just speak to Kaya alone?" he asked her.

"Um, okay," I heard her say.

"It's just me and you now, honey," he acknowledged.

"Please, stop calling me that," I expressed harshly.

"Why? You're acting strange," he remarked.

"Can I just explain why I called?"

"Go ahead," he said.

I took a breather just before I started so that I could process what I wanted to say but no thought process came. I was just really really angry.

"I know what you did, Dad," I began.

"Did when?" he asked, starting to sound defensive.

"No, you're going to let me finish and when I'm done then you can speak. Please, don't interrupt me or I will just cut the call," I argued.

"O-okay," he stuttered.

"I know what you did to Mama; how you abused her, raped her and nearly abused me too. I know how you treated Gogo even though she let you live with her out of the kindness of her heart. I know what kind of man you truly are deep down and how much of a front you put up to people when on the inside you're rotten and disgusting.

"Mama told me everything and I feel sick to my stomach to know that I hated her all those years for keeping me from you when she was just protecting me from the monster you really are. I'm so angry at you; so so angry. I want to shout and scream at you until the anger leaves but, even if I did that for a hundred years, I don't think I could get all of the anger out. How could you have pretended to be a good man to my face knowing that you literally tried to kill me in Mama's womb? What do you have to say for yourself?"

"Goodness. I-I don't know what to say," he stuttered again.

"Well, you better say something or you'll never hear from me again," I returned.

"Okay, okay. Well, to start, I'm sorry," he tried.

"Not good enough. I'm giving you less than a minute," I remarked bitterly.

"I need you to know I'm not that man anymore," he started.

"Oh, cut that out," I hissed.

"Please, hear me out. I really am not that man anymore. I sought help when your mum kicked me out and I really reflected on my actions. I didn't mean to do all those things to her, or *to you*; I was just a very broken man on the inside. I hated myself and I was so angry with my life so I took it out on her. I was a terrible husband and an even more terrible person. I don't know if you will believe me but I really do love you, Kaya, and I would never hurt you now, never," he said. I could hear his voice breaking. I felt like he was crying.

"I don't believe you, and it still doesn't change what you did. You ruined Mama's life," I contended.

"What can I do to make you believe me?" he asked hopelessly.

"Nothing. I just needed to tell you how I felt so I could begin moving forward with my life," I declared.

We were silent for a while as I began to happily bask in my personal atmosphere of resentment.

"Don't make the same mistake I did," he said quietly. "This is exactly how it starts."

"Excuse me? I will *never* be like you," I cackled.

"Do you think I just woke up one morning and decided to hit a woman?" he said, beginning to sob.

"I don't know. Probably," I vented, softening my tone as I realised my words had been extra harsh.

"Anger always leads to bitterness which drives you to commit actions you regret. I hate to say it but, Kaya, you know that the drug business has done that to you; you've said it yourself. Anger always turns you into the person you said you wouldn't become. I grew up with a dad who relentlessly abused my mother until he killed her," he confessed.

"W-what?" I whispered.

"I became the man I swore that I would never become."

"I don't know what to say," I said as my heart began to soften.

"I'm not asking you to forgive me for my own sake, Kaya. I'm asking you to forgive me for *your* own sake. Don't make the mistake I did."

"I'll…think about it. I've got to go now," I replied bluntly and quietly.

"Will I ever hear from you again?" he asked with desperation in his voice.

"I don't know, Dad. I don't know," I said, cutting the call.

I didn't know what was happening to me in this moment but my heart just felt like it was being smudged and softened in so many different directions; it was like someone was kneading it. It just felt like somehow I was feeling *sorry* for him. Why would I feel sorry for him when he did all those things? Yet, I just felt an overwhelming sense of sorrow for him. I couldn't believe his dad did all those things. My grandfather did that to the grandmother I never knew. That could have been Gogo.

Just as I got up from my seat and started to head back inside, I heard my ringer ping.

Strange. My phone is always on Do Not Disturb.

It was a text from Underwood. I thought about reading it later but something prompted me to take a quick look at it. It read:

I don't know why, but I feel like you should go and read the scripture, Luke 7:47 :)

I went straight to my Google search, typed in Luke 7:47, and began reading it out loud. *"Therefore I say to you, her sins, which are many, are forgiven, for she loved much. But to whom little is forgiven, the same loves little."*

I sank to my knees and began weeping; in fact, I was literally wailing. How could I not forgive my dad when God had literally forgiven me for everything I'd done? Families had been killed on my watch, children's lives destroyed, and mothers taken from their babies. I am a hypocrite.

25

2021

I fell asleep last night reading the scripture that Daniel had sent me again and again. This morning, I got up early and started my day by reading the scripture again, praying that my heart would change; thankfully, I felt less resentful and angry towards my dad since our phone call and I didn't want to leave things where they were.

I still have to be honest with myself though; I'm not yet at the stage where I can say I can forgive him, but I can say I do eventually want to get there. I hope I'll get there anyway.

I looked over to my wall cabinet and suddenly remembered that I'd kept the letter my dad had given me on my 18th birthday. I needed to read it again to remember why I'd chosen to find him in the first place; why I used to believe he loved me.

I walked over and took it out carefully, unfolding the letter with extra care and kindness. For a while, I didn't read anything, I just stayed there staring at the paper and remembering how life-changing this day had been for me. I remembered the emotions of sadness, anger, excitement and hatred; I was just a desperate kid looking for love.

Eventually, I plucked up the courage to begin reading and read over every single word in detail so that I didn't miss anything.

Dear Kaya,

I'm sorry yet another year has gone by without me being able to see you. As you know, I never forget your birthday and I will continue sending you letters each year without fail even if you never stop being angry with me. I'm hoping that now that you're 18, we can be reunited. I hope you will forgive me and let us build a relationship. I love you, my precious girl.

Happy birthday.

Dad.

Those words, 'I hope you will forgive me', struck such a cord inside of my heart. I wasn't even angry with him then yet it's almost like he could see into the future.

He *did* love me. He *did* regret his actions. He *did* want to be in my life.

The only way I could think of responding to him right now without exploding in emotion was to write back to him after all these years. That was exactly what I was going to do—write him a letter.

I made my way over to Mama's office, took out some papers from the printer and one of her fancy fountain pens and just began to write. I didn't want to overthink it; I just wanted to write.

Dear Pops,

I'm writing back to you from the letter you sent me ten years ago.

I'm sorry that life was unfair to you from the beginning. I'm sorry that your innocence was taken away from you as you learnt what abuse was before you could even learn your name. I'm sorry that the only love language you were taught was violence.

I have to be honest with you, when I first heard what you did to Ma, I wanted you to disappear from the face of the earth and suffer for everything you'd done. Don't get me wrong; I'm still angry, but there's something working on the inside of my heart that has made me realise that I'm no better. I realise that we're all just broken people screaming out for love and we don't just wreck our own lives in the process, but everyone else's as well.

What I do ask of you is that you apologise to Mama as I believe that is the least you can do. It can't ever make it right but you know how wrong it was for you to treat her the way you did. She is worthy of much more.

I don't want us to rush back into a relationship because I'm still recovering, but I do want us to have a healthy relationship one day. I also want you to know that

I'm no longer a drug dealer. I'm living my life for good and for purpose now; I hope you will choose to do the same. God has forgiven me and God has forgiven you too.

I'll be praying for you.

With love,

Kaya.

I sealed up the letter, put it in an envelope and didn't think twice before running down to the postal office to send it to him. It was done, and I felt like a huge burden had been lifted off of my shoulders; unforgiveness and anger requires so much energy and it was energy that I didn't have. The only energy I wanted was the energy to love people unconditionally; therefore, there was no room for hate.

***

The evening came a lot faster than I expected as I was so engrossed in reading the Bible; however, I was also excited for this fellowship at Genesis' house. I was elated to be able to finally understand why Genesis and her family loved God the way they did because I was beginning to share in this same love for God.

I showered, put on some jeans and a blue crew neck t-shirt, sprayed myself with some of Mama's perfume (as I didn't bring any with me from Joburg) and left the house.

"Hey friend. Just on time," Genesis smiled brilliantly at me as I yet again appeared on her doorstep.

"When am I ever late? Don't push your African timing complex on me," I laughed.

"No, but girl, African timing is *real*. I question whether it's just a part of our DNA," she giggled.

"It's true. Even when Africans try to be on time, it's like something still makes the clocks work against them," I continued, laughing alongside her.

"Kaya! Wow, it is so good to see you darling," Genesis' mum said. "You look beautiful as always, shining like the sun."

"Thank you, Ma. It is good to see you too; thank you for having me in your home."

"Oh, stop it; you're always welcome here. You're family," she said, beaming at me.

"We're just about to start praise and worship," Genesis said, pulling me inside.

"Okay. What should I do?" I whispered to her anxiously.

"We love to free-flow here so whatever you feel like doing. You can sing, close your eyes, pray, dance…whatever you want," she assured me.

"I see. Okay," I smiled nervously.

I followed closely behind Genesis into the living room and found a place for myself in the corner, out of the view of everyone. The worship leader had already started to lead the worship with Luke playing his guitar and Cindy accompanying him on the keyboard— everyone seemed to be comfortable and happy in this atmosphere and it made me feel alive after such a heavy day.

Straight ahead of me was Luke's dad on his knees with his hands raised to the ceiling, completely in his own zone. The more I looked around, the more I realised that no one cared and everyone was literally doing their own thing, worshipping God individually. I actually felt a bit prideful to think that I thought everyone's attention would be on me because I'm a newcomer.

I closed my eyes and just began to take in the atmosphere very gently. I pictured the words that were being sung in my mind: "Holy, holy, holy," and I just felt my mind begin to dance with ideas of what 'holy' could look like. First, I imagined Jesus in a white robe standing in front of me silently, and then I began to imagine white doves flying all around me. I could feel that feeling of peace rising up in me again; the same peace that came over me when Luke and I went to grab coffee weeks ago. It could only be God.

Without even realising it, I began to sing the words alongside everyone else. I didn't feel self-conscious or embarrassed; rather, I just felt comfort inside of me, knowing that I was in an atmosphere free of judgement and full of love. It dawned on me that Luke and Cindy knew of my past mistakes yet fully accepted me to join them in this fellowship meeting; it could only be a heart full of love that would allow them to look at me in this way.

I continued singing and clapping with the music for who knows how long but I was being carried in this presence. It could have been two minutes or three hours, I wasn't even sure.

"Good evening, everyone," Luke's dad said as he beckoned the lead worshipper to end the worship. "It's great to be with you all again. Also, I feel honoured to have my son and his beautiful wife in our midst this evening. I've missed their presence. Welcome both of you. I am also aware that we have someone new with us." Everyone looked in my direction which was exactly what I hoped wouldn't happen this evening. "Could you maybe introduce yourself?" Luke's dad added.

"Um, yeah. Hi everyone. I'm Kaya," I said awkwardly.

"Hi Kaya," they all said in unison.

"I think I recognise you, Kaya; did you come to this fellowship many years ago?" a man in dungarees and glasses asked me.

"Um, yes, I did. I was much younger," I admitted.

"It's great to have you, and it's wonderful that you have come to know Jesus," he smiled at me.

"Welcome, Kaya," Luke's dad continued warmly. "Tonight, we have one of my oldest friends here who is going to share some things the Lord has dearly laid on his heart. He's travelled all the way from Pretoria to be with us just for today as he believed that God wanted him to be here this evening. Please, welcome Jeff Basson."

A man in a very simple outfit stood up and hugged Luke's Dad as he was welcomed up to the front. He wore a washed out forest green t-shirt, beige cargo trousers and some climbing shoes. He looked a little scruffy but he smelled *amazing*. It's like his whiff just filled up the whole room.

"I'd like to begin by honouring the Lord and his goodness to each and everyone of us. He's a good, mighty, and faithful God, who has gifted us all with his wonderful grace. Can we just take a minute or so to lift up our worship to him," Jeff said.

I looked around for what I was supposed to do next and saw everyone with eyes closed and muttering words that I couldn't understand. What were they saying? Was this some made-up Christian language that I'd have to learn? What was going on?

Anyway, I just closed my eyes and began to pray in my head, thanking God for life and for his love towards me.

"Amen," Jeff concluded.

"Amen," everyone repeated in unison.

"Can we all turn our Bibles to the book of Luke, chapter seven," he said.

I took my phone out and clicked on the Bible app, turning to the book that Jeff asked us to turn to. I was relieved to know that most people were also using virtual Bibles and I wasn't the odd one out. I'm not sure what I expected of Christians, but I didn't think they used their phones to read the Bible.

"There are a few things I want to speak about this evening, but the main one is our faith as believers. If we look at the lives of all of the different characters and stories across the scriptures, the one thing that speaks the loudest to all of us is the faith that they had in God. Now, it could have been a lack of faith or an abundance of faith but the one thing that God always seems to highlight is the level of faith a person has.

"God cannot operate without someone having faith. We enter into all of God's blessings via faith and one of these blessings is forgiveness. Did you know that we cannot accept forgiveness from God without faith? The reason this is so is because we must have faith in the finished work of Jesus to understand that we have been forgiven. If we read Luke chapter 7 verse 47—and I'm reading from the King James Version—it says, *'Wherefore I say unto thee, Her sins, which are many, are forgiven; for she loved much: but to whom little is forgiven, the same loveth little.'*

These are actually two different dimensions of faith: you can see the one who had a high level of faith to know that Jesus had forgiven them much, and the one who had little faith as they didn't have faith in the forgiveness of Jesus. Now, to go deeper into this, let's start at the very beginning of this chapter."

I completely zoned out of his continuation of the chapter as I was stunned at how exact his message was; it was literally directed at me. This was the *exact* scripture that Underwood had sent me yesterday. It was like God was not trying to leave me be about this forgiveness thing; he wasn't letting me forget about it.

I could feel the tears about to flow—God could *really* see me and wanted me to understand how loved I was.

"Excuse me, your name is Kaya right?" I looked back up as I snapped out of my own world and saw Jeff looking right at me as he asked me the question.

"What? Sorry; yes, my name is Kaya," I replied, feeling a little startled and embarrassed that I didn't know what was going on.

"Can I just prophesy over you right now? There are some things I feel the Lord wants me to share with you," he said.

"Y-yes, sure," I said, beginning to get anxious again.

"The Lord says over you that you are like a flower blooming in this season. I feel as though you are in the midst of a lot of confusion and you don't quite know what is going on, but the Lord says, *'Peace, be still and know that I am God.'* He is right beside you and is holding your hand through it all. Can I ask that everyone begins to pray over Kaya as I continue to prophesy? Come over here, Kaya, so everyone can stretch their hands out towards you," Jeff beckoned me to come over.

I came into the middle of the room where he was and knelt down and closed my eyes.

"You are marked with purpose and have such a heavy call on your life. You are one that will leave a legacy in this generation because of your story. I can see that you have a past that has left you with such guilt and shame and regret, but God has given you a new name. He calls you *My beloved daughter.*

"I also see that even before you accepted Jesus as your Lord and Saviour, he has been revealing himself to you in your dreams over the course of your life. You've had many encounters with God and, even though you were unsure of who he was, he has constantly been trying to show you how much he loves you. To specify, I see a dream in which he was helping you sort out your dirty laundry. He was trying to show you that your sins have been forgiven—he has taken them all away. Kaya, you are very special and unique and from today, your life will never be the same. You are marked with purpose."

I could feel the tangible presence of God falling upon me. I began to shake and cry and finally, all of the puzzle pieces were coming together. The man that had been appearing in my dreams and showing me overwhelming and reckless love was Jesus. God loves me. He's always seen me and he's always cared.

I am loved. I am forgiven. I am not condemned.

I am chosen.

Epilogue

2023

A *lot* has happened in the past two years. To start with, I got married this year. Who would have thought that I would get *married*? I guess good men do exist. The good man who happened to exist in my life was Daniel Underwood. Yes…Mr 'I Don't Trust Him' Underwood. I guess we women do need to get a grip on our mouths at times. I'm definitely still getting my head around the fact that Daniel and I used to be business partners on the completely wrong side of the law and ended up getting married.

Anyway, sure enough, we fell in love and did the whole engagement and wedding thing. He's wonderful, really. I feel like I should give him a lot more credit, especially because I know how hard it was to finally win me over—I gave him a lot of stress as I'm sure you would know.

Now, we're still business partners, but we are very, *very* much clean. Together, we coach people from all around the world on how to run successful businesses (ironic really, isn't it?). I also personally coach and mentor women to help them overcome all of life's challenges: mentally, physically, emotionally and spiritually.

Johannesburg is still our home and we hope it will be for a long time because we have a great love for this city and would love to raise a family out here. Yes, a family! I hope to eventually become a mum to little *Kayas and Daniels*. Thankfully, I'll have a lot of help on my hands because Blessing is back with us, and Mama and Pops will be there on standby. Additionally, we are faithfully committed to our faith as Christians and attend Luke and Cindy's church here in Joburg.

Each and everyday feels like a blessing waiting to be walked in, and I'm forever grateful for the opportunity. Don't get me wrong; it comes with its challenges, but thank God that now I am more than a conqueror.

Also, I've finally accepted that I can be a very stubborn person.

With love,

Kaya Imka *Underwood*. (Ahh! Still getting used to saying that.)

Printed in Great Britain
by Amazon